MW00330959

Tattered Stars

Stars

THE TATTERED & TORN SERIES

CATHERINE COWLES

Editor: Susan Barnes
Copy Editor: Chelle Olson
Proofreading: Julie Deaton and Janice Owen
Paperback Formatting: Stacey Blake, Champagne Book Design
Cover Design: Hang Le
Cover Photography: Michaela Mangum

Tattered Stars

Prologue

Everly

BE BRAVE. FOR SIXTY SECONDS. TWENTY BREATHS. I could do anything for twenty ins and outs. The springs on my mattress squeaked as I swung my legs over the side of my bed. I froze. And listened.

There were lots of things I hated about growing up here. But there were things I loved, too. Things I was grateful for. Like how attuned I was to every whisper. I'd know in an instant if a sound didn't belong.

I waited. Heard the screen door rattle in the wind. The call of an owl. Even the hum of our refrigerator in the kitchen. I didn't hear my brother or dad. Mom had been gone for days, helping a baby come into the world. But I wished for her now. She was the only one who had a chance of stopping the craziness. But she wasn't here, and I wasn't sure what tomorrow would bring.

I pushed to my feet, praying my mattress would stay quiet and not give me away. The springs didn't betray me again. I moved to my closet, careful to avoid any floorboards that creaked. Pulling a pair of worn jeans from a shelf, I slipped them on. I tugged the nightgown over my head and reached for a t-shirt.

The breeze picked up through my open window. It had been unbearably hot today but just a few hours into the night and a chill had settled. I grabbed a flannel just in case. Slipping on socks, I picked up my boots. I knew better than to put hard soles on this floor.

My dad had taught me how to move without a sound to avoid any kind of predator. And tonight, I was thankful for each and every lesson—even the ones where I'd had to roll in mud to disguise myself.

I reached for the doorknob, but my hand stilled on the metal. I could just go back to bed. Forget my attempt at being brave and wait for Mom to come home. To bring my dad down from his paranoid state where everyone was the enemy and we were at risk from it all—the government, neighbors, even my teachers.

I'd watched as our lives got smaller and smaller, with fewer and fewer people to trust. I didn't remember a lot of the normal. But I remembered some. The second grade and Miss Christie before Dad had pulled Ian and me out of school. Visiting Mom's family in Portland before he'd decided they were heathens. The town fair before he became convinced that it was evil.

I closed my eyes and turned the knob. Stepping out into the hall, I listened again. Nothing out of place. I created a dance to avoid every problematic board in my path, sometimes tiptoeing, other times stretching my legs to the point I worried I'd tip over.

Finally, I reached the front door. Our old dog, Bruiser, raised his head, but I held a single finger to my lips, begging for silence. Feeding him table scraps must've paid off because he lay back down and let out a soft snore.

I eased open the door and stepped through to the first

true rebellion I'd ever embarked on. One that might make me like my older sister—an outcast. I closed the door behind me with a soft snick, but it was deafening to my ears, echoing off the mountain itself. I let the screen door fall closed, too, only a small rattle in my wake.

I hopped over the porch steps entirely, knowing each and every one would give me away. I landed with an oomph but held in my cry of pain. Slipping on my boots, I glanced at the shed in the distance. The motion lights on its exterior meant I didn't dare try for it. So, I started for the barn instead.

One of the doors was open a hair to let some of the night air in, and I pulled it a bit more, just wide enough so Storm and I had a path. As I moved down the aisle, our few horses nickered or lifted their heads to see who was about. I paused at the tack room, picked up a bridle, and then continued until I reached Storm's stall.

She must have scented me coming because her head was already over the stall door. I gave her nose a rub and then urged her back. "Gotta let me in." She did as I asked, and I left the door open, knowing she wasn't going anywhere…not without me.

I eased the bridle over her head, and she accepted the bit without complaint. "What do you say we go for a ride?" She seemed to nod her head in agreement. It would've been so much simpler if we were just taking off for one of our afternoon adventures, exploring the mountains.

I led her out of the stall and towards the exit. We made our way out, and I hoisted myself onto the fence so I could climb onto her back. She stayed steady as I threw a leg over and adjusted my grip on the reins. "Nice and easy."

I guided her down the path that stayed far away from the house. One that led to the mountain switchbacks. I glanced up at the sky, thanking the heavens for a nearly full moon. I just prayed my sense of direction was as good as I thought.

I'd never ridden all the way to town before. It was at least fifteen miles, and several paths ebbed and flowed. But I knew where I was headed. I'd memorized these mountains every day of my life. They were both a refuge and a prison. Solace and tormentor.

Tonight, they were on my side. Each trail's crossroads seemed to give me the next logical step until switchbacks turned to wide, worn paths, the dirt packed by hikers and riders. Soon, I reached the road into town. I stayed just off it, my heart hammering against my ribs as the forests turned to neighborhoods.

I adjusted my grip on the reins, seeking out a peek at the lake on the outskirts of town. The moon made the water almost glitter. "Just a few more minutes," I whispered to myself. I could be brave for a little longer.

I moved Storm onto the blacktop, her hooves echoing against the buildings along Aspen Street. Every store was dark with limited streetlights so residents and visitors alike could see the stars. Normally, I loved seeing them, too, but tonight I fought a shiver. Wolf Gap felt like a ghost town.

I slowed Storm as we approached the street I knew held my next battle for bravery. I wondered if I was already past the point of no return or if I could guide Storm back up the mountain and go home. I turned her onto Spruce.

The light from a building poured out into the night. It wasn't harsh, more like a soft beacon, guiding me home. Only if I walked inside, I had a feeling I'd never see *home* again.

I halted Storm in front of that soft light and slid off her back. My hands trembled as I tied her reins to a lamppost. Patting her neck, I nuzzled in close. "I'm doing the right thing. Right?" She pushed into me as if to agree. "I'll see if we can get you some water."

I didn't want to step away from Storm's warmth and comfort. I wanted to stay there forever and ignore the rest of the world.

Instead, I took a giant step back and turned. "Twenty more breaths." It would all be over in just twenty more breaths.

I felt the harshness of each concrete step through my boots. I paused as I reached the glass doors, glancing to my left, seeing a bulletin board with all sorts of notices. Missing pets. Town functions. An event at the library. But one piece of paper made my chest tighten.

I reached out and plucked it from the board. My empty hand reached for the door, but when I pulled, I found it locked. A young man behind a desk looked up at the rattle of metal and glass. His eyes widened for a moment, and then he must've pushed a button because the door made a sound.

I pulled again, and it opened with ease. The soles of my boots echoed on the linoleum floor. Just a few more breaths.

"Are you okay?" the man asked.

I laid the paper on his desk, the photo on it staring up at us, the stark letters—*Missing*—a glaring accusation. The face on it was only a little younger than mine, but it was smiling and carefree. It had been a long time since I'd been that. It was too exhausting trying to read Dad's moods or being on alert for one of his *drills* that could happen at any time.

I touched a finger to the side of the photo, not wanting to get dirt on the girl's face. "I know where she is."

The man's mouth opened and closed. "Where?"

"At my house. In the shed with the green roof."

His eyes narrowed on me. "How old are you?"

"Eleven."

His gaze traveled over my shoulder, out the glass doors. "Did you come here alone? This isn't something to joke about. Is that a horse?"

A side door opened. "What's all the fuss out here, Nick?"

A man with tanned skin and salt-and-pepper hair appeared, and his gaze immediately moved to me. "Now, who's this?"

Nick scowled. "She says she knows where Shiloh Easton is. Probably a prank. You know how these kids are."

The older man came towards me and crouched. "What's your name, little one?"

"Everly. Everly Kemper." I did my best to keep my voice from shaking.

The man shared a look with Nick. "You live up on the mountain?"

I nodded. "The girl. She's there. My dad...he said he had to save her from the evil and that she would be in our family now. But she doesn't want to be there. She wants to go home. And Mom's gone. She had to go midwifing, and no one can talk Dad down when he's like this. But it's been five days, and the girl... she won't eat or drink. And Dad keeps getting madder. I didn't know what to do."

All the words tumbled out of me. It wasn't anything like I'd practiced on my long ride into town. I fisted my hands, my nails biting into my palms, to keep from letting everything else fly.

The man's jaw looked as if it were carved out of granite, but he patted me on the shoulder. "Everything's going to be just fine. I'm Sheriff Hearst. I'll figure everything out." He turned to Nick. "Let's call in our team. As fast as they can get here."

Nick jumped on the phone, and Sheriff Hearst guided me towards the side door, but I halted halfway there, looking towards the doors. "Storm, my horse. She needs some water."

"Did you ride all the way here?"

I nodded. "She's probably thirsty."

"And I'm sure you are, too." The sheriff waved at Nick. "Get the horse some water." Nick gave a lift of his chin, and the sheriff looked down at me. "Let's get you something to drink and maybe a snack, too."

He seated me in a room with two vending machines and a little kitchen. "Have a seat."

The chair made an ugly sound as I pulled it back, and by the time I sat down, the room was getting a little fuzzy. I barely registered Sheriff Hearst placing an array of items in front of me. Water and a soda. Some crackers, and a candy bar.

I couldn't remember the last time I'd had packaged food. Maybe when I was seven? About the time Dad pulled me and Ian out of school. He'd demanded that we live off the land as much as possible. Nothing store-bought. Those companies were trying to poison us.

But I remembered the chips Mom used to pack in my lunch, and they were my favorite. My hands trembled as I went for the crackers. But I could barely taste them.

Everything went in and out of focus as a female deputy came to sit with me. I watched from my spot at the table as officers assembled in the main room. They donned vests and guns. My stomach cramped, and I squeezed my eyes closed. *I did the right thing.* I said it over and over in my mind, just hoping I might believe it.

When I opened my eyes, the armed men and women were gone. I toyed with the crackers as the woman asked me questions. "Has your dad ever hurt you?"

I shook my head. He'd been strict, but his punishments were training. Teaching us to go without because we might not always have access to the comforts of home.

The woman shifted in her chair. "Has he ever touched you anywhere that made you feel uncomfortable?"

I blanched. "No. He's not like that. He just…" I didn't know how to finish the sentence. "His mind plays tricks on him."

It was the best way I could think to explain him. His brain told him lies. Like the one that decided a family was evil because they were going to a town fair, but their daughter could be saved because she hadn't wanted to go. So, he'd stolen her away.

I tuned the deputy out and stared into the main room, letting my eyes go unfocused. That same side door opened, and a group of people filed in—a family. The mother was red-eyed and panicked, while the father tried to calm her and hold onto the girl in his arms, who couldn't have been more than six or seven.

Two boys followed, looking around the room. The oldest was probably in high school. His fists clenched and flexed, and anger lit his eyes. But the younger wasn't more than a few years older than me. Worry lined his face. He looked from the room back to his parents, taking his mother's hand and squeezing it.

It had to be the little girl's family. *Shiloh Easton.* I said the name in my mind, shaped it with my mouth. She would go home to this family who loved her.

I watched as the mom kissed the boy on his head. He didn't dodge away like Ian did when my mom showed him affection. This boy let her love on him, seeming to understand that she needed it.

Our gazes locked from across the room. There were a million questions in his eyes. I wasn't sure I had any of the answers he needed, but I couldn't look away. I stared into those dark depths as if he held me hostage.

The bang of the door against the wall broke our trance. The entire Easton family was on their feet in a flash, surrounding Sheriff Hearst. He held Shiloh in his arms. I couldn't hear what he said, but the mother wept, and I caught tears streaming down the father's face, as well. The siblings hugged their sister tightly. But the boy with the haunting eyes kept looking back at me where I sat. All alone.

Chapter One

Everly

MY HANDS TIGHTENED ON THE WHEEL AS I GUIDED MY SUV onto Aspen Street. Everything looked remarkably the same. The slight Old West feel still clung to the buildings and antique lampposts. Many of the institution spots like The Cowboy Inn and Wolf Gap Bar & Grill were still here, just with a fresh coat of paint.

But while it looked as if there were some new restaurants and shops, as well, I knew hoping for a spot to order my favorite Thai dishes might be too much to ask. There was no question that coming back to eastern Oregon meant I'd be giving up some things.

My older sister, Jacey, thought I was crazy. Sure, that I'd step back into town limits and get sucked back into all the drama that surrounded our family. I understood her fear. Especially since she'd been more mother to me than a sister, taking custody of me after my father went to jail, and I'd begged my mom to let me leave this place.

All that determination to break free, and here I was, a decade and a half later, coming right back to where I started. My pulse picked up speed as I drove past Spruce Street and caught sight of the sheriff's station. I knew Sheriff Hearst had to be far into retirement, but I wished I'd have at least one friendly face to count on.

It didn't take long for me to pass through downtown. No more than twenty of those brave breaths I'd come to rely on. I'd need them now more than ever.

I thought about stopping at the hardware and grocery stores but knew I needed to get the lay of the land first. I'd called the water and power companies and had them check the lines to our old property, making sure things were still in working order. After a few repairs, they assured me that all was good on their end.

That meant the rest was up to me. The letter from my mother burned a hole in my pocket, but I hadn't been able to simply keep it in my purse. It was as if the words inside could give me the final kick I needed to finish my task.

I hadn't been crazy enough to think that Jacey would help. She had two children and a husband who had a solid job in Seattle. They'd given me more than I'd ever expected. A safe and stable home. One where I was free to go to school and didn't have to fear being woken up in the middle of the night to practice for a raid. They'd made sure I knew that I was loved and cared for. But I wasn't *theirs*.

As soon as Jacey became pregnant, I'd started to feel like an interloper. They were building their family, but they were still stuck caring for me. I'd tried to be helpful. Cooking and cleaning. Babysitting when they needed a break. But I always felt like a guest. Like I never truly fit. It was as if I didn't quite belong anywhere. It was part of the reason I was back. To see if I could finally lay it all to rest and find my place in the world again.

The main road turned into a two-lane highway, and within a

few minutes, I was looking for my turnoff. Street signs on these kinds of roads weren't exactly common, and I was sure the landmarks I'd known as a child had changed. I almost missed the large boulder, the young pine tree in front of it having grown wider and taller over the years.

I braked and made a hard turn. Gravel flew as I hit my mark, but it wasn't the hairpin turn that had my hands dampening on the wheel—it was all the memories. The countless times we'd taken this road to venture into town or to The Trading Post. The afternoons my father had made us run its steep inclines to *prepare*.

My SUV jostled along, exposing new potholes and old, familiar ones. The pines towered alongside the road, almost creating a tunnel. The only thing that hadn't changed was the mountain herself. The blue planes and snow-capped peaks welcomed me with a reassurance that there was good here. I only had to look for it. The only real grounding point I'd ever known.

As I veered off my gravel path onto an even narrower road, I was glad that I'd thought to go ahead and get all-terrain tires before I left Seattle. The winters here could be vicious. There were times we hadn't been able to get off the mountain for weeks at a time.

When I took in the final climb my SUV needed to make, I wondered if getting a snowmobile might be a good plan. I'd managed to get a job at the local vet's office with my same vet tech title and only a slight pay dip. I imagined they'd frown on me not showing up due to snow.

I pressed on the accelerator to make it past the final rise, and as I did, the property came into view. My heart seemed to take up acrobatics in my chest, flipping and tumbling, expanding and contracting. My hands gripped the wheel harder as my foot eased off the gas.

The house itself was in worse shape than I'd expected. One of the walls had a gaping hole in it. But the small guest cabin didn't look too worse for wear. The cottage had been in my mom's family for generations, but the house had been my father's construction after they married. She hadn't stayed long after he went to prison, choosing to move us down to the flats to live on some land my uncle owned.

While the generations-old construction of the cabin had held steady, the barn and paddocks hadn't fared nearly as well. The entire structure seemed to lean to one side, and a storm had taken down more than half of the fencing. My back hurt just looking at all the work that needed to be done.

I sighed and pulled to a stop in front of the cabin, releasing my hold on the wheel. My phone dinged, and I sent up a mental thank you to the gods of technology that it seemed I had service up here.

Shay: *Are you there yet? Text me the second you arrive.*

I smiled down at my phone, feeling a little less alone, knowing that I had someone who would drop anything to have my back.

Me: *Just pulled up outside. Cabin looks okay. The house and barn are a disaster.*

Shay: *Are you sure you don't want Brody and me to come help you get settled? We can be there in two days.*

God, I was lucky to have her as a friend, but I wasn't ready to open all the doors I'd need to if they came to stay. There were too many skeletons I didn't want to let out into the light.

Me: *Thank you, but I've got this. Let me get settled, and then you can come for a visit.*

Shay: *I don't like that you're there all alone.*

Me: *I won't be alone for long.*

Soon, I would have this place crawling with animals. It had always been my dream to build a home for neglected or abused animals of any kind. A sanctuary. It was simply coming more quickly than expected.

I turned off my SUV, rolled down the windows, and the pine air swept in. It was different than any other type, the Ponderosa pines. And as it filled me, tears sprang to my eyes. I'd missed this, more than I'd realized.

I leaned back in my seat and pulled out my letter.

Dearest Everly,

I know much of this will come a day late and more than a dollar short, but better that than not at all. Even once the doctors told me the cancer had a hold, I couldn't bring myself to call you, to tell you these things face-to-face as I should've. So, I'll take the coward's way out. That won't be anything new. There were so many times I should've stood up but didn't.

But that's not you. You've always been the bravest person I've ever known. Even before that night. I should've told you, but I didn't—I'm so proud of you, beautiful girl. You made yourself into this amazing warrior all on your own, without any help from your dad or me.

I wish I had a chance to truly see you shine now. That's the price for my sins. To miss all of your beauty and light shining on this world.

This should've come so long ago, but I'm sorry. For not being there for you. For not getting your father the help he needed. For not taking you and your siblings away when things went sideways. I'm so very sorry that I wasn't stronger. That I wasn't more like you.

I don't have much I can give you, but the land's still mine. I know a lot of pain's been poured into the dirt there, but there was good once, too. When I spent summers there with your grandparents. As your father and I made it our home. The babies that grew there. The animals we raised.

Maybe you can find your good there, too.

I understand if you can't. Or don't want to. But I know if one person is strong enough to do it…it's you.

I love you forever and always, my little warrior.

Mom

A single tear splashed onto the page. She'd been gone before I even knew she was sick. Buried before I even knew she was gone. My family hadn't wanted me there. Not my brother—who I was sure still blamed me for everything—my uncle, or any other vast network of relatives still rooted in the area.

To them, I was the enemy, the outsider. And now, I'd returned. The only one who might be happy to see me was my cousin, Addie, but I wasn't even sure about that. We hadn't spoken since I'd left. All of my letters came back, marked as *Return to Sender* in her father's handwriting.

My mother thought I was a warrior, and I hoped she was right. I would need all my armor if I was going to face them again. Because no one would be happy that I was here. And they'd be downright livid when they learned I was staying.

Chapter Two

Hayes

"I'M TAKING LUNCH," I called to one of our newer deputies.

Young nodded, her ink-black hair not moving from its tight bun with the motion. "Calls forwarded to your cell or no?"

"Only if it's truly urgent." I paused when I reached the door. "That does not include one of Ms. Pat's cats going missing."

Young's cheeks pinked beneath her tanned skin. "Sorry about that. She was really insistent that you would want to know."

"She always is. Don't worry about it. You'll learn the frequent flyers from the true emergencies with time."

Her shoulders eased a fraction. "I hope so. I just don't want to make a mistake."

I turned to face Young fully. "You're going to make one, so just let that go right now. It's how you recover from it that counts. The best officers are the ones who own their mistakes and learn from them."

"Thanks, Sheriff. I'll try to remember that."

"And if you have questions, you only need to ask."

She nodded, and I headed out the door. I could've gone for

my SUV, but I needed the walk. I always got itchy this time of year, my skin a little too tight, and muscles aching for a long run. That was on the agenda for tonight, just Koda, me, and the trails for at least ten miles.

I pulled out my phone and typed a text.

Me: *Lunch at the bar and grill? If you can steal away from your precious pole for an hour.*

A second later, my phone dinged.

Calder: *It's amazing you cops can even walk down the street with your heads as big as they are. See you in ten, just finishing up some paperwork.*

Me: *It's Sheriff. There's a difference.*

I chuckled and slid my cell back into my pocket. Making my way down the street, I could just make out the lake through the trees. The view never got old, and I couldn't imagine wanting to live anywhere else. I'd done the college thing a few hours away but couldn't wait to get back home.

Not everyone felt that way. My older brother certainly hadn't. He'd run out of this town like his feet were on fire. Trading ranch life for every adrenaline-fueled adventure he could find. But I'd been more than happy here.

"Hayes," a voice called from the florist and gift shop up the street.

"Afternoon, Ms. Honeyman. How are you?"

"I've told you time and again, call me Charlene. You're grown now."

I gave her a grin. "It's hard to break old habits."

"That's because your mama raised you right."

"She did her best, anyway. What can I do for you?"

She looked back at her shop and then out towards the streets dotted with tourists and residents alike. "I'm wondering if you have any plans for all of the shoplifters. They're bad this summer. It's the tourists, no doubt."

I'd call my summer a good one if my worst calls were shoplifting and missing cats. Unfortunately, we got our share of car accidents and near-drownings. But, thankfully, things stayed fairly mellow with a community as tightknit as Wolf Gap. "I'm asking the officers and deputies to make their rounds on foot. They'll be stopping by the shops and will be a visible presence on the street."

"I hope that helps. You know it's a fine line to stay in the black."

Charlene wasn't wrong. When your town relied on tourists, a rough winter or summer with bad forest fires could mean businesses closing and people hurting. I patted her shoulder. "We'll do everything we can. And you just call the non-emergency line if you see anything suspicious."

"I'll do that. You're a good boy. Always were."

I waved her off, doing my best to hold in my laughter. It didn't matter that I'd turned thirty this year. I'd forever be a *good boy* in her eyes. I picked up my pace, hoping to avoid people stopping me at every shop along the path. I nodded at tourists and waved at familiar locals. By the time I reached the Wolf Gap Bar & Grill, I wished I'd taken my damn SUV.

Pulling open the door, the air conditioning hit me in a refreshing wave. "Hey, Cam."

The hostess's smile turned up a few notches. "Hey, Hayes. Calder's already here." She gave a little pout as she led me towards a table where Calder was already seated. "Ignoring me as usual."

I swallowed back a chuckle. "How are your parents?"

"Everyone's good. We're taking the boat out on the lake this weekend…" She shot Calder a grin that spoke of things beyond her years. "Maybe you wanna come with?"

He rubbed at the back of his neck. "I've gotta work. But thanks."

"You know what they say about all work and no play…"

"That it makes Calder boring as hell?" I cut in.

Cammie laughed and waved me off. "He's not boring. Calder just needs someone to show him how to have a little fun." And with that, she sauntered off with a sway to her hips.

I let out a low whistle. "She's not messing around trying to get your attention."

"It's bizarre. I feel like Hadley was babysitting her just yesterday."

"When my little sister has been someone's babysitter, I feel like it's an automatic no-go."

He gave an exaggerated shiver. "Let's make that one a rule."

"Adding it to the book." I picked up the menu and set it at the edge of the table. I'd memorized its contents decades ago, and it barely changed. Even the specials on the chalkboard were predictable. Thursdays would always be chicken-fried steak, and Saturdays some sort of pasta. "Everything quiet at the fire station?"

Calder nodded to his radio on the table. "So far. We had to grab Tommy Bixley off his parents' roof yesterday. He'd made himself Batman wings that he wanted to try out."

"Sounds like something we would've done."

His mouth pressed into a thin line. "Maybe, but he could've been hurt."

My friend of thirty years had lost his desire for mischief when his ex-wife, Jackie, had almost cost him his girls. Now, he saw the world through a much more serious lens, and as much as I tried to get him to let loose, I understood. He had sole custody of the girls now, and that came with a weight I hoped I never had to shoulder. "How are Birdie and Sage?"

"Giving me a head of gray hair."

"Wouldn't be doing their job if they weren't. Why don't you bring them over for dinner on Sunday?"

"Sounds good to me. Ask your mom if I can bring anything."

I grunted. "You know what she'll say."

"*Just bring you and those two angels.*" Calder grinned. "She doesn't live with them when they're about to tear each other's hair out."

"Maybe not, but Hadley and Shiloh could get into it pretty good growing up." My two sisters had fought like cats and dogs, and they could still dip into it now and again.

Calder adjusted the silverware at the side of his paper placemat. "That's true enough."

"What?"

His nervous fidgets were a dead giveaway that Calder was holding something back. His gaze lifted to meet mine. "I heard someone was moving into the old Kemper place up on the mountain."

I stilled, my hand tightening around my water glass. "I hope whoever was insane enough to buy it levels the place." I'd like to be the one to go after it with a sledgehammer. Maybe burn up the pieces.

It was crazy how a single piece of property could hold so much pain. Five days that had changed my family forever. There was no way it could be any different. I knew from all the cases I'd worked that mere seconds could change everything. But for us, it had been five days.

We'd gone to the fair as a family, and five days later, we were unrecognizable. For months, my mother had cried every time she had to let one of us out of her sight. My dad had spent his days trying to console her and give us some sense of normalcy. And my siblings had coped—however they could.

But every time I saw Shiloh take off into the wilderness by herself or leave mid-conversation because something triggered her, that anger in me built. I knew Howard Kemper was sick, but that knowledge didn't help soften my rage.

"Hayes. You okay?"

I cleared my throat and focused on my friend. "Fine."

"Don't bullshit me. You've been with me at my worst."

"And you've been with me at mine."

Calder had kept my head above water when guilt was eating me alive. When all I could see was Shiloh's hand. The one I was supposed to hold on to but had let go of to play a stupid fair game.

He jabbed his finger into the table. "Then don't give me some dumb party-line. Give me the truth."

That was the kind of friendship we had—one full of ugly truths instead of pretty deceptions. And I wouldn't spit on that by lying now. "I hate what having someone there will bring up for my family."

"I get that. But they're strong. So much stronger than they were fifteen years ago."

"We're functioning. There's a difference. But Shiloh still runs off into the woods. Hadley and Mom can barely talk without one of them storming off. And I've lost track of where Beckett even is."

"No family is perfect. Everyone has their baggage."

Calder was right. The Eastons just had more than our fair share. "I'll take a drive up there after lunch and see what's what."

He eyed me carefully. "Let me see if I can get someone to cover my afternoon shift, and I'll come with you."

The corners of my mouth tipped up. "I'm not going to start brawling just because someone bought the old place. I've got a little more self-restraint these days."

"It wouldn't be the first time I had to pull you out of something."

"I'm not fourteen anymore."

Calder held up both hands. "I just want you to know that someone always has your back."

"Appreciate it, man. But I can handle this one." At least, I thought I could. It had been fourteen years since I'd set foot on that property. I'd gone once when I was sixteen.

I'd needed to see it. The place that had stolen so much from my family. Calder had driven me up there, and he was the one who'd stopped me from doing something stupid like burning the whole place to the ground. Most of our community completely ignored it. As if by doing so, they could erase what Howard Kemper had done. Erase the knowledge that we were all more vulnerable than maybe we thought.

But I didn't have that luxury. I knew all too well that you were always just one breath away from having your life ripped out from under you. Mere seconds from your whole world changing. Five days out from becoming an entirely different person. And I didn't need a shed on a mountain to remind me.

Chapter Three

Everly

I MUTTERED A CURSE WHEN A CLOUD OF DUST ENGULFED ME as I opened a closet door. The bones of the cabin might have been in good shape, but that didn't mean it was pristine. Far from it.

I'd spent last night on an air mattress in one of the two bedrooms in the cabin, trying to adjust to the deafening quiet, interrupted by sounds that had once been familiar. The old owl. Crickets. Wind rattling the screen door.

I had a couple of days before my furniture arrived. The contents of my small apartment wouldn't fill the space, but it would be good enough for now. Creating a sanctuary wouldn't come cheap, and even though I'd been saving, I needed to pinch pennies wherever I could.

But that was one of the things my mother had taught me that I'd held onto. How to repurpose broken things or stuff others had thrown away. How to make the old new again. She'd also taught me how to live from the land. What things grew heartily here, and what needed the protection of a greenhouse.

I peeked through the large front window at the glass building that had lost many of its panes to winter storms. Those would be a challenge to replace. I added it to my mental list as my gaze shifted past the greenhouse to a green metal roof.

The one I'd told the sheriff about all those years ago. The structure where a little girl had pounded on the door, begging to be set free. I gave my head a little shake. Of course, it hadn't been one of the things the storm took down. It would've been easier if it had.

I turned away from the window and refocused on my sweeping. I brushed the bristles of my broom across the wide planks of the floor and then moved into the open closet. I let out a high-pitched squeal as a furry critter shot out of the dark space. My hand flew to my chest as my heart hammered against my ribs. "Not a monster, just a little…" Chipmunk?

The knowledge startled a laugh out of me. I'd almost lost it over possibly the cutest and least intimidating creature on this mountain. And now I could see that he was limping. He made his way over to the corner, shaking. "I'm sorry, little guy. I think we scared each other."

I moved towards the kitchen that opened to the larger living and dining areas. Pawing through the totes of groceries I'd brought and still hadn't put away, I found a bag of almonds. I picked out a handful of nuts and crossed back to within just a few feet of the little critter.

I sat on the floor and tossed out an almond so it was just a couple of inches in front of him. The chipmunk eyed me carefully and then slowly reached for the nut, shoving it into his cheek.

"Want another one?" I repeated the action but dropped it just a little closer to me, trying to check the critter's movement.

He scurried forward with that same gimp and grabbed another one, stuffing it into his other cheek.

"Those chubby little cheeks are pretty dang cute. Bet you've been hungry living in that closet."

I held out another almond, this time placing it flat on my palm. The chipmunk looked at me as if I were crazy.

"I promise, I won't hurt you."

We stayed in a silent standoff for a moment, and then Chip made a lopsided dash forward, grabbed the nut, and ran away to his corner.

"See, that wasn't so bad, was it?" I dumped the rest of the nuts onto the floor and rose to open the door. "You can have those."

It was official. I was losing it. Talking to a chipmunk as if he could understand every word that came out of my mouth.

Well, it would likely be a pretty lonely existence living in Wolf Gap. I needed all of the friends I could get—even if one of them was a chipmunk.

I returned to my sweeping, and Chip devoured his feast. My broom grabbed something that I realized was Chip's nest. I crossed back to the kitchen and snagged a pair of gloves, pulling them on. I ducked into the closet and found the nest. Guilt clawed at me for disrupting the little guy's home. I didn't think he would do well outside; he moved too slowly and would likely get snapped up by something larger.

I searched the room for any sort of answer. The old built-ins on the opposite side of the living space seemed like as good an idea as any. I opened one of the bottom cabinets and carefully set the nest inside. Three nuts fell out as I did so.

"Apparently, you're not so hard up for food."

Chip hopped and scampered inside, his new bounty stuffed in his cheeks.

Just as he did, the sound of tires crunching on gravel filled the empty room. My heart gave a healthy lurch, and I moved to the corner where I'd placed my gun safe. I plugged in the code and pulled out my shotgun. If my family was making an appearance already, I was in for a battle.

I stood to the side of the large window, angling myself so I was protected but also had a view of whoever was coming. I caught sight of the lights fixed to the top of an SUV, then the sheriff's star. I wasn't sure if the vehicle made me more or less nervous. But at least I knew I didn't need my gun.

I placed it back in the safe and tried my best to brush the dust off my clothes. It was a lost cause. Crossing to the entryway, I pushed open the screen door as a sheriff's department SUV came to a stop in front of the cabin. I swallowed against my suddenly dry throat as a man climbed out.

He was younger than I'd expected. Dark hair and broad shoulders. Thick scruff gracing his jaw. But it was the eyes that stole my breath. Not because of how gorgeous they were but because they were familiar. The same pair that had haunted my dreams for the past fifteen years. Ones that still held fierceness but also untold pain.

I grabbed hold of the porch rail to keep myself upright, and the man who I'd only ever known as a boy circled his SUV. He tipped his head in greeting. "Afternoon, ma'am. I'm Sheriff Easton. I heard we had a new resident and wanted to introduce myself."

He wasn't simply an officer or a deputy, he was the sheriff. And Hayes Easton didn't remember me at all. I cleared my throat. "Hello, Sheriff. I'm Everly Kemper."

He froze, his foot halfway to the bottom step of my porch. "Everly."

I nodded. "I know, it's been a long time."

His parents had protected him from the trial, but my uncle had demanded that Mom, Ian, and I go. He said the jury needed to see that Dad had family. Support. So, I'd been forced to hear every argument and detail, to watch as my dad lost it during closing arguments, yelling about evil and righteousness.

But Hayes hadn't been there. He'd only come one day with his older brother. They'd attended the verdict reading. I'd watched as his mother kept a protective arm around him the entire time. How his father had ruffled his hair and tried to cut the tension with a joke. And his eyes had called out to me, so serious and full of pain.

His foot settled firmly back on the dirt. Apparently, he was no longer coming up those front steps. "You getting the place ready to go on the market?"

"No. I'm moving in."

Those eyes lit with something entirely different now. Hot anger. It felt as if flames were swirling in their depths. Ones that could lash out and burn me without a second's notice. "Hasn't your family put mine through enough? Why the hell do you need to come back here and stir everything up again?"

Each word was a carefully placed blow. It wasn't that I hadn't expected some blowback. I guessed I'd simply thought I would have more time to prepare. And it wasn't as if my family had disappeared from the area. My uncle's ranch was just a few miles down the road in the flats. I was sure Hayes and his family saw them now and again.

"My mother left this to me in her will." I wasn't sure what else to say. I didn't owe Hayes an explanation. Yet, somehow, I felt I did. I'd be paying for the sins of my father for the rest of my life—especially if I lived here.

"Sell it."

"Excuse me?"

Hayes' fingers wrapped around the railing, his knuckles bleaching white. "Sell the damn property. Maybe someone will buy it and finally tear everything down. Build something fresh here that doesn't remind my sister and the rest of us of the hell we all went through."

My knees began to quiver, but I locked them to keep steady. "I'm trying to build something fresh here."

"You're a Kemper. Whatever you build here will still be laced with the pain your father wrought. Do everyone a favor and go back to wherever you've been for the past fifteen years."

I stiffened my spine. "I'd like you to leave now. Unless you have a warrant, that is."

A muscle along Hayes' jaw ticked. "Think about what I said. You won't receive a warm welcome here."

I watched as he retraced his steps and climbed into his SUV. I had known I wouldn't receive any warmth from this town. Yet, somehow, I'd hoped. That I could atone for something that wasn't even mine. That I could make things right. Find a home again in the mountains that had always soothed me when life was roughest. Maybe even find peace after all of these years. But I'd been naïve in my hope. And Hayes Easton wasn't going to let me forget it.

Chapter Four

Hayes

I BROUGHT MY SUV TO A STOP OUTSIDE MY PARENTS' RANCH house. Turning off the engine, I simply sat there, staring at the place that had always been *home*. The immaculately painted white siding, and rough, exposed wood beams. It had been in my mother's family for generations. And you could feel the history as you walked from room to room.

It held so many of my happiest memories. Christmas mornings. Looking out my window to the first snow of each season. Epic games of hide and seek with my siblings. The time my dad had brought home a new puppy.

But it held pain, too. My mother in hysterics as the sheriff promised to do everything in his power to find Shiloh. Seeing my dad breaking down on his way to the barn, unable to hold it together and feeling the need to hide that from my family. Shiloh's screams as she woke from a nightmare.

Koda stuck his head between the two front seats, pressing into my arm as if he could sense the progression of my thoughts. I scratched between his ears. The German shepherd had failed out of the K-9 program for being too friendly, but he was the perfect companion to come home to every night.

"What do you say we go in and find ourselves some dinner?"

Koda gave a half-whine, half-bark. I chuckled and gave him another rub. "Okay."

Climbing out of the truck, I opened the door to the cab, and Koda took a flying leap. He went straight for the front door and then looked back at me as if to say, "*Hurry up, would you?*" I shook my head and trudged up the porch steps.

My feet might as well have been dragging. All afternoon, I'd thought about how to tell my parents and Shiloh what I'd learned. I still hadn't found the right words.

Just as my foot hit the top step, the front door opened. Koda did a happy leap as my mom appeared. She grinned at the dog and bent to give him a good rubdown. "Well, isn't this a pleasant surprise? I didn't think I would lay eyes on you until this weekend."

I crossed the space and pulled her in for a hug. My mom's small form was deceiving. She was petite but could rope cattle with the best of them. She could run a fence line and soothe a skittish colt. I pressed a kiss to the top of her head. "I hope you don't mind me showing up without warning."

"You know I don't. I'm happiest when all my chicks are home." She pulled back and surveyed my face. "Come inside and tell me what's got those worry lines popping up on your forehead."

I should've known I couldn't hide anything from her for long. "Are Dad and Shy here?"

Mom held open the door for Koda and me. "They're on the back deck grilling the chicken. This serious?"

I nodded and wove through the open ranch house. A large living and dining area spilled into a kitchen that would make any chef jealous. And the entire back wall was dotted with massive windows, making it feel as if the house were open to the fields behind it. Cows and horses grazed on land that went on for miles. Property that ran right up to the mountains.

It had been more than a little disturbing that we could almost see the shed where Shiloh had been held for five nights. The mountain seemed to taunt us, even now. But the range was still beautiful—that beauty was simply haunted.

I opened one of the French doors, and Koda bounded over to Shiloh. She sat on the end of a lounge chair, and Koda put his paws on her shoulders. She'd always loved animals, but after her kidnapping, she'd started to spend more time with them than anyone else. Koda licked the side of her face, and Shiloh laughed.

There wasn't a better sound than my sister laughing, a confirmation that she was happy and safe. And now I had to ruin it.

My dad's hand clamped down on my shoulder in greeting. "What're you doing out here? I thought you were on duty tonight."

"I switched my shift to tomorrow."

Mom joined us on the back deck. "Hayes has something to tell us, and it's serious."

Dad's gaze turned assessing. "What's going on?"

I shot a sidelong look at Shiloh, who picked up on it immediately, her spine stiffening. She'd developed this built-in radar for people looking at her or whispering, an ability finely honed over years of living in a small town where she was the biggest story to gossip about. My jaw worked back and forth as anger heated in me again. "Everly Kemper is back. She's living at their old property."

My mom froze, her gaze drifting to the Kemper property up on the mountain. "I didn't think she'd ever come back."

"Neither did I." The words came through clenched teeth, and Mom's gaze drifted back to me.

"There could be a lot worse news."

I glanced at Shiloh, who seemed lost in a world of her making, imagination or memory taking over. "This is pretty damn bad in my book," I hissed at my mom, inclining my head towards Shiloh.

My sister startled from her haze and sent me a death glare. But as usual, she didn't say a word, simply took off for the barn, my dog following in her wake. I muttered a curse. "That was what I was worried about."

My mom rubbed my back like she'd done when I was a little boy. "Nothing about the path Shy has had to walk has been easy. The gossip mill is bound to kick up, and that pisses me right off. But since you've given her a heads-up, Shiloh will steer clear of town for a bit."

"She shouldn't have to," I gritted out.

"You're right, she shouldn't. But life isn't fair. It certainly hasn't been for Everly Kemper."

I bit back the words that wanted to escape. Dad watched as Shiloh disappeared into the barn. "I can't imagine how scared that little girl must have been. Only eleven. Riding down that mountain in the dark to do the right thing. And her whole family turned on her."

I tried to push the image out of my mind. I didn't want to see Everly as a little girl, scared and alone. I didn't want to think about her or her family at all.

My mom took hold of my arm, giving it a squeeze. "How'd you hear about this, anyway?"

"Calder heard that someone had bought the place, but I guess he was wrong. I went up there to introduce myself, and there she was."

She gripped my biceps harder. "Hayes Easton, please tell me you were warm and welcoming to that girl."

Heat crept up the back of my neck. "She doesn't need warm and welcoming. She needs to go back to wherever she came from."

Dad set his barbeque tongs down with a clang and turned

around to face me dead-on. "That girl saved your sister's life. A couple more days and she could've died of dehydration. She risked everything for someone she didn't even know."

"Her father kidnapped Shiloh!" I couldn't believe my parents were taking this in stride. So happy to have the memory dug up and salt poured into every wound.

"Hayes…" My mom's voice grew quiet, thick with emotion. "It kills me that Shy will never be the same because of the actions of a sick man. But none of it was Everly's fault. You need to open your eyes a little more. You've always seen things in black and white, but life is shades of gray."

I pulled my keys out of my pocket, fisting them so the bite of pain would keep me in check. "I just wanted to give you a heads-up. I'm going to head back to town now."

Mom laid a hand on my forearm. "Hayes, don't do that. Stay. Have dinner. Shy'll be back when she's ready, and we can all eat together."

I couldn't refuse. Not when there was so much hurt in my mother's voice. She might not recognize it, but that pain was there because Everly had returned. Stirring things up just like I'd feared. We'd be lucky if Shiloh had only retreated to her loft above the barn. If it was a bad episode, she'd grab her horse and her pack and disappear for days, leaving us all worried half to death.

I just couldn't see Everly as a hero. Couldn't erase her ties to the man who'd destroyed so much of the heart of my family. I simply wasn't built that way.

Chapter Five

Everly

Pulling into a parking spot outside the hardware store, I kept my hands firmly on the wheel. I'd mentally donned my armor all the way here, bracing myself for any ugliness that might come my way. If Hayes' reaction was anything to go by, I'd have to get used to it.

I rolled my shoulders back and turned off the engine. More than a few projects around the cabin needed my attention. Drawer pulls that needed replacing. A few warped cabinet doors. A bedroom door that needed to go. And paint. I needed lots of paint.

I'd decided that paint was the solution to ushering out the old and bringing in the new. Fresh colors on the walls to bring in light and drown out memories. I still hadn't been able to bring myself to venture inside the main house. Making the cabin mine would have to do for now.

Climbing out of my SUV, I shut the door and beeped the locks. As I strode towards the old-timey store, the same one my father had taken us to so many times before, my steps faltered. I hadn't seen her in fifteen years, but I would've recognized her anywhere. The long braid down her back, the high cheekbones tinged pink.

"Addie," I called.

My cousin whirled around, her eyes going wide. "Evie?"

I didn't think, I simply launched myself at her, wrapping her in a hug. "I missed you."

She stiffened in my arms, pulling away. "What are you thinking coming back here?"

"Mom left me the mountain property."

Addie's gaze jumped around the parking lot. "You should sell it. Go home to Seattle."

Her words stung—a hell of a lot more than the ones from Hayes. "I knew some people wouldn't welcome me back, but I honestly didn't expect that from you."

She grabbed my arm. "That's not what I mean. I'm so glad to see you. But not everyone will feel the same."

"Adaline. Step back from that traitor."

The voice cracked like a whip through the asphalt, and Addie immediately dropped my arm.

My gaze rose to meet the cold eyes staring back at me. "Uncle Allen."

He spat at my feet, thankfully missing my shoe. "I'm not your uncle. If it were up to me, I'd take payment for your betrayal with a switch."

Addie flinched behind him, and heat rose to my face. Anger for everything I knew he put Addie through with his fear tactics and cruelty. "You forget," I said in a low voice, "I'm not a child anymore. I know how to fight back. Don't start something with me that you can't finish."

Addie paled as Allen's face turned a shade of red I'd never seen on a human before, but I stood my ground. When I went to live with my sister, I'd felt powerless. I was so terrified that I barely slept. It didn't help that my uncle and brother had shown up to Jacey's home and my school multiple times to make a scene. They couldn't simply let me go. In their minds, I needed to atone for my sins.

Even after Jacey and Kevin had moved us to a place that Allen and Ian didn't know about, I was still on edge. I'd felt as if I were losing my mind, piece by piece. Jacey had finally sat me down and told me that I needed to find things that would make me feel safe.

I'd built that wall of safety, brick by brick. I'd thrown myself into self-defense training with a single-mindedness that I knew sometimes scared Jacey. I'd begged Kevin to continue the firearms training my father had started. Dad's fixation on preparedness and self-reliance had been the one gift he'd left me with. When my classmates were all building profiles on the newest social media app, I refused to be in a single photo.

I'd become obsessed with making sure my family never had a way to find me again. I'd relaxed over the past five years, easing my restrictions, living life more freely, and no longer constantly looking over my shoulder. But I hadn't relaxed a single thing about preparing for something bad to happen. The events all those years ago had taught me that bad things could happen to anyone.

And as I looked at my uncle, who spluttered and raged, I hoped he'd take a swing. He had no idea what would be waiting for him if he did. My eyes focused on looking for the signs. The weight shift. The angle of a shoulder. The retreat of an arm.

Allen's hands balled into fists, his knuckles bleaching white. "You will have to face what you've done. I can't believe you had the audacity to come back here. Just wait until Ian hears."

The sound of my brother's name made me flinch. My hand wanted to curve around my ribs protectively. I could still hear the crack of bone. Feel the steel-toed boot meeting my torso time after time. I could taste the blood in my mouth. But for all the pain I'd endured that night, I wouldn't wish it away. Because it had been the thing that'd freed me. The last straw that gave my mother the push she needed to send me to Jacey. The final breaking point that let me let go of every last tie to my family.

At least, that was what I'd thought. Until the letter. A collection of words on a page that had made me realize I hadn't moved on. There were ghosts I still needed to exorcise.

I didn't look away from my uncle's face. "If Ian wants to come for me, let him come."

Addie shook her head. She stayed silent, her eyes begging me to stand down, to be quiet. But those things had never been my strong suit, and now I was even better equipped to fight my battles.

Allen sneered. "You think you're better than us, with your fancy education and worldly ways. You haven't lived here in a long time. That mountain can bite, girl. And we might just help it along."

"I don't think I'm better than you. I *know* I am. But not because of anything I have. Because I don't prey on those weaker than me. That doesn't make you strong. It makes you an asshole."

Allen's hand lashed out, aiming for my cheek. I was ready with my block, my other hand poised for a palm strike to his nose, but Allen's palm never made contact with my skin. Tanned fingers wrapped around Allen's forearm. I followed the limb up to a face with dark, haunting eyes. Eyes that had held so much judgment just yesterday. Now, they were full of anger, but that rage wasn't directed at me. It was solely focused on my uncle.

"That, Mr. Kemper, is attempted assault."

Allen ripped his arm from Hayes' grip. "I was trying to teach the girl some respect. You don't need to intrude. It's a family matter."

"It's a matter of law." Hayes inclined his head to a female officer. "Deputy Young, please take this man into custody."

A woman whose face spoke of her Native American heritage stepped forward, and she began reading Allen his rights as she placed him in handcuffs. Allen blustered and threatened. When none of that worked, he turned his head towards Addie. "Get Ian. Now."

Addie quickly nodded and headed towards Main Street, barely sparing me a glance, her eyes wild with fear. I wanted to reach out, to pull her to me. To tell her to run in the opposite direction. But she wouldn't have heard a word I said. Allen had her just where he wanted her, under his thumb.

I glared at Hayes as his deputy placed Allen in a squad car. "Was that really necessary?"

His eyes flared. "You would've preferred he hit you?"

"Yes. Then I would've been within my rights to kick his ass."

Hayes was silent for a moment. "Or you could've been seriously hurt."

"Which probably would've had you dancing a jig."

A cool heat filled Hayes' eyes. "I may not want you here, but I take my job seriously. That means if any citizens of this county are at risk, I'm going to step in."

I searched his face, looking for any signs of deception. There were none. This town was lucky to have someone who cared so deeply for its people—even those he despised. "Well, you'll be happy to know you can take me off that list of people to worry about. I can take care of myself."

A muscle ticked along Hayes' jaw. "You haven't been here in a long time. Your uncle's and brother's beliefs have only intensified. They think the law doesn't apply to them."

I swallowed against the lump in my throat. We'd been raised to be self-sufficient. To survive without help from the outside world. To rely only on the people in our small little community. Sometimes, I wondered if the obsession with preparedness had fed my father's illness. It certainly hadn't helped.

There was beauty in that world, too. People who chose to live off the land and treat it with care. Those who wanted to create self-sustaining communities where everyone was looked after. But the Kemper family looked at everyone with distrust— as a potential enemy or thief.

I met Hayes' hard gaze. "Trust me, if anyone knows what my family is capable of, it's me."

Chapter Six

Hayes

"Hell," I muttered as I watched Everly weave through the parking lot towards the hardware store.

"Looks like my big brother finally met a woman who will put him in his place."

I turned to face Hadley, who grinned from ear to ear. "It's not funny, Hads."

She only smiled wider. "I'm pretty sure it is. Who is she, anyway?"

I scrubbed a hand over my jaw and wanted to let a slew of curses fly. I hadn't had time to fill Hadley in on the latest developments. "Everly Kemper."

The grin slipped from Hadley's face as her eyes widened. "*That* Everly Kemper? The one who…?" She let her words trail off as she watched Everly disappear into the store. "I can't believe she's back."

"It's not a good situation." It was more than that, though. After watching the encounter with Allen, I knew things were volatile. A powder keg just waiting for a spark.

Hadley's gaze turned shrewd. "Please tell me you weren't a giant asshole to her."

I blanked my expression. "What do you mean?"

She let out an exasperated sigh. "You know I love you. The kind of love that means I'd do anything for you."

"But?"

"*But* you have taken what happened completely on your shoulders."

My gaze drifted away from my baby sister towards where they'd be setting up the fairgrounds any day now. "I was supposed to be watching her."

"You *were* watching her. You turned your back for a few minutes to play a game."

"And because of that, Shiloh will never be the same."

"Bubby…"

At the use of her childhood nickname for me, I looked back to Hadley. "It's the truth."

She shook her head. "If it hadn't happened right then, it would've been some other time when someone else had their back turned. He was a sick man, and he was obsessed."

"But it wasn't some other time. It was when *I* was supposed to be watching her."

Hadley gripped my arm. "You have to figure out a way to let this go. You're letting it eat away at you. It's not your fault, and it's certainly not Everly's."

I let out a groan. I knew it wasn't her fault, but Everly was a reminder. Not just to Shiloh and my parents but also to me. If I'd been paying more attention, all of this heartache and pain could've been avoided. Everly was a reminder of my greatest failure. One I'd been working to make up for ever since.

"I know she's not to blame."

Hadley arched a brow. "Does she know you feel that way?"

Uneasiness slid through my gut. Everly had known she would have to face a family that hated her, but me piling things on had likely been a surprise blow. "I'll make it right."

The corners of Hadley's mouth tipped up. "I know you will, Bubby. You always do."

I scowled at her. "Stop calling me that."

"But I love the way it makes your eye twitch."

I wrapped an arm around her neck, bringing Hadley in for a noogie. "What are you doing here, anyway? I thought you were on duty today."

She shoved at my chest, extricating herself from my hold. "Another EMT asked to switch shifts. So, I'm using my free afternoon to fix my leaky faucet. Aren't you proud?"

"Why didn't you call me? You know I would've come over and fixed it."

Hadley rolled her eyes. "You know I am capable of doing things on my own, right?"

"You've made that clear." A little too clear. Hadley was always running off on some new daring adventure. Hiking a range of the Pacific Crest Trail, completely alone. Rock climbing. Trekking Machu Picchu. Riding her bike down mountains. She'd almost given our mother a heart attack more times than I could count.

She stuck her tongue out at me. "Take a breath, brother dearest, it's not the end of the world to have a sister who can take care of herself."

I wrapped an arm around her shoulders, pulling her in for a hug. "I'm proud of you. You know that, right?"

"Doesn't hurt to hear you say it."

"I am. The work you do. The person you are. I'm damn lucky you're my baby sister."

She pinched my side. "You make me cry in public, and I'll put your hand in warm water the next time you fall asleep on the couch after family dinner."

And she would, too. I gave Hadley a quick kiss on the head and released her. "Try not to get into too much trouble."

"I'll do my best."

Her mischievous tone had me groaning. "Don't forget family dinner on Sunday."

"I might have to work a shift."

"Hads…"

She'd do anything to avoid spending concentrated time with Mom. I kept hoping they'd come to an understanding, see where the other was coming from, but the relationship just seemed to grow more strained.

Hadley twirled her keys around her finger. "I'll try to make it."

"Don't try, do."

"Yeah, yeah. Don't you have a world to save?"

I glanced at my watch. I'd spent far too much time in this parking lot. And I needed to talk to the prosecutor about pressing charges against Allen. Somehow, I didn't think Everly would be much help, but I had to try.

I gave Hadley a chin lift and headed for my SUV. "See you Sunday."

Hadley simply waved and started towards the store.

Keeping my family together would be the death of me.

The sun hung low in the sky, even though it was already seven. I was grateful for the light as I wound my way through the mountain roads. The absence of any streetlights and the frequent steep drop-offs meant navigating them in the dark could be treacherous if you took a turn too quickly.

My back teeth ground together as I imagined Everly doing just that. We still had months before the time change and winter came upon us, but I couldn't stop the image in my mind. It came on the heels of another picture of Everly that had been haunting me all day.

The rise of her chin, the glint in her eye. So prepared to take that hit. She'd been ready to go to war. It made me see her just a little differently. As more than just a reminder of the worst time in my life. The knowledge made me twitchy, as if my skin were too tight for my body.

Koda whined from the cab. I pressed a button to roll down his window. "Happier now?" His tongue lolled in response, and I couldn't help but chuckle.

I turned off the main gravel road and onto the steep incline of a lane I wasn't sure even had a name. I knew for certain the post office didn't deliver out here. Everly would have to come into town to get all of her mail. I was shocked she even had power.

The cabin appeared as I crested the last bit of the hill, the dilapidated house and barn, and past it, the shed. That familiar desire to tear it all down flared to life. I swallowed it down, just like every other emotion I didn't want to look at too closely.

Everly straightened from where she was bent over the railing of the porch steps, sanding block in hand. I just had to hope she wouldn't throw the thing at me. Bringing my truck to a stop, I turned off the engine. Koda let out a whine. "You can come. But only if you're on your best behavior."

My dog seemed to almost nod. Climbing out of the truck, I opened the door to the cab. "Heel, Koda." But my damn dog didn't listen for a second. He took off, tearing around the vehicle and making a beeline straight for Everly. I muttered a slew of curses. "He's friendly, I swear."

Koda was massive, and if you weren't used to dogs, he could be intimidating as hell. But Everly didn't miss a beat. She crouched, setting her sanding block on a step, and met my beast of a dog with open arms. Koda let out a happy yip as her hands sank into his fur. His tongue lashed across Everly's cheek, and her head tipped back as she laughed.

The sound, the image, they stopped me in my tracks. Blond hair cascading down her back, blue eyes shining. And that laugh.

So uninhibited and carefree. Gone was the guardedness that had engulfed Everly the last two times I'd seen her. She was an entirely different person as my dog fell head over heels in love with her.

I cleared my throat, and Everly looked up, that blank mask slipping over her expression again. I wanted the other woman back. The one who was free and unchecked. "I take it you like dogs."

She didn't say a thing, just stared at me as if I were a bug. I toed a piece of gravel with my boot. "Have any more trouble since you left the hardware store?"

"What are you doing here, Hayes?"

It was the first time she'd said my name, and it sounded good on her tongue. Different, somehow. I gave my head a small shake as if I could dislodge the sound from my ear. "The district attorney wants to know if you'll press charges against your uncle."

"No."

"You protecting him?"

She looked up, meeting my gaze without an ounce of hesitation. "I'm trying to find a way to live in the same town as them. I'm not afraid anymore. I'm prepared."

I wished there was even a hint of fear in Everly's eyes. Because fear made you careful. "The D.A. won't move forward with the case unless you're on board." She shrugged a shoulder as she kept scratching behind Koda's ears. Her casualness about it all only ratcheted the tension running through me. "You should at least file a restraining order. With my testimony, you'll get one."

"Why do you care so much?"

My back molars ground together. "I told you. It's my job."

"You're dedicated. I'll give you that," she muttered.

"Look. I don't want it on my conscience that Allen came up here and killed you in a rage. All I'm asking is that you take reasonable precautions. File charges so it's on the record."

Everly stood from her crouch. "I absolve you of any guilt if I get dead. Now, you can go on with your life in peace. It was never my goal to mess that up for you."

She strode up the steps and through the entrance, the screen door slamming in her wake. Koda turned accusing eyes on me. I let out a growl of frustration. "That didn't come out right."

I started back to my truck, motioning for Koda to follow. He paused for a moment, letting out a little whine. "Koda, come." He trotted over to me and jumped into the cab, but he wouldn't meet my gaze.

Great, everyone was pissed at me.

Chapter Seven

Everly

I HELD OUT MY HAND WITH A COUPLE OF ALMONDS. CHIP grabbed them and skittered across the floor in his odd gait, taking the bounty into his new home. I'd cut a small hole in the cabinet door so he could easily get in and out. My only friend in Wolf Gap was warming to my presence. Taking nuts straight from my hand and sometimes coming out to watch me work.

I turned back to the kitchen. All of the cabinets had been painted and new hardware affixed. The oven would likely need to go in the next few months, but it was functional for now. The refrigerator was in surprisingly good shape, and after my thorough cleaning, I was no longer scared to put food inside.

My gaze traveled around the space. My couch, armchair, and coffee table fit surprisingly well. But I desperately needed chairs and a table for the back deck. I had managed to find two rocking chairs for the front porch for a steal, though.

The sound of tires on gravel had my spine stiffening. If it was Hayes again, I was going to give him a restraining order, all right—against him. I moved to the window, slipping behind the curtains I'd just hung earlier that day. One hand went to my shotgun in the safe, and the other pulled back the linen fabric just enough that I could look through.

An unfamiliar truck crested the hill and came to a stop in front of my cabin. The glare of the sun meant I couldn't see who was behind the wheel. I lifted my shotgun so the butt rested in the crook of my shoulder, but the barrel pointed down.

A woman climbed out of the cab, petite and middle-aged with just a hint of gray weaving through her blond hair. She reached into the cab for something, and I stiffened but relaxed a fraction when I saw the covered dish.

Placing my shotgun back in the corner, I crossed to the door. As I opened it, the memories hit me with a force that nearly knocked the air out of me. The grief and panic. The sobs of relief. Her pain had been the most visceral that night, all those years ago. It had clogged the air and nearly choked me.

She must've read the panic on my face because Mrs. Easton upped her smile. "Hello, Everly. It's so nice to see you." A small chuckle escaped her. "That sounded ridiculous. I'll just say I'm really glad to see you."

"Hi." It was the only word I could seem to get out.

Mrs. Easton climbed the steps and handed me the casserole dish. "I hope you eat cheese. This is my famous spinach lasagna. Even my meat-loving family can't get enough of this recipe."

"Thank you, Mrs. Easton." I paused for a moment. "Hayes didn't tell you to poison me, did he?"

She barked out a laugh. "Even if he had, I wouldn't have listened." She sobered. "He hasn't given you the warmest welcome, has he?"

"He's not offering to hold a parade."

Her lips pursed. "I'm sorry about that. He's…well, we'll talk. Get that in the fridge, and let's have a seat in those pretty rockers you have out front."

I nodded, moving into the cabin, but Mrs. Easton didn't follow.

I caught sight of her glancing past the cabin to the house and the shed that lay beyond, pain flashing through her eyes. God, maybe everything on this property *did* need to be burned down. It caused hurt to so many and healing to none. I closed my eyes for the briefest of moments. I was going to change that. To make this place a haven. Then, maybe it could have a whole different effect on the people of this community.

I slipped the lasagna into the fridge and pulled out a pitcher of lemonade. Grabbing two glasses, I filled them and headed back out to the porch. I handed one to the woman who was staring out at the land around us. "Here you go, Mrs. Easton."

"Thank you, hun. It's Julia to my friends. Mrs. Easton was my mother-in-law."

I nodded, unsure if that was an invitation. I certainly wasn't her friend.

She took a sip of the lemonade. "This is delicious. Fresh-squeezed?"

"I think it always turns out better that way."

"I agree. And it doesn't hurt to drink it looking at this view."

I raised my gaze to the expanse in front of us. Forest that dropped off so you could see the land go on forever. Ranches and farms. The lake and the rolling hills. I'd missed it, this view. When I moved to the city, I'd missed the peace it had given, the knowledge that I was so small in the grand scheme of the world. "I'm glad to see it again."

Julia raised her glass towards the fields dotted with cattle and some horses and pointed at a cluster of buildings we could just make out. "That's our ranch. Been in my husband's family for generations."

I'd always wondered about the people who lived there. What their lives were like. Did their dad wake them up at all hours for *training*, to prepare for an attack that he was sure was coming? Were the kids who lived there allowed to go to school? "I didn't know that. I always wondered growing up."

Julia looked in my direction. "How has it been, being back?"

Something about the warmth in her tone had me wanting to spill all my secrets and pain. To lay them at her feet and ask if she could heal them. "It's been…what I expected. I know this town doesn't want me here."

"Oh, hogwash. I'm this town. I want you here."

"You can't. Not really. I know that what Hayes said is true. I bring up bad memories for all of you."

Julia took my hand and squeezed hard. "Yes, bad memories are bound to pop up. But you're also a reminder of my best memory. Being reunited with my girl, my family whole again. *You* gave me that."

The back of my throat burned. "I'm so sorry for what he put you through. I'm sorry I wasn't brave enough to come sooner."

"Oh, Everly. No. That is not yours to take. You were a baby yourself. And so incredibly brave. I thank God for you every night."

A single tear slid out of the corner of my eye. "How's she doing?"

"Shiloh's good. She'll always be a little different. I won't lie. That experience and everything that came after, marked her. She hates attention and marches to the beat of her own drum. But she's happy. Loves helping Gabe and me run the ranch. Has a real gift with horses."

"I'm glad she's okay."

Julia patted my hand and released it. "Me, too. She'll probably come up here before long. I get the sense she's curious about you."

"She's welcome anytime." I couldn't imagine what it would be like to see that little girl grown. But I needed to. There were things I needed to say. Words similar to what I'd given her mother, but different, too.

"Shy will be glad to know that. And I know Gabe would love to officially meet you, too. Hadley, as well."

I couldn't help but notice that she'd left off Hayes and his older brother. I guessed those two weren't Team Everly. But, honestly, four out of six was way more than I thought to have.

Julia seemed to read my thoughts and gave me a sad smile. "Beckett's in Venezuela right now, treating patients and likely driving his motorcycle on crazy mountain passes. And Hayes… it's not you. He blames himself for Shy's kidnapping. And he's turned that into this need to protect us all."

"He blames himself?" I couldn't put that together. He'd barely been a teen at the time.

"He was supposed to be keeping an eye on her. He turned his back to play one of those Duck Hunt games, and when he was done, she was simply gone."

My chest constricted, empathy curling around my heart that I didn't want to feel. It was easier to think of Hayes as a jerk rather than someone trying to protect his family and shouldering baggage that wasn't his to carry. "I'm sorry he's going through that."

Julia's lips pressed into a thin line. "I am, too, but it doesn't give him the right to be an ass."

I barked out a laugh. "It wasn't that bad." She arched a brow. "Okay, it wasn't *good*."

"That's what I thought. I'm sorry he hasn't treated you fairly. He's got a good heart in there, and once he pulls his head out, he'll see the light."

I wasn't so sure about that, but I wouldn't give voice to my disagreement.

"So, tell me what your plans are for this place?"

I traced a design in the condensation of my glass. "I'm creating an animal sanctuary." I didn't say "*I wanted to*" or "*I hoped to*," because failure wasn't an option. And not just because it had been the last thing my mother had asked of me, but because I needed it, too.

"What a wonderful idea. Even though you're on the mountain, you're low enough to have some good grazing spots."

"There are definitely a lot of inclines, but there are some flatter areas, too. It's going to be a lot of work to get everything ready, and I'll have to start small—"

Julia cut me off with a look. "Even taking in just one animal changes the world for that creature."

My mouth curved but my ribs constricted. This was what I'd missed from my mother—gentle encouragement. I had flashes of her guiding me through the planting each spring and helping to gentle a skittish horse, but they were almost sepia-toned, aged and worn. "I've got to figure out what to do about the barn first. It's a mess."

Julia glanced towards the leaning structure, her lips pursing. "I don't want you in there. It looks like it could go down with a strong gust of wind. And the house doesn't look much sturdier. I'll have Gabe come out and take a look. He's overseen all the construction projects on the ranch. Usually works alongside whatever crew we bring in."

"Oh, you don't need to do that."

"I want to. *We* want to help. And I know Shy will love the idea of a sanctuary." She nibbled on the corner of her mouth. "She'll make her way up here for sure. Don't be offended if she walks off mid-conversation, it's just how she deals with things she doesn't want to talk about. Or if she's simply had enough people for a while."

"She's free to be whoever she needs to be with me." I could barely get the words out, knowing the reason she handled life the way she did was because of my father.

Julia patted my hand. "That's one of the greatest gifts a person can give another. The freedom to be who they truly are."

I hoped she was right because I didn't have anything else to give to the woman whose life my father had broken, leaving it tattered and torn.

Chapter Eight

MY MOM DRUMMED HER FINGERS ON THE COUNTER AS she glanced at the clock for the dozenth time in the past twenty minutes. "Maybe you should call your Search and Rescue team leader."

I laid a hand over hers. "She's fifteen minutes late. That's not a call for S&R."

"She isn't answering her phone."

Dad wrapped an arm around her shoulders. "You know how Hadley is when she's hiking. She's on her own schedule."

Mom's mouth thinned. "She should have the courtesy to let us know she's okay, if that's the case. Calder told us he couldn't make it, so we're not worrying about him and the girls."

I winced and stole a glance at Shiloh, who was on the floor with Koda. Shy didn't look the least bit concerned. But then she knew her sister, and this was one area where they were incredibly similar—their need to break free and be out in nature alone. It drove my mom nuts. I'd done everything I could to alleviate her worry and make sure my sisters were safe. Given them emergency kits, even satellite phones. But it still put Mom on edge.

Tires on gravel sounded, and Mom hurried to the front window. I could just make out Hadley's SUV. As soon as my mom caught sight of her youngest daughter, she turned and retreated to the kitchen, busying herself with dinner prep. The slightly frenetic energy told me that we were in for it.

I sighed and squeezed the bridge of my nose where a headache was forming. The front door slammed, and Hadley called out. "Sorry I'm late. I went longer than I'd planned."

Mom chopped a carrot with a bit more force than necessary. "Would a phone call be too much to ask when your family's expecting you?"

Hadley's steps faltered. "I didn't know that I still had to report my movements now that I'm an adult."

"Okay, ladies, I think that's enough," my dad began. "Hadley, your mom was worried. I think you know why. Julia, let's give the girl some freedom. She's grown."

Mom huffed and turned back to the salad. "The lasagna's done so everyone can sit."

Hadley went to the sink to wash her hands, and I came up alongside her, bumping my shoulder into hers. "Your phone was off."

"The battery died, and I didn't have my car charger."

"Hads, that's not safe."

"Quit it. I don't need you on my case, too. You're my brother, not my keeper. You know, people lived their lives before cell phones."

I bit back every retort that wanted to fly from my mouth, every statistic about what could happen to a woman alone. "I'll get you another charger and an external battery for your pack."

Hadley simply rolled her eyes and crossed to the table, sitting as far away from Mom's chair as she could. Shiloh gave Koda one last rub and then followed suit. I turned to Mom. "Want me to carry the lasagna?"

"That would be good. Thank you."

I squeezed her shoulder and then grabbed hotpot holders and the casserole dish. I set it carefully on the risers on the table's surface just as Hadley muttered, "Kiss-ass" under her breath. The tension between my eyes throbbed.

Mom set a salad and the garlic bread down and then slipped into her seat. "So, how was everyone's day?"

Silence met her query. I hurried to fill it. "Three calls from Ms. Pat about her missing cat."

Dad chuckled. "It might be worth some taxpayer money to get that cat a tracker."

"It always comes back," Hadley muttered. "She should just leave it be."

Mom's hand tightened on her water glass. "She's worried about her."

"I bought a new horse," Dad interjected, steering the conversation in a different direction.

For the first time in the evening, Shiloh's gaze sharpened, focusing in on Dad. "Where?"

"Ramsey Bishop."

I set down my beer. "He let you come out to his place?" Ramsey brought the term *loner* to a whole new level.

"No, he brought the gelding here."

"There aren't any new horses in the barn," Shiloh argued.

Dad smiled. "I'm not hiding him from you. Ramsey wants a few more weeks to finish the training."

"No one has a way with horses like he does. Especially the wounded ones," Mom said. "I might want to connect him with Everly."

My spine stiffened. "Why?"

"Because Everly's going to turn that property into an animal sanctuary."

"How do you know that?" It prickled something in me that

my mother had more information than I did about the woman I'd somehow become fascinated with.

"I went out to see her today." She shot a pointed look in my direction. "Someone had to make up for how rudely my son treated her."

Hadley choked on her water as she laughed. "I think Everly can handle herself. She was ripping Hayes a new one the last time I saw her."

Mom's eyes hardened on me. "Really, Hayes? That girl has been through enough. I expect you to get a new attitude, young man."

Hadley snickered. "Uh-oh, she brought out the *young man*. You're in trouble now."

Before my mom could turn her ire on Hads, I cut in. "I know I messed up." Both women turned their gazes on me. "I know it's bound to bring up some tough stuff." I looked at Shiloh, whose eyes narrowed. "I didn't want anyone getting hurt. Especially you."

Shy shoved back from the table, taking her plate and not saying a word. Koda trailed after her.

"Shit," I mumbled.

"Let her go," Mom said, patting my arm.

Hadley's mouth pressed into a hard line, but she didn't say a word.

"So, she's making a sanctuary." I couldn't quite wrap my head around that. It was certainly needed. The sheriff's department got called out on all sorts of animal abuse and neglect cases, and there weren't a lot of options for where those animals could go afterwards.

"Makes sense," Dad said. "I heard she got a job with Miles, working as a vet tech."

Mom assembled the perfect bite of salad on her fork. "From what I can tell, he'll be lucky to have her."

A vet tech. It made perfect sense, yet it was still a surprise. From the few interactions I'd had with Everly, I knew she was tough as nails. But I'd seen a glimpse of her softer side with Koda. Dr. Taylor would be more than lucky to have her.

"Maybe I should get a dog," Hadley mused.

Mom set down her fork. "That means you'd have to be home on a regular basis. No taking off whenever the mood strikes."

I sent an urgent look at Dad, but before he could come up with a way to divert the conversation, Hadley cut in. "And the problem with that is?"

"Nothing, but it's not exactly responsible or safe, either. You know that."

"Yet you have no problem with Shy taking off into the woods for days at a time, no one knowing where she is. You just tell us to let her go."

Mom's jaw worked back and forth. "It's different, and you know that."

Hadley pushed back from the table, tossing down her napkin. "It always is. I should've learned by now that what's acceptable for Shy will never be okay for me."

"Hadley," Dad called as she headed for the door. But Hadley's steps never faltered. He turned his gaze to Mom. "Julia…"

"What?"

"Was that really necessary?"

Her eyes glinted in the low light of dusk. "I'm allowed to be worried about my daughter when she disappears. I worry about them both. But I know with Shy it's because she can't handle something. With Hadley, it's simply because she doesn't care. It's selfish. And I'm allowed to say as much." With her final words, she shoved back from the table and headed for the back deck.

I looked across the table at my dad. "Some family dinner."

He tried to lift the corners of his mouth in a grin but couldn't muster it. Neither of us could. Because those five days all those years ago were still tearing us apart.

Chapter Nine

Everly

"THANK YOU AGAIN FOR TAKING ME ON."

The man in his fifties gave me a kind smile, the dark skin around his mouth forming grooves that told me he made the motion often. "I am beyond thrilled to have someone with your experience on my roster."

Dr. Taylor—Miles, as he'd insisted I call him—seemed as if he would be a dream boss. He was kind, knowledgeable, and ran a tight ship. We'd had several phone calls and a video conference before he made me the job offer, but something about meeting someone in person was the real test. And Miles was a dream.

"You're sure you don't need me this week? I can work a couple of shifts if you do."

He shook his head. "You get settled. There's plenty of work to come. Take some time and get to know the town again. I'm sure a lot has changed since you were here."

"There are definitely some new restaurants I'd like to try."

"I highly recommend Spoons. They opened this year and have a revolving menu of soups, salads, and sandwiches."

"That sounds perfect. I think I'm going to head there now."

He extended a hand to me for a shake. "Sounds like a good plan to me. Welcome aboard, Everly. We're so happy to have you."

"Thank you." I released his grip, picking up my purse and heading for the door. I waved at the receptionist, Tim, who seemed to remember me even though he was a few years younger. But he'd been warm in his greeting, no instant hatred because of who I was related to.

I took a deep breath as I stepped outside, letting the clean air soothe the nerves that had been running rampant since I'd stepped out of my SUV. The first meeting was over, and it hadn't been a disaster. Everyone at the office had been kind.

That knowledge gave me the most dangerous of feelings… hope. That I would be able to make a life here. Possibly have a community. Friends. My phone buzzed in my purse.

Shay: *How's it going? I've been trying not to hover, but I'm dying to know every detail.*

I grinned down at the screen. Even if I didn't make the best of friends in Wolf Gap, I still had Shay. Our friendship was one borne of running from our pasts. Hers had just been more violent than mine. The fact that she'd found a true home gave me another dose of that reckless hope.

Me: *It's been pretty good. How about a catch-up tonight? I'm heading to pick up lunch and then need to run a few errands.*

Shay: *Sounds good. Call me whenever.*

I slid my phone back into my purse. As I looked up, I stumbled back a step. Familiar whiskey-colored eyes met mine. Just as hard as the last time I'd seen them. I straightened my shoulders. I would not cower from him now. I might still be years younger than him, but I was smarter now. Stealthier. And I knew half of Ian's power came from his mind games.

I kept my face perfectly blank. "Hello."

His lip curled in a sneer. "You have a lot of nerve showing your face around here."

"Good to see you, too, brother dearest."

He spat on the ground between us, a move so similar to my uncle's that it cramped my stomach. But that had been the only real influence Ian had over the past few years. "You're no sister of mine."

I wished it was that simple for me. That I could sever every tie with a flick of a knife or a carelessly tossed-out word. But I couldn't. I felt every tether as if it were made of the heaviest chain. It seemed like I'd never be rid of them. "Then I guess there's nothing left to talk about." I moved to step around him, but Ian mirrored the movement.

"When are you leaving?"

My heart rate picked up a fraction, but I did my best not to let the panic show. "I'm not."

"That land isn't yours."

"The deed says otherwise."

Ian's hands fisted and flexed. "I'm the oldest in this family—"

"Actually, that would be Jacey."

"A woman. I'm the leader. By rights, that land should fall to me."

I rolled my eyes. Uncle Allen had clearly been hard at work, inundating Ian with his twisted thinking. The same mindset that meant Addie was never allowed to show her shoulders or knees. "I don't know what to tell you. According to the courts, it belongs to me."

"I don't submit to those courts. Those laws mean nothing."

A faint wave of nausea slid through me. It sounded so familiar—the kind of tirade our father used to go on. "If you live in this country, those laws apply to you."

"Your mind's been warped. You don't remember where you come from. But you will."

He was wrong. I remembered all too well. At times, it felt as if it were burned into my bones and I'd never be rid of it.

Ian smiled, but it had an ugliness to it that had me fighting a shiver. "You could always plead your case to come back into the fold. Signing the land over and submitting to whatever punishment Allen deems right for you would probably do the trick. You might even con Ben into marrying you since his wife died in childbirth."

Nausea swelled and strengthened. I would never go back to that life, but my chest tightened at the mention of Ben's name. The third piece of my and Addie's trio. My best friend. I hated that I hadn't even known he'd gotten married. And now his wife was dead? Probably because of a refusal to take her to a hospital. The knowledge made me rage...for this anonymous woman, for Ben. "I'm afraid I'll have to pass."

"Ian." Uncle Allen's voice boomed across the street. "It's time to go." The hatred pouring from his eyes felt like a living, breathing flame that could burn me alive.

Ian knocked into my shoulder as he walked away. "Watch your back."

I swallowed the bile that crept up my throat, watching as they drove off. Suddenly, lunch didn't sound appealing at all.

Chip sat on the coffee table with a bowl of nuts as I did my best to scrub the oven. The amount of baked-on grease was enough to make me lose the meager amount of food I'd been able to consume this afternoon. It had been more of a battle of wills. I hadn't wanted to give my brother the power to take away my appetite. So, I'd forced a sandwich down once I got home.

Home. I leaned back to rest on my heels. Would this place ever truly feel that way? Chip let out a happy little sound as he nibbled away, and I couldn't help but smile. "Taste good?"

He gave a series of squeaks as if to agree.

I groaned and rubbed at my temples. "I'm losing it. Talking to a chipmunk."

I heard the now-familiar sound of tires on gravel. Taking a long, steadying breath, I made a promise to myself not to kill whoever was coming up the drive. But I wasn't sure I'd be able to live up to that promise. This day had burned away the last of my patience.

I pushed to my feet and took up my usual vantage point at the window, where my shotgun was within reach. Peeking through the curtains, I muttered a curse as I saw the light bar on top of the SUV. "Great, just great." I had half a mind to bring my shotgun out with me, but I resisted.

Crossing to the door, I pulled it open just as Hayes climbed out of his sheriff's department vehicle. Unfortunately, there was no gorgeous dog to temper his visit this time.

I leaned against the porch railing. "You know, you come here a lot for someone who hates the sight of me."

Hayes scowled, the movement somehow making his dark blue eyes shine in the afternoon light. "I don't hate the sight of you."

"That scowl on your face says otherwise."

He let out a long sigh as he came to a stop at the bottom of my porch steps. "I was surprised that it was you when I showed up here. I thought someone from out of town had bought the place."

"And being surprised turns you into an asshole?"

The corner of his mouth quirked up. "It might. I certainly do better when I know what I'm getting myself into." I was silent for a moment, simply taking the man's measure. He shifted on his feet. "I'm sorry. You didn't deserve the greeting I gave you. I was trying to shield my family, but I didn't need to be a jerk to do it. Think you can forgive me for not handling myself well?"

I gripped the railing, my fingers digging into the freshly stained wood. It turned out Hayes could be a charmer when he needed to be. Which meant it was my turn to scowl. "Oh, turn that grin off. I'm not gonna fall at your feet because you flashed those pearly whites at me."

He chuckled. "A smile never hurts when you're trying to get your point across."

"I've always been a believer that actions speak louder than words."

"Let my actions speak, then."

"And what actions would those be?"

Hayes was quiet for a moment, his gaze traveling over the property. "My mom said you were turning this place into an animal sanctuary."

"That's what I'm working towards." Unfortunately, the process was moving as slow as molasses. I still wasn't done with the repairs and renovations on the cabin.

"Let me help you get this place into shape."

My mouth fell open. A fly could've swooped right in. "You… want to help me make repairs on this place?"

He rubbed at the back of his neck. "Why not? My dad said he's coming out this weekend to check out the barn. I can help him. I grew up on a ranch. I know my way around hard work."

I snapped my mouth closed, swallowing the million and one retorts that wanted to surface. Ones that lashed out and told Hayes to get off my property. I took a deep breath. "Okay."

The word was out before I could think better of it. Before I could remember the hatred I'd seen flash in Hayes' gaze that first day. I closed my eyes for a moment, reminding myself that I could take it, whatever his emotions. Because if he didn't let them out, they'd simply fester. To move forward, we had to look at this head-on.

"Okay?" Surprise lit his tone.

I nodded. "You can help on the weekends."

"I have some afternoons off—"

I shook my head, cutting him off. "Weekends are enough." I

couldn't deal with him all week, too. Two days would be more than enough.

"All right, then. I'll see you this weekend. Let me know if there are tools you think I'll need to bring."

"I guess I could send you some smoke signals."

His lips twitched, and the movement stirred something in me that I didn't want to look too closely at. "All right, smartass. Take my number."

I pulled out my phone and unlocked the screen. I typed his name into my contacts. "Ready." He listed off the digits, and I plugged them in. "Prepare for some prank calls."

Hayes groaned. "I guess I'd deserve that."

"You would."

His gaze met mine, freezing me to the spot. "Call me if you need anything."

I wouldn't. "Okay."

He shook his head as if he knew I was lying and turned towards his SUV. "I'll be seeing you."

The words felt like both a promise and a threat. There'd be no escaping Hayes now.

Chapter Ten

Hayes

A KNOCK SOUNDED ON MY DOOR, AND I LOOKED UP FROM the pile of paperwork on my desk to see Calder standing in my doorway. "Look what the cat dragged in after he got it out of a tree."

"After all the calls you get from Ms. Pat, I'd say missing cats are your wheelhouse, brother."

I leaned back in my chair and glared at him. Because he was right. I'd had two this morning already.

Calder barked out a laugh. "She called you today already, didn't she?"

"It's been a long Friday, and it's only nine a.m."

He slid into one of the chairs opposite me at my desk and set down some coffee in a to-go cup. "Maybe this will help."

I eyed him cautiously. "You're bringing me coffee…"

"Yes…"

"You need a favor, or something bad happened."

Calder rolled his eyes. "So suspicious of everyone."

"I'm suspicious of *you* because I've known you my entire life."

"Can't a guy check up on his friend? Make sure he's hanging in there?"

I picked up the cup and took a sip. "Mom told you Everly's back?"

"Hadley took the twins to the park yesterday."

Hads adored Birdie and Sage and loved stealing them away for adventures whenever she could. I scrubbed a hand over my face. "She talk to you about Mom at all?"

"No. They get into it at family dinner?"

"Understatement." Over the years, Calder had become one of the family and had seen more than a few dustups between Hadley and Mom.

His gaze drifted out the window as a muscle ticked in his cheek. "Hads needs to understand that she can't just take off to climb a mountain by herself and expect no one to worry."

"I know that, and you know that, but Hadley's yearned to stretch her wings from the time she was seven. Mom and Dad were protective after what happened to Shiloh, and Hadley took the brunt of it for the longest."

Calder looked back to me. "I get that she needs freedom, but it's not worth her getting hurt or killed."

His words alone caused my chest to constrict, made breathing just a little more difficult. Calder muttered a curse. "Sorry, man. I shouldn't have said it like that. I know you worry about her."

"It's fine." But the tension in my voice argued otherwise.

He studied me for a moment, likely taking in the lie. "Want to come fishing with me and the girls tomorrow? Should be the perfect day for it."

"Can't."

"Helping out at the ranch?"

I picked up a pencil and rolled it between my fingers. "Dad and I are going up to Everly's to assess her barn. It looks like it's one gust of wind away from collapsing."

Calder's brows rose practically to his hairline. "You're going to help out up there?"

I wasn't setting foot near that damn shed. But I didn't mind helping stabilize the barn, run some new fence line—whatever else she needed. "She wants to start an animal sanctuary, and I'm trying to make up for being a total asshole to her when I showed up at her place the first time." Well, the first and the second times.

Calder snorted. "You never did handle surprises well."

"Shut up."

"Sounds like a good use for all that land. And it's something the community could get behind."

"More than a few animals in this county could use a good home."

He took a sip of his coffee and then rested it on the arm of his chair. "You think she'll give them that?"

"I do." Everly had a stubborn determination that meant she wouldn't back down from a challenge. But there was gentleness, too. The way she'd sunk to the ground to engulf Koda in a hug. "She was good with Koda."

"Probably the only way she could've gotten you on her side—being good to that dog of yours."

"Sides have nothing to do with it. I'm just trying to make things right after biting her head off."

Calder's expression sobered. "You gotta let this go, Hayes. The only person responsible for what happened is in jail. He'll be there for a long time. It wasn't Everly's fault, and it sure as hell wasn't yours."

My back molars ground together. "I know that."

"You may know it in your head, but your heart sure as hell doesn't. That guilt is going to eat you alive."

It wouldn't. Not if I didn't let it catch me. It was why I stayed so busy. And why I went on such long runs. "Every time I see someone from that family, it's a reminder of how I failed. Of all the ways my family is still broken. So, I get angry. Not because it's any of their faults, but because when I see them, I have to remember."

"If you're going to be helping Everly, you're gonna need to figure out a way to come to terms with this. It's not fair for you to hold on to all this anger and make her deal with it."

"I know, it's not," I growled. It made me feel like the lowest of the low that anger had been my reaction to seeing the woman who had saved my sister's life when she was a girl. But there was more than anger in the mix now, too. There was also a healthy dose of admiration.

"Okay."

"I'm working on it."

Calder's mouth twitched. "She flusters you. Is she pretty?"

"Pretty?" No, Everly was heart-stoppingly gorgeous. She had the kind of beauty that could bring a man to his knees. I bit the inside of my cheek to stop that train of thought.

"Yeah. Is she attractive?"

I spun the pencil between my fingers. "I guess you could say that."

Calder barked out a laugh. "Oh, man, this is going to be so much fun to watch. Maybe the girls and I should ditch fishing and go up the mountain to watch the show."

"Don't make me deck you. You know I'll do it."

"I'm not scared of you. I know all your tells."

My eyes narrowed at my lifelong friend. "I still have some tricks you've never seen."

"But I'm quicker. That's what happens when you have to do your job with forty-five pounds of gear on your back. That desk you're riding has made you lazy."

"I do not ride a desk," I said through gritted teeth.

Calder inclined his head to a stack of paper on my desk. "What's that? Looks like a whole lot of paperwork to me."

"It's called being the boss. It comes with strings."

"Sure, but just remember what the nail in your coffin was when you try to take a swing at me."

I had half a mind to do it simply to prove Calder wrong. "Get out of my office before I throw this coffee at you."

He chuckled but pushed to his feet. "I have to get to work anyway."

"Enjoy riding that pole."

"Always do, desk jockey."

Just as Calder disappeared, Deputy Young stepped into my office with an amused smile on her face. "Did he just call you a desk jockey?"

"Yes," I growled. "He's an ass."

"He's a firefighter. They're all pompous."

"You're not wrong there. What can I do for you, Young?"

Her feet shuffled as she gripped the back of the chair Calder had vacated. "I, uh, saw something yesterday I thought you might want to know about."

"Okay…"

"I was picking up lunch for my mom and me from Spoons, and I saw Everly Kemper."

Young stopped talking. I waited for a moment, but she didn't say anything else. "She does live here now. You'll probably see her in town."

"I know. It's just… It looked like her brother was threatening her. I was about to step in and see if she needed help when her uncle called Ian off. I've got a bad feeling about those guys, boss."

The coffee in my gut soured. I did, too. And Everly hadn't said a single word when I showed up at the cabin yesterday afternoon. "He touch her?"

"He knocked into her when he walked away. She stood her ground, didn't let him see her scared. But I saw her shaking a bit when she walked to her car."

I bit back a slew of curses. I didn't want to feel this pull to make sure Everly was okay. I tried to justify in my mind that it was simply because this was my job—to protect the citizens of this county. But I worried it was more.

Chapter Eleven

Everly

I LEANED ON THE FENCE AND PULLED. WITH A GROAN, IT gave way in an almost comical domino effect. Post after post, and board after board went down. That answered whether any part of the fence line was salvageable. It looked like an entire new one was on my list. I stepped on a rail with my boot. The wood itself seemed sturdy. That meant I might be able to reuse the materials, but it also meant I'd have to assess each piece.

The sound of an engine caught on the breeze, and I turned to see an old pickup truck cresting the hill. I stiffened, my hand going to the holster at my back and resting there. If my brother thought he'd catch me unaware, he had another thing coming.

But it wasn't Ian who climbed out of the truck. It was a face as familiar as his, but one that had matured over the years. The rest of him had, too, broad shoulders and a leanly muscled form. I froze in place, my body warring with itself. Part of me wanting to run to Ben and engulf him in a hug. The other part felt the need to protect myself from whatever might be coming my way.

"Hey, Evie."

His voice was different, yet the same. And it had tears burning the backs of my eyes. "Hey, Ben."

"Ian said you were back."

I did my best not to stiffen at my brother's name. "I'm sure he had lots to say about that."

"Ian has a lot to say about any topic. Even when he doesn't know anything about it."

His words startled a laugh out of me. "I guess some things never change."

Ben took a step closer. "You have, though."

"Bound to, I guess."

"You gonna take that hand off your gun, or still making up your mind?"

Of course, he knew what my hand rested on. We'd practically grown up together, his family having the ranch next to my uncle's and being just as involved in the prepper community as we were. We'd formed this insular almost-family. Homeschooled together, raced horses, swam in the lake. But all of that had disappeared in a blink.

My hand flexed. "That depends on why you're here."

"To see my best friend."

I studied Ben's face. I didn't see any deceit in it, but that didn't mean it wasn't there.

He took another step closer. "I'll never forgive myself for not protecting you. For not stepping in when Ian—"

The look on my face stopped Ben cold, and his words fell away. The echoes of pain had entrenched themselves there. I usually kept them well disguised, but I couldn't hide them when he brought *that* up. "Someone should've stepped in. I'm not sure it was your job, though."

The feel of Ian's steel-toed boot in my stomach, ribs, and shoulder resurfaced. The pain bloomed as if it were yesterday, not sixteen years ago. I released my hold on the gun, my hands fisting so my nails could dig into my palms as if that small bite of pain could distract from memories of so much worse. It couldn't.

Ben kicked at a rock. "It *was* my job. I'd been looking out for you practically since you were born."

It was true enough, but it only hurt more to hear him say it aloud. "I can't go there. Please, don't make me."

"All right. But I need you to know I've regretted it every day since."

I nodded, unable to get any other words out for a moment. "Why did you stay?"

"It's home."

It was such a simple answer—the ties that bound us to family, the roots that made up our pasts, they were powerful. Far more than I'd given them credit for when I was just eleven years old. "I get that."

"Are you okay? I don't know that you should be staying up here all alone. If I talk to Allen, he'll let you come back. He won't do anything—"

"I can take care of myself." My spine locked tight. It didn't matter how many precious childhood memories I shared with the Ben I'd known as a boy; he was a man now. And he was tied up with a group of people who wanted nothing more than to put me in the place they thought I belonged and deserved—which was likely under their boot.

"I know that you're a capable woman. I admire that. But—"

"But nothing. I'm fine here. And I'm more than protected. You can report that back to Allen and Ian."

"I'm not reporting—" The sound of another vehicle cut off Ben's words. Another unfamiliar truck appeared, and Ben surveyed the driver. When he saw that it was a woman, he turned back to me. "I should get going. I'll come by later and—"

"I don't think that's a good idea."

The hurt that flashed across his face cut, but I just dug my fingernails deeper into my palms. I had to draw a line in the sand because as much as I'd missed our friendship, I wouldn't let Ben try to drag me back to that life. Not now, not ever.

"Okay, then. When you change your mind, you know where I'll be."

My throat burned as I watched him walk back to his truck and drive away. As his taillights disappeared, I tried to convince myself that it was for the best. A door slammed, and I looked at the woman who was standing in front of a dusty truck.

I would've recognized her anywhere. The image of the missing person's poster was seared into my mind. Even a decade and a half of time passing and growing up didn't disguise her.

Shiloh raised her chin and met my gaze. "Who was that?"

I wanted to laugh. She asked the question as if we were life-long friends, and she had every right to know who came and went from my life. "Someone I used to know."

"Friend or foe?"

"I'm not sure. Maybe a little of both."

"Those are always the most complicated ones."

My mouth curved. "You're not wrong there. It's good to see you, Shiloh."

She shifted on her feet. "Is it okay that I came?"

That slight hesitation made my ribs tighten around my lungs. "You're welcome anytime."

The set of Shiloh's shoulders relaxed a fraction, and she surveyed the land around us. Her gaze caught on the shed in the distance. The building that held all of our ghosts—or most of them, anyway. I needed to tear the thing down. Burn it and bury the ashes. Put something worthy in its place.

Shiloh's face shut down, her gaze dropping to her feet as her hands clenched and flexed at her sides. She seemed to be counting silently. I didn't say a word, wanting to give her all of the time and space she needed. After a minute or so, she straightened, turning back to face me. "Thank you. For what you did. I've thought a lot about you over the years. I never had a chance to say that, so I'm saying it now."

"You don't need to—"

"I do." Her eyes blazed with a fierce heat. "The doctors said I probably wouldn't have made it another couple of days. Thank you."

The invisible vise around my torso tightened another notch. How could my family not see? That this sickness in my father had almost cost another family everything? "Are you okay?"

Shiloh lifted one shoulder then dropped it back down. "I'm as good as anyone can be, I think. People might think I'm a little weird. But that's okay with me."

"All my favorite people are a little weird."

The corner of her mouth kicked up as the wind made the long braid down her back swing. "Good taste." She was quiet for a few moments, seemingly not feeling the need to fill the space. "Mom said you're turning this place into a sanctuary."

"That's the plan. As you can see, it's going to take a while."

"Might go faster if you had help."

I met Shiloh's stare. "True enough."

She steeled herself, those hands clenching again. "I'd like to help."

"You would?" I couldn't imagine it was easy for her to be here. Yet she stood steady as a rock.

"Yes."

"I can't really afford to bring anyone on." It would take a wish and a prayer to get this place off the ground without going bankrupt.

"I've got money. Don't need any more from you. And I like animals...a hell of a lot more than people. It would be nice to build a home for ones who could use it."

I studied the woman in front of me. The face that had haunted so many of my dreams. The person I'd wondered about, time after time. "What do you know about fences?"

She grinned. "Dug more than my share of post holes."

"We still have an hour or so of light. Let's tear this down so we can build it back up."

Chapter Twelve

Hayes

DAD GUIDED HIS TRUCK UP THE MOUNTAIN ROAD. "She's gonna have a hell of a time when we get a good snow."

"I had the same thought when I first came up here."

"Should talk to her about snow tires and good chains. I can call Greg about putting her on the plow list for winter. Maybe even get a snowmobile in case of emergency or—"

"Dad."

He glanced quickly at me. "What?"

"It's gonna be okay. She's nice."

He nodded, adjusting his grip on the wheel. "I know that."

"Then I think you can stop chattering about every type of plan for snow."

Dad scowled in my direction. "I wasn't chattering. Didn't anyone ever teach you to respect your elders?"

"Apparently, not."

"I'm rethinking my parenting approach."

"Understandable. You raised a bunch of hooligans."

He snorted. "Ain't that the truth?"

Koda pushed his head between the two seats as the cabin came into view. I gave him a scratch under his chin. "I know you're excited, but you need to behave yourself. You were an embarrassment the last time you were here."

"He jump on Everly?"

"No, just didn't obey a single command."

"Koda," my dad said, leaning his shoulder into the dog, "you're gonna get yourself into trouble one of these days."

"Not with Everly. She loves dogs."

We came to a stop in front of the cabin, and I caught sight of the woman stacking what appeared to be fence posts. Her hair was piled in a messy array on top of her head, blond strands gleaming in the sun. She moved with an ease that said she wasn't a stranger to hard work. Her tank top and worn jeans showed the lean muscles and curves beneath.

"That her?" Dad whispered.

"That's her." I forced my gaze away from the woman I was beginning to worry could drive me to distraction. "Come on, Koda." I slid out of the truck and opened Koda's door as I shut mine. Everly looked up at the sound, but I had a feeling she'd already known we were there. "Incoming," I called as Koda leaped down.

He made a beeline for his new best friend, and Everly dropped her post so she could meet Koda on the fly. She sank to a crouch as Koda's front legs went to her shoulders. He licked her face, and Everly's head tipped back as she let a laugh free. The sound punched me right in the gut, and I almost had to take a step back.

"Well, I'd say those two have hit it off," Dad said, coming to stand next to me.

"Something like that," I muttered.

Everly stood, pulling a treat out of her back pocket. Her gaze met mine. "Is it okay if I give him this?"

"Sure."

She sobered, looking Koda in the eyes. "Sit." With a singular motion of her hand, Koda's butt plunked right on the dirt.

"Well, I'll be. I've never seen him sit so quickly for you when he's this excited."

"Shut up."

Dad's mouth pressed into a firm line as if he were trying to hold back a smile. "It wasn't an insult."

"Sure, it wasn't."

Everly gave Koda the little bone and rubbed his head. "Good boy." She looked up at me. "I was hoping you'd bring him."

"So you were prepared."

A hint of pink flushed her cheeks. "There were some treats by the checkout at the hardware store. Thought it wouldn't hurt to have some on hand."

I adjusted the ballcap on my head to block the sun. "You've made his day."

"A little spoiling now and then doesn't hurt."

"He gets more than a little of that," Dad cut in, taking a step forward. "I'm Gabe. It's wonderful to finally meet you. Thank you for everything you've done for our family."

Everly slid her hand into my father's open one for a shake. "I'm glad to meet you, too. And thanks for coming out here to check out the barn. I'm afraid it might be a total loss."

I didn't miss that she avoided the thanks from Dad. I studied her carefully, trying to figure why that was. I was sure it brought up bad memories at the very least.

Dad inclined his head towards the leaning structure. "Let's go see what's what, and we can take it from there."

"Sure."

Everly led us towards the barn. "I haven't been inside."

I looked up at the building—if you could even still call it that. "That's probably a good idea. It looks like the snow did a number on it."

Dad let out a low whistle. "We'll take a walk around the outside first. I'm guessing it might not be sound to go inside."

Everly's steps slowed as she worried the corner of her lip between her teeth and stared up at the structure. I could see the mental calculations eating up her mind. I doubted she'd been gifted a massive pile of cash to go along with the property, and taking care of animals got expensive when you did it right.

My fingers tapped out a rhythm on my thigh. The urge to reach out and provide some sort of comfort took me by surprise. It seemed incredibly unfair that she had so much stacked against her. "Why did you come back?" The words came out a little more abruptly than intended, and my dad cut me a glare.

Everly stiffened, her lip dropping from between her teeth. "You know you don't have to help, right?"

"I didn't mean it like that. I just meant…I'm curious, why. You've never been back before. Wouldn't it be easier to sell this place and use the money to start your sanctuary somewhere else?"

"Ignore my son. His manners leave something to be desired, and he often puts his foot in his mouth."

Everly's lips curved, and her eyes got back a little of that sparkle that had fled once my dad said the barn might be a loss. "I've learned that about him."

"Hey, two against one isn't fair," I said.

She met my gaze. "Life rarely is."

That was the truth. I learned it day after day. Those who deserved a break, rarely got one. That familiar marching band of guilt picked up its tune inside me. Everly deserved a break, and I hadn't given her a single one. "Sorry. I shouldn't have stuck my nose where it didn't belong."

"You and your dog have that in common. He's just a little friendlier about it."

Dad snickered. "She's got your number."

"Yeah, yeah. I'm sorry, okay? Forget I asked."

"Fair enough." She turned back to the barn. "I think the worst of it is around the other side."

My phone buzzed in my pocket, and I pulled it out. Seeing the dispatch number on my screen, I hit accept. "Easton."

"Sheriff. We've got a call. There was an attempted abduction over by the lake."

I stilled, the world seeming to tunnel, my gaze traveling to that damn shed. What were the chances of getting a call like this when I was standing where I was? "Who's the vic?"

"Cammie Sweeney. She's okay. Ruiz and Young are already there and told me to call you."

"I'm on my way. Probably twenty or thirty minutes out."

"I'll let them know."

I hit end without another word. "Dad, I need your keys. I got a callout."

"But it's your day off."

I abruptly shook my head. "I need to go. Can you keep Koda?"

He tossed me his keys. "Of course. I'll have your mom pick me up, and you can come get him at the ranch when you're done."

Everly's eyes were sharp and assessing as if she could already read my tone and movements. "Everything okay?"

"I don't know yet. I'm sorry I have to bail. I'll come back to-morrow if I can."

"No need, if you're busy. I can handle this on my own." She turned away and started around the barn, my father and Koda following her.

Why the hell did it feel like I'd let her down? I muttered a curse as I picked up my pace to a jog. In less than a minute, I was heading down the mountain. But the look on Everly's face stayed with me.

As soon as I hit the two-lane highway, my foot pressed the accelerator. I'd only worked one kidnapping since I'd started working for the sheriff's department. I'd been a deputy sheriff at the time, and it had rocked me. It had turned out to be a custody dispute, a man simply taking off with his son. But my mind had been full of all the worst what-ifs.

I adjusted my grip on the steering wheel, turning onto a back road to avoid going through town. I worked my jaw back and forth as I slowed my breathing. By the time I pulled to a stop by the lake, I had my mask firmly in place.

A number of squad cars and SUVs littered the small parking lot, and an ambulance sat with its back doors open. Tourists and locals alike gawked at the scene. I slid out of the truck and looked at one of our youngest officers trying to hold them all back. "All right, you guys, back up. Please move to the picnic area at the other end of the beach." I motioned for another deputy. "Sergeant Ruiz will be with you in a moment to take your statements."

I got a few scowls but far more sheepish looks as if people knew that what they were doing was just a little heartless. Officer Williams sighed as he turned my way. "What is wrong with people?"

"They're just curious. Want to know what happened."

"It's not their business."

"You're right there." I glanced towards the assembled group and caught sight of Cammie's tear-streaked face. "If anyone comes back, send them on their way. If they refuse, arrest them."

"Okay, Sheriff."

I strode towards Young and Cammie. I was glad Young had been the one who responded to the call. She was green but had a way with victims that made them feel more at ease. Cammie looked up as I approached, and I caught sight of what would soon be a hell of a shiner. I swallowed back the curses I wanted to spew. "You okay, Cam?"

She nodded, the movements jerky. "I just want to go home."

Hadley appeared next to her fellow EMT partner and popped an instant ice pack. "Let's get this on that eye now that it's clean."

I watched as she gently placed the ice pack in Cammie's hand and guided it to her face. "Does she need to go to the hospital, Hads?"

"I don't think so. No sign of a concussion. But she's a little shocky. Some juice wouldn't hurt."

Cammie's best friend, Katie, shot up from where she was sitting on a bench nearby. "I have some Gatorade in the back of my car from when I do my long runs. Would that help?"

Hadley gave her a gentle smile. "That would be great."

Once Cammie had a few sips of Gatorade, I bent forward to meet her gaze. "Can you tell me what happened?"

"S-sure. Katie and I paddleboarded across the lake with a picnic. It's the perfect day for it, but we wanted to avoid the tourists. We ate lunch and then, uh, I had to pee. So, I walked off a ways. I was just looking for a good spot. But someone grabbed me. H-his hand went around my mouth before I had a chance to scream."

Cammie shuddered, and Hadley wrapped a blanket around her shoulders. "I was so scared. I just froze. He started dragging me off, and that's when everything kicked in. My dad makes me take a self-defense class every summer. I always thought it was so stupid." She let out a laugh, but it was almost manic. "I guess parents really do know best."

"A lot of the time, they do. Then what happened?" I asked.

Cammie's gaze went a little unfocused. "I bit down on his hand and threw my elbow back. It stunned him, but he recovered quick. He caught me with a punch as I was trying to run away, but he lost his balance, I think. I heard a crash, and I just kept running. I screamed the whole way.

"Katie met me halfway back to our spot, and I told her to run. We both got onto her paddleboard, and she rowed us back. I left everything there. I couldn't… I was too scared. What if he came back? I shouldn't have left our stuff there like trash. Am I going to get a fine?"

I took Cammie's hand and squeezed it gently. "You did everything just right, and your dad's gonna be so proud of you. I'll send some deputies to get your belongings. Don't you worry."

Young stepped forward. "Ruiz sent techs that way just before you got here. They can retrieve everything."

"See, already being dealt with." I patted her hand. "I need you to think really carefully. Can you describe the man who attacked you?"

Cammie's eyes flared, panic setting in. "I-I don't know."

I met her gaze. "Squeeze my hand." She did as I ordered. "I'm with you. No one's going to hurt you. Just close your eyes and tell me everything you remember. There's more there than you think. Was he bigger than you? What about his hair?"

"Dark, I think. There was dark hair on his arms."

"Good. That's really good, Cam. What about his build?"

Cammie's eyes stayed closed, but she trembled beneath the blanket even though it was almost ninety degrees out. "Bigger than me. Really strong. And fast. I…I didn't see his face. I didn't want to. If I saw it, I was scared he would kill me." Her eyes flew open, tears spilling over her lashes. "I'm sorry. I didn't see anything else."

I laid my free hand over hers as her nails dug into my palm. "It's okay. What you gave us helps. We're going to do everything we can to find him."

"Cammie!" Her father charged past Officer Williams, headed towards us. "Oh, God, are you okay?"

"I'm okay, Dad. Really."

He pulled her into a hug. I stepped away but I couldn't seem to move my gaze. Sobs wracked Cammie's body as her father held her. The only thing I could see was my father holding Shiloh as EMTs inserted an IV. He'd had to lie on the gurney with her because she refused to let go of him.

Ruiz appeared to my left. "Boss? You okay?"

I shook my head and turned to him. "I'm fine. Do we have anything yet?"

"Nothing much. Techs think they found the site of the attack, but they haven't found any sign of the attacker."

I checked my watch. Whoever did this could've made it around the lake by now. "Has anyone come off the trails?"

"I don't think so. No one has been able to leave the parking lot, at least."

"Okay. I want two four-person teams. One takes the north side trail, the other the south. If he's coming back out this way, I want us to get him. And check all the male onlookers' hands. He could've slipped into the crowd."

"You got it." Ruiz looked up at me, trying to choose his words carefully. "I can take point if you need me to."

My back molars ground together. "I'm fine. But thank you."

Ruiz nodded hesitantly as if he didn't believe a word coming out of my mouth. But I was fine. I had no other choice.

Chapter Thirteen

Everly

I WASHED DOWN THE LAST BITE OF MY EGG SALAD SANDWICH with a drink of my soda. I had a feeling Spoons would become the lunch spot I treated myself to whenever I needed a pick-me-up. I needed to bring lunch from home as much as possible, but today being the first day of my new job meant that I deserved a little treat.

A young woman who'd introduced herself as Jill gave me a warm smile as she stopped at my table. "Are you all finished?"

"I am. That was delicious. Thank you."

"I'm so glad I didn't steer you wrong. The egg salad is my favorite."

I looked down at my empty basket as she picked it up. "You certainly didn't, and the focaccia it's served on is amazing."

She beamed. "We make it right in-house."

"I'll definitely be back soon."

"We'll be glad to have you. Welcome to town."

Jill hadn't recognized my name when we'd engaged in idle chit-chat as I ordered, so I figured she was newer to Wolf Gap. But I was grateful for a friendly face, and a spot where I knew prying eyes wouldn't greet me. "Thank you. I hope you have a good rest of your day."

I pushed to my feet and headed back towards the vet's office. I had time to meander if I wanted to. Maybe pop into a shop or two. But as I peeked into windows, my mind traveled to the same place it had dozens of other times over the past few days.

Hayes hadn't returned to the cabin this weekend. And he hadn't called or texted. I felt a flare of disappointment that was completely irrational. I barely knew the man, and he didn't even like me. His father, on the other hand, was a complete charmer. He'd made me laugh, even after he'd informed me that we needed to tear down the barn. And he'd helped me take down the rest of the dilapidated fencing.

Yet, I couldn't stop myself from worrying about Hayes. The call he'd received. I'd never known anyone who ran straight towards danger every day at their job. And it was clear why. Hayes was a protector. And he'd likely become that way because of Shiloh's kidnapping.

That familiar swirl of guilt, anger, and grief swept through me. That potent array always seemed to be nearby. My brain knew that my father's actions weren't mine to take responsibility for, but the rest of me had a harder time recognizing that fact.

A shadow fell across the sidewalk in front of me. "What the hell are you wearing?"

I lifted my head to see Ian glaring at me in disgust, Ben just a few paces behind him. Instead of answering, I did my best to step around the man who used to be my brother. But he blocked my path. "I'm talking to you."

"And I'm walking away."

Ian grabbed my elbow, yanking me back. "You don't walk away when I'm speaking to you."

I tore my arm free. "Touch me again, and I'll make it so the possibility of you having children is non-existent."

He chuckled, throwing a look at Ben. "Isn't that cute? She thinks she can defend herself."

"Quit it, Ian," Ben barked, pushing him back.

"What? I can't hit her with the cold, hard truth?"

Ben looked at me. "Are you okay?"

"I'm fine," I gritted out. "I can take care of myself."

Ian stalked towards me, the flare of rage in his eyes so familiar that it sent memories hurtling at me one after the other. "You need to be taught some manners, Everly."

Ben stepped between us, pushing my brother back. "Enough. You need to cool off, Ian. Evie, get out of here."

I didn't argue. I simply left. I didn't run, but I fled, just like I had all those years ago. I hurried down the street and slipped inside the vet's office.

Tim looked up from his desk. "Hey, how was lunch?"

"Good," I choked out and went straight for the break room. I knew Miles was gone for the afternoon, and the other vet tech, Kelly, had gone to lunch with her boyfriend.

I sank into an empty plastic chair and put my head between my legs. Flashes of light and memory slammed into me: Ian dragging me by the hair as I clawed at his arm and begged him to stop, the slap of his open palm against my face, the taste of blood in my mouth.

I struggled to breathe as tears slipped out of my eyes. I'd thought I was so much stronger than this. Yet here I was, falling apart. My lungs trembled as I willed them under control.

"Hey, Everly? Tim said you were back here. I wanted—" Hayes' words cut off as he caught sight of me. He was the last person I wanted to see me this way. He crouched in front of me. "Hey, what's going on?"

I forced myself to sit up, but I couldn't disguise the shaking. "Nothing, I'm fine."

His concern morphed into a scowl. "You're not *fine*. You're shaking like a leaf, and your face has no color in it at all."

I closed my eyes for a moment as if I could make it all

disappear. The run-in with Ian. Hayes witnessing my weakness. I wanted to simply float away.

"I can't help if you don't tell me what's going on."

My eyes fluttered open at his words. He hadn't disappeared, and I hadn't floated away. "It's not your job to help."

"It's exactly my job. And I'll do it wherever I can."

I studied the man in front of me. The angular jaw that always betrayed Hayes' frustration. The rough stubble and planes of his face. Those eyes so dark and deep, I felt as if I could sink into them and get lost for days. Nothing in him spoke untruths. Maybe Hayes truly was one of the good ones. Someone determined to make the world better for everyone around him. "You don't need to take care of me."

He pushed to his feet and started for the door. I thought I'd finally sent him running. But instead, he only poked his head out. "Tim, we need twenty."

"We don't—"

Hayes ignored me and simply shut the door. He began moving around the small kitchenette without another word to me, opening cabinets until he found two mugs. Then he riffled through drawers until he found a box of something. Within a few minutes, he was easing into the chair opposite me and handing me a steaming mug.

I didn't touch it. "What if I don't like tea?"

"Then just wrap your hands around the mug. It'll help."

I had the burning urge to stick out my tongue at him. But as I wrapped my hands around the ceramic, and the heat sank into my palms, something in me eased. "You're very overbearing, you know that, right?"

He shrugged and blew on his tea. "Everyone has to have a character flaw."

I snorted. "I'd say you have a few."

"Never claimed to be perfect."

I stared down into the swirling liquid. "Perfect's boring anyway."

"Very true." Hayes was quiet for a moment, letting the silence swirl around us the same way the liquid in my cup did. "You going to tell me what happened?"

I sighed. It was clear he wasn't going to leave me alone until he got some pieces of the puzzle. "I had a run-in with my brother. Just brought up some bad memories."

"Okay…" He was quiet and, for a moment, I thought he wouldn't push. "What's the status with your family?"

"What do you mean?"

"Have you been in touch with them since you left Wolf Gap?"

I dunked the tea bag a few times before taking it out and resting it on a spoon. "I lived with my older sister in Seattle until I moved out for college. But, no, I haven't talked to the rest of my family since I was twelve. Allen and Ian paid a couple of visits to Seattle when I first moved there."

Hayes' jaw worked back and forth as if he were working out a math problem in his mind and having trouble. "They harass you?"

"They made their presence known. But once we moved, they didn't put any real effort into finding us."

"And your mom? She didn't put a stop to it?"

I gripped the mug a little tighter, my mother's face flashing in my mind. "I think she lost her fight."

"You were her daughter."

"And I cost her the love of her life."

Hayes' gaze bored into mine. "Was that really how she saw it?"

"I honestly don't know. All I know is that she couldn't break free of that life. My sister, Jacey, tried to get her to come with me, and she wouldn't. She didn't want that freedom for herself."

"I don't think I'll ever understand your family. The people they've tied themselves to."

I traced an invisible design on the table. "I won't lie, there's some ugliness. Hate. But some of the paranoia comes from how they were raised. My grandparents on my dad's side were the same way. They've been preached to about the government being out to get them. Other preppers wanting to pillage and steal. It skewed their outlook. But there's good in that community, too."

"I know that. Some folks simply want to live off the land or protect their families in case the worst happens. But that's not…"

His words fell off, but I finished Hayes' sentence for him. "That's not what my family is." I looked up to meet his gaze. "My childhood wasn't all bad. And my parents taught me things that I'll forever be grateful for."

There was heat in those dark eyes. It blazed as he swallowed. "But you're different from them. Always were. Or you wouldn't have ridden that horse into town all alone."

I'd tried time and again to think back and see what might've made me do that. To break free of everything around me. I'd never exactly figured it out. "While my dad always looked for danger, I saw beauty—in the land, in other people. In all of it. As much as he tried to school me, I could never get my mind to work that way." Not even after Ian's attack.

Hayes took a sip of his tea. "Shows a strength of character."

I let out a mock gasp, my hand flying to my chest. "Hayes Easton, was that a compliment? Careful, I might start to think you actually like me."

That familiar scowl returned. "I never said I didn't like you."

"Mm-hmm."

"I didn't." He adjusted the collar of his shirt. "But I did make you feel unwelcome. And for that, I truly am sorry. Do you think we could have a do-over?"

"A do-over?"

"We're fond of them in my family. If someone messes up, they can ask for a do-over to start fresh."

A fresh start. Wasn't that exactly what I was trying to foster here? For myself. Hopefully, for a whole lot of animals. So, who was I to deny Hayes the same? I extended my hand. "I'm Everly Kemper."

Hayes' large hand engulfed my smaller one, the rough calluses on his palm sending a skitter of sensation up my arm. "I'm Hayes Easton. It's a pleasure to meet you, Everly. Welcome back to Wolf Gap."

He made it seem as easy as taking an eraser to a chalkboard. But I knew it wasn't quite that simple for either of us.

Chapter Fourteen

Hayes

I STARED DOWN AT THE REPORT IN FRONT OF ME. I'D BEEN poring over our cases from the past couple of months, and the closest thing we had to abduction was a botched mugging a few weeks ago that had left a female tourist with a shiner. I couldn't help feeling like we were missing something. A piece of the puzzle that would at least give us a direction to go in. I scrubbed a hand over my face. Maybe it was because I'd slept like shit last night that things weren't adding up in my mind.

I'd tossed and turned and had finally given up sometime around three. The same image haunted me over and over. Everly curled over as she struggled to catch her breath, fear wafting off her.

I didn't know much, but something bad had happened with her family. Something beyond her father's mental illness and him kidnapping Shiloh. I'd wanted to sit with her all afternoon, to pry every last secret out of her. But I'd barely gotten that fresh start. I didn't want to ruin it with too many questions, too quickly.

I had to hope that she'd open up with time. And I'd give her that time. I'd be helping her on my weekends off whether she wanted me to or not.

My mouth curved at the memory of her calling me on my crap. I'd never thought I would be drawn to that, but somehow, I was. Maybe I'd been going after the wrong kinds of women all these years. Most of the ones I'd dated had been softer somehow, not willing to rock the boat. I liked that Everly didn't back down.

I blinked at the words on the paper as everything in me locked. Thinking about pursuing anything more than a friendship with Everly wasn't in the cards. There was too much painful history there.

A knock sounded on my open door, and I looked up to see Young. Grateful for the distraction from my spiraling thoughts, I motioned her in. "You're early for your shift."

She came to a stop behind one of the chairs opposite my desk, shuffling her feet. "I wanted to run something by you."

"All right. Hit me with it."

"I went back out to the crime scene first thing this morning."

I straightened in my chair. "Alone?" She winced, and that was all the answer I needed. "I thought you were smarter than that. A woman a few years younger than you was taken from just that spot, and you thought it was a good idea to go out there alone?" Just saying the words made me realize I needed to have a conversation with both Hadley and Shiloh. Everly, too. None of them should be going off alone until we figured out who was responsible.

"I have training."

"None of which protects you from a blitz attack."

Her shoulders slumped. "I'm sorry. You're right, it was dumb. You've taught me better than that. But something was troubling me."

"Sit." I pointed to the chair, and Young slid into it. "What doesn't feel right?"

"I don't think he could've hiked out of there. We put officers at all the nearby trailheads, and he didn't come out at any of them. He either lives out there, or he had another mode of transportation."

Her thoughts were exactly what my scattered brain had been struggling to put together. "I agree. So, what'd you find?"

"Horse poop."

I raised a brow in question.

"That, and some tracks. I think whoever did this got out there on horseback. Maybe he saw her, and it just flipped some switch."

"An opportunistic offender."

"Yes."

I'd been thinking the same thing. This didn't fit the modus operandi of someone who stalked their victims. This was a crime of opportunity. It didn't make it any less dangerous, but it was good news for Cammie. "So, where do we go from here?"

Young blinked at me a few times. "Don't you want to tell me?"

"You're the one who took the initiative to go out there on your own time to investigate. And even if you could've done it safer, I appreciate you going above and beyond."

She straightened in her chair a fraction. "Thank you. I really love this job, and I want to excel at it."

"You're getting there." I met her gaze to hammer my point home. "But that means you have to be responsible."

"I promise, no more going off on my own."

"Good. Now, tell me what's next."

She was quiet for a moment, putting together pieces in her mind. "Two things: I'll ask around on the reservation, see if anyone has seen a single guy that fits our description riding alone. We should do the same around town. But I also think we should head out to The Trading Post. It's not too far down the highway from the lake, and they could've had someone come by who fits."

I pushed back from my desk. "I think we need to hold off on putting the word out in town or on the reservation. I don't want to start a panic or people looking at everyone as potential violent attackers. But I think The Trading Post is a great idea."

"I didn't think about the panic piece of things."

"Don't be too hard on yourself. I've learned my lessons the hard way. A huge part of this job is making people feel safe. That means being careful about what we share and how we share it."

Young followed me out the door. "What about at The Trading Post? That's gossip central."

She wasn't wrong there. The Trading Post was just what it sounded like and more. It was a place where people could exchange goods, but there was also a general store of sorts inside, and a small bank of mailboxes for people who lived way out of town. Basic groceries and hardware supplies. There was even a small farmer's market on the weekends during the spring and summer. It was so far out of town that it was frequented mostly by those who lived out that way. And it catered to those who liked to stay off the grid.

"We're going to tread carefully." I led the way through the desks in the main room, passing the same bench my family had waited on all of those years ago. This time when I passed it, Everly's eleven-year-old face flashed in my mind more clearly than it had in years. The pain ravaging it struck like a whip. God, I was an asshole. So focused on my family's pain and mine, mixed with a healthy dose of guilt, that I couldn't see her clearly.

I hadn't wanted to if I were honest. I hadn't wanted to think about what she and her family might have been going through. I'd wanted to cast them all into the darkness along with her father.

I beeped the locks on my SUV, and Young and I climbed in. On the thirty-minute drive out to The Trading Post, I updated her on the latest reports. There hadn't been a hell of a lot so far. Unfortunately, Cammie hadn't scratched her attacker, so there was no DNA under her nails. And there simply hadn't been much forensic evidence to find.

I pulled into the dusty lot of The Post. There was an older truck parked behind the store and a few other vehicles in front, but it looked quiet enough that we might have a shot at real conversation with the owner. I glanced over at Young. "We go in easy. Friendly."

She gave me a sharkish grin. "I can be friendly."

"God help us," I muttered.

"What? I can."

I slid out of the SUV, Young following suit, and headed towards the store. I passed a couple of trucks with stickers showing intertwined snakes. One with a makeshift license plate that claimed the vehicle belonged to a Sovereign Citizen. Young's brows rose. I shook my head. We weren't after traffic violations today.

I held the door open for Young. She passed, giving me a smirk. "Such a gentleman."

"What can I say? My mama taught me right."

The store was a bit rundown but it had character. The aisles were arranged in a way that only made sense to Sue, the owner. A handful of tables were gathered in a corner where folks could sit and eat the food that was prepared in a small kitchen in the back. One of those tables had three grizzled men sitting at it. They eyed us warily as we walked by, one outright glaring as we passed.

I ignored them and headed for the counter. Sue looked up from her book. A woman in her seventies, her long, salt-and-pepper hair was woven into a braid that hung down her back. She wore jeans, a t-shirt, and perfectly worn boots. "Sheriff. Deputy. To what do I owe the pleasure?"

I gave her my most charming smile. "Can't I just come for a visit? Maybe I missed you, Sue."

"I wish you missed me." She gave Young a wink. "This one is nothing but trouble, but he's pretty to look at, so I don't mind."

Young tried in vain to hold back her laugh. "All the most dangerous ones are that way, don't you think?"

"Truer words have never been spoken." Sue's expression sobered a touch as her gaze drifted to the men assembled at the table. "But since you're both in uniform, I'm guessing you don't need a quart of milk."

I leaned a hip against the counter, shifting my body so I had a side-eye view of the men at the table. All three were carrying, and I had a feeling if I asked them for permits, we'd have a problem. "You hear about the young woman who was attacked at the lake?"

"The Sweeney girl, right?"

I nodded.

"She's okay, isn't she? I heard she got away."

The men at the table seemed to shift with the conversation's focus, stopping their card-playing altogether. I drummed my fingers against my thigh, my hand itching to rest on the butt of my gun. "She's going to be just fine, thanks to the self-defense class her dad made her take."

"Smart man. Brave girl."

"That they are." I focused in on Sue. "You see anyone come through here on horseback that day? Lone rider. Man. Over six feet."

Her face carefully blanked. "You know if I start answering questions about who comes through here, I'm going to lose more than half my business."

I raised my voice so the men at the table could easily hear. "Do you really think your customers want to protect a kidnapper? Probably a rapist?"

The largest man at the table, one who looked vaguely familiar, stood. "This about that girl?"

"It is." My hand itched and strained, but I forced it to stay loose at my side.

"You find who did this, and we'll be happy to take care of it for you."

I gave him an easy smile. "I appreciate that, but I think we're gonna do this one by the book."

He shrugged. "Those books don't work for a lot of folks."

"You're not wrong there. But I do my best to make them do their job."

The man studied me for a moment, seeming to take my measure. "What do you want to know?"

"Looking for a lone man on horseback, around this area or the lake. You guys see anyone?"

A slender man, still sitting, snickered. "I see them all the time. Lots of folks around here prefer horseback to a car or truck."

He was right. It was far from abnormal for someone to ride to The Post for a few groceries. Or just take off into the national forest for some time alone in nature. I scanned the men's faces. "What about anyone who seemed off to you?"

The third man, who hadn't said a word yet, sneered. "You seem pretty damn off to me. Sticking your nose in where it don't belong."

My fingers twitched. "Well, that's a matter of opinion, isn't it?"

"My opinion is that pigs aren't wanted here."

Young stiffened next to me, her hand going to the butt of her gun. The third man's hand did the same with his. Just as I was afraid things might take a turn we couldn't come back from, the saloon doors to the kitchen swung open.

A young woman with her blond hair dreaded and wrapped in a scarf appeared with two plates in hand, oblivious to what was going on around her. "I've got that breakfast burrito, extra steak, and the special. Who's winning this morning?"

The appearance of the woman seemed to take the tension

down more than a step immediately. The surliest of the men smiled at her. "You know I'm kicking their asses."

She beamed at him. "It might be nice to let someone else win once in a while."

"Don't listen to him, Dahlia. I'm cleaning up," the skinny man said.

"Let's get to cleaning up these breakfasts. I'll be back with yours, Jim."

The men went back to ignoring me and started shoveling in their breakfasts. Sue snorted a laugh. "Hippies. They save my ass every time. And they grow the best herb."

I ran a hand through my hair. "I'm going to pretend I didn't hear that."

Sue leaned back on her stool. "I'm sure they have a license." She was quiet for a moment. "I didn't see anyone like you described the day the Sweeney girl was attacked."

"What about before or after?"

"Too many to count."

I muttered a curse. "Thanks, Sue."

"Don't go spreading around that I answered your questions."

"Your secret's safe with me." I inclined my head towards the door, and Young and I headed out as Dahlia appeared with the last plate.

She smiled at us. "Have a beautifully blessed day."

Young's lips pressed together to keep from laughing. She held it together until we made it outside. "What was that?"

"This county is full of interesting characters."

"I thought for a minute it was going to go bad in there."

"It could've. Don't place your hand on your weapon in a situation like that unless you're ready to use it."

Young flushed. "Sorry."

"You don't have to be sorry. Just learn with each callout." I sent her a grin. "Maybe I should think about hiring Dahlia as a crisis negotiator."

"Wouldn't be a bad idea." She glanced over her shoulder. "I just don't get guys like that."

I beeped the locks on the SUV, and we climbed inside. "They don't think rules and laws apply to them."

"Think they could have something to do with what happened to Cammie?"

"Honestly, no. But there are bad apples everywhere. We just might have to turn over the whole barrel to find what we're looking for."

Chapter Fifteen

Everly

I SHUT THE DOOR OF MY SUV WITH MY HIP AND PRESSED THE button on my key fob to lock it. It was a habit after living so long in the city. But given the latest run-in with my brother, it was probably a good idea to keep it up. I wouldn't put it past Ian to rig my SUV to blow.

I trudged across the gravel drive, my boots almost dragging through the dirt. The day had been nonstop from beginning to end. A full roster of appointments and then a handful of emergencies. Luckily, all of them had a happy ending.

I pulled my keys from my purse and found the one I was looking for. Shiny new silver for my brand-new lock. It was one of the first things I'd done after moving. You never knew how many old spare keys were floating around.

Sliding the new key into the slot, I listened for a moment before heading inside. As soon as the door shut behind me, Chip skittered out of his hidey-hole, chattering away. I grinned down at the chipmunk. "Good to know you missed me." He kept right on talking as if I could understand every word. "Or maybe you're just hungry."

I hung my purse on a peg I'd put by the door and moved

towards the kitchen. Opening a cabinet, I poured a small amount of the nut mix into a little dish. I sat it on the floor, and Chip pounced. I couldn't help but laugh.

Letting the sound free released some of the tension in my muscles. I rolled my shoulders back and turned the oven on to four hundred. Tonight was a frozen-pizza kind of night. I moved to the window to peek outside.

It looked like Shiloh had been here today. The remaining dilapidated fencing had been taken down and arranged in piles: keep and use for firewood. At least, I wouldn't have to split logs anytime soon. I really should've gone out to get a few hours of work in—the summer light would last until after eight—but I just didn't have it in me.

Instead, I opted for the hottest shower known to man while my pizza cooked and then climbed into bed with a book it was taking me far too long to work my way through. The long days I'd pulled lately meant I nodded off before I'd read more than a few pages.

I looked around the room before I switched off the light. It was starting to feel more like home. In the last week, I'd made it more mine—a purplish-gray paint on the walls and gauzy white curtains that lifted in the breeze. I took a deep breath as I switched off the light, letting the fresh mountain air soothe me—hoping it would keep the nightmares away.

It certainly helped me fall asleep faster. It seemed like moments after my head hit the pillow, I was slipping under.

A foreign smell tickled my nose. It was the fact that my nose scrunched in repulsion, the scent invading the calm of my pine air, that woke me. I lay in bed for a moment, blinking awake into the darkness. As I inhaled again, I jolted upright. Smoke.

I flew out of bed, grabbing my phone on the way. I ran down

the hall and out into the living room. I slipped my feet into muck boots and threw open the front door. Flames greeted me in the distance, fully engulfing the barn.

I dialed nine-one-one in a haze.

"Sheriff's Department. What's your emergency?"

My voice cracked as I struggled to get the words out. "My barn is on fire."

"What's your address?"

I listed it off as a particularly violent gust of flames surged.

"Are you in a safe place away from the fire?"

I looked at the distance between the barn and the cabin. The flames could easily catch on the trees and then jump to my cabin. "Safe enough. I have to go." I hung up without another word, running for the hose. The barn was a lost cause, but my cabin wasn't.

I turned on the water as far as it would go, thankful I'd picked up the hose and spray nozzle at the hardware store. I aimed the stream of water at the cabin's roof, coating the side closest to the blaze as much as possible. When it was thoroughly doused, I moved around to the front and aimed for the opposite side as I heard sirens in the distance.

I stayed fully focused on my task, glancing at the barn and the surrounding forest every minute or so. My stomach dropped when two nearby trees caught. "Hurry up," I begged to no one in particular.

Lights poured across the drive as two fire trucks crested the ridge. They paused in front of me, and a window rolled down. A handsome man with dark hair stuck his head out. "Water?"

"There's a line to the pasture."

He nodded and motioned for the driver to move forward. When the trucks parked, they moved in what almost looked like a choreographed dance. Everyone knew their places and went to work immediately. One hose hooked on to the property's waterline, and others came from the trucks themselves.

I kept my pathetic hose pointed at my little cabin. I moved in a slow pattern, doing all I could to prevent the fire from jumping. A series of shouts sounded as a tree fell. My heart stopped as it sent a cascade of embers flying. It would've been beautiful had it not been so deadly.

I breathed a sigh of relief when I saw everyone was free of the destruction. More sirens cut through the night as an SUV came to a screeching halt in front of me. Hayes jumped out in jeans and a tee that molded to his chest. "Hi," I croaked.

"You need to get out of here. That fire could jump at any minute."

"I need to water down the cabin." If I lost my place to live, that would be it. I wouldn't recover from the blow.

Hayes moved towards me, trying to take the hose from my hands. "I'll do it. Just get out of here."

I held firm. "I'm not going anywhere."

He muttered a slew of curses. "Is there another hose?"

"Around the other side."

Hayes jogged to retrieve the second one. Soon, we were working in tandem as the firefighters battled the other blaze. We didn't say a word, but after an hour, by some silent agreement, we turned off the water. The fire department was slowly getting the barn fire under control. Hayes and I moved to my steps and sat, watching them slowly cut back the blaze until only embers remained.

The same man who had asked about the water walked towards us. He'd lost his helmet and jacket, now wearing a white tee streaked with dirt. He jerked his chin at Hayes. "They drag you out of bed?"

"Something like this, you know they have to."

I pushed to my feet. "Thank you so much."

He nodded, holding out a hand. "Glad we made it in time. I'm Calder, by the way. It's nice to meet you."

"Everly."

His grip and expression were warm. Friendly. But Hayes scowled at the man, only making Calder chuckle. He turned back to me. "It'll take us a bit to fully suppress the fire."

"No problem. Do you have any idea what caused it?"

Calder flashed a quick look at Hayes. "Our fire investigator will come out tomorrow and have a look. He's the one who determines that kind of thing."

I took a step closer to him, watching every flicker of his expression. "But you have a guess."

Hayes came to stand next to me. "Just tell us what you know."

Calder ran a hand over his head. "I smelled gas. You store that out there?"

"No. There was nothing in the barn. Not even old tack."

A muscle in Hayes' jaw ticked. "Dad went through it not a week ago. There was no gas inside."

Calder looked back at his crew, currently stomping out the last dregs of the blaze. "Then I'd guess our investigator will find arson."

A man on the crew yelled something I couldn't quite make out, and everyone moved back. The structure let out what almost sounded like a groan. Seconds later, the last of it collapsed to the ground.

Calder winced. "I'm sorry about your barn."

Tears burned the back of my throat. Not because of the building, but because someone had intentionally done this. Wanted to hurt and destroy. "It needed to be torn down anyway."

"Not like this, it didn't," Hayes growled.

He was right. But I'd learned long ago that life rarely went as planned.

Chapter Sixteen

Hayes

I couldn't handle the devastation in Everly's eyes anymore. The need to give her some sort of comfort clawed at my insides. She looked so damn alone, sitting on those porch steps. She didn't have anyone. I hadn't seen a sign of a single soul who was on her team. I couldn't fathom that. I'd been through hell, but I'd had countless people there to prop me up along the way. Everly had no one.

I sat down next to her and leaned into her a bit, almost bumping her shoulder with mine. She startled as if she'd been in another world. "You don't have to stay. They're almost done. I'm fine."

"What if I want to stay?"

She gave me a look that called bullshit.

I shrugged. "Looks like a good spot to watch the sunrise." The sun was just peeking out over the horizon, turning the sky a pinkish-purple.

Everly met my gaze dead-on. "What do you want?"

"Wouldn't mind a cup of coffee. Maybe a donut. I'd like to take a Ferrari for a spin one day. Maybe own a private island in the Caribbean. Have a private jet to take me there."

There was no flicker of humor on her face. "You know what I mean."

I leaned back, resting my elbows on the step behind me as I turned back to the sunrise. But I kept sight of Everly in my peripheral vision. "You're alone. And no one should have to deal with something like this alone."

She bristled. "I don't need your pity."

"It's not pity. It's friendship."

"And that's what we are? Friends? Even though my father is the one who hurt your family beyond measure, you want to be my friend?"

Each word punched into that reserve of rage that always simmered in the background. But I didn't let it catch fire. Not this time. "Yes. You aren't your father."

"But I remind you of him. What he did. I remind everyone."

The words tumbled out, almost as if she didn't have control of them. Broken and full of so much pain. They did something to the rage inside me. Changed it somehow. Shocked it into submission. "You have to give people time to build different memories of you. The longer you're here, the easier that'll be."

The corner of my mouth quirked up. "Now you'll remind me of a firefighting badass in muck boots and—" I leaned forward to examine her pajama shorts. "Avocado boxers."

Her face flushed. "I'm a fan of guacamole."

"It works for you." It worked a little too well. Those damn tiny shorts exposed what felt like miles of golden skin. I forced my gaze up to her face.

"I don't know what to do with you. I want to give you that fresh start, but I keep waiting for the blow you're going to deal me."

My fingers tightened around the lip of the step I leaned against. That fear was more than fair. I'd been cruel the first two times I'd come here. "I'm sorry." The word felt so damn lacking.

"I hope with time I can prove to you that I'm not that guy—or that's not me at my best."

Everly slumped against the steps. "I understand not always being who you should, who you're capable of. I'll try not to have my back up every time you show. I just…after I've experienced it once, I'm used to learning to watch for the snap."

My gut soured at the thought of what'd taught her that lesson. "Appreciate you trying. That's all I can ask."

She tucked her hair behind her ear and, as she did, revealed some delicate script there. I couldn't resist moving her hair out of the way to read the words. *Twenty breaths.*

I didn't release my hold on the silky strands, but my gaze locked with hers. "What does it mean?"

"Anyone can be brave for twenty breaths. And in that time, you can do almost anything. Or at least take the first steps you need to get there."

I didn't move, just stared at the words. I wanted more. All of it. The whole story. But to get it, I'd have to earn Everly's trust. And that was an uphill battle.

She ducked away, moving her hair from between my fingers. "It's just something that's meaningful to me."

"Twenty breaths. I like it."

Officer Williams waved from the front desk. I lifted my travel coffee mug in a halfhearted greeting. "Anything that needs my immediate attention?"

"Nope, but Calder is waiting for you in your office."

I glanced at my watch. I'd barely had a chance to grab two hours of sleep, but I'd bet Calder hadn't had any. "Thanks."

I moved through the main room, trading greetings with officers and deputies, trying my best not to act like a grumpy asshole. Pulling open my door, the smell of something amazing hit me.

Calder looked up from an open box of donuts. "I thought this might help get you through the day."

"You are officially my favorite friend. Hell, I'll let you replace Beck as my brother."

"How is that asshole?"

I eased into my desk chair and plucked up a chocolate old fashioned. "Who knows. I haven't heard from him in over a month. But that's not exactly new."

"Where is he again?"

"Venezuela. They're getting a few clinics up and running and training the staff."

Calder set his donut on a napkin. "He's doing good work."

"And breaking my mother's heart." I didn't remember the last time Beckett had been home. Maybe at Christmas four years ago for a total of forty-eight hours.

"Julia likes all of her chicks home to roost."

"But it'll never happen with him. Too much of a restless spirit." I took a sip of coffee. "You get word from your investigator yet?"

"He called just as I was dropping off the girls. It's arson. Not a professional job. If it hadn't been so damn dry, it might not have spread so quickly."

"Hell." I dropped my donut onto a napkin and leaned back in my chair.

"You got some ideas?"

"Her family, to start." Ian and Allen were at the top of my list.

Calder scrubbed a hand over his jaw. "That girl has more to deal with than anyone should."

He wasn't wrong. I looked longingly at my donut. "I'm going to have to take this to go." I paused, taking in my friend and the dark circles rimming his eyes. "You okay?"

"Fine. Could just use a few more hours of sleep. You know how that goes."

"Why don't you let my mom take Birdie and Sage for one of

their sleepovers next weekend? She's always asking for more time with them."

Calder broke off a piece of his donut but didn't eat it. "Your mom does more than enough for us already."

"And she loves every minute of it. You know she's ready to throttle her kids because she doesn't have grandchildren yet. You take some of the pressure off."

He chuckled. "She playing matchmaker again?"

I stood from my chair and wrapped my donut in a napkin. "Thankfully, she hasn't ambushed me lately, but I know it's coming."

"That's one good thing about my parents moving to Florida. I only have to deal with their in-person meddling a couple of times a year."

I scowled in his direction. "Rub it in, why don't you?"

Calder stood to follow me out of the station. "You wouldn't give up your family for anything."

I wouldn't. As many issues as we had, I couldn't imagine living across the country from them. And it pissed me the hell off that Calder's folks had up and left when they knew he needed help. But my parents had simply brought him into the fold. He was an honorary Easton now, and he'd eventually learn that being one of us meant someone was always there to help—or meddle.

I gave him a chin lift of farewell as we headed down the department steps. "Grab a nap today."

He paused. "You taking backup?"

"Not for this."

"You sure that's smart? If they had something to do with this, they might not take kindly to you saying as much."

My back teeth ground together. I'd accused Young of being reckless, and I was about to do the same damn thing. "You might have a point."

He grinned. "Are you saying I know what I'm talking about?"

"Don't push it."

Young pulled into the small parking lot in her cruiser, waving as she stepped out. "Hey, boss. Smoke-eater."

Calder nodded in her direction. "Donut-pusher. Why don't you go with Hayes and make sure he doesn't get himself into trouble he can't get out of?"

She turned to me. "Sheriff?"

"Come on, let's go. Call Mom, Calder."

"Yeah, yeah." He waved as he took off down the street.

Young climbed into the passenger side of my SUV. "Where are we going?"

I set my coffee in the cupholder and balanced my donut on my thigh as I started the engine. "We need to pay the Kemper family a visit."

"What happened now?"

"That fire that started at Everly's last night? It was arson."

"Shit," she whispered. "How is she holding up?"

"She's fine. I can't say the same about her barn."

"Is there anything I can do to help?"

I glanced across the vehicle. "You like her, huh?"

Young's mouth curved. "She was going to take a punch so she could lay her uncle out. That makes her a badass in my book. And my gram brought her cat to the vet because she wasn't eating. Didn't have an appointment, but Everly worked her in and was really kind. That makes her good people, too. So, if I can do something to help, I'd like to."

"I'll let you know."

"Thanks."

For the rest of the drive, we talked over what had happened last night. The likely timeframe we were looking at. I wasn't exactly sure what I hoped to gain by talking to the Kempers. They sure as hell weren't going to give me any sort of truth. But I needed to see a reaction, at least.

My SUV bumped and jostled as I navigated the potholes in the dirt road. There was no sign overhead, like most of the other ranches. Only a gate propped open with a log.

"I kind of expected locked gates and armed guards," Young muttered.

"I don't think they've gone that far." But it didn't mean they couldn't. I kept a close eye on any FBI reports about militia activity in the area. It certainly wasn't unheard of. Most of the people out here wanted a peaceful life away from the trappings of the city. But some thought it was the Wild West, and they were certified outlaws.

I guided my SUV down the road until a cluster of buildings came into view—an old, large farmhouse, a smaller guest cabin, and a series of barns and outbuildings. As I came to a stop, Allen stepped out of the barn, Ian on his heels. A couple of other men followed behind.

I parked so I faced the road, just in case things went south. "Remember, play it cool."

"I'm not sure Allen is a friend of mine after I took him in."

He glared at my SUV. Allen wasn't a fan of any woman putting him in his place. I checked the gun at my hip. "Hold steady, and we'll be fine."

Young and I slid out of the SUV, and I nodded at the group of men. "Morning, gentlemen."

Not a single friendly face greeted me. Allen took a few steps forward. "You're on private property, and you're not welcome here. Leave."

"You're free to request that, and I'll abide, but then I'll have to take you and Ian in for questioning."

"What the hell for?" Ian asked.

A door clapped against a wood frame, and I looked to see Everly's cousin and another older woman appear on the porch. "Ma'am. Ma'am," I greeted.

The older woman scowled at me, but Adaline looked panicked. Young eyed her carefully, looking as if she wanted to go over and ask her if she was okay. I gave a slight shake of my head. That would take things from bad to worse.

"My nephew asked you a question," Allen gritted out.

"Does that mean you'd rather answer my questions here?"

He straightened. "We don't recognize your authority here. This land is sovereign and not under your corrupt power."

"Is that a yes, or a no?"

Allen spat onto the dirt. "I'm curious enough to see why the hell you're bothering me."

"Need to know where you and Ian were last night."

Ian stepped forward, shoulder to shoulder with his uncle. "Why?"

Young and I had turned our backs towards each other slightly so our positions protected us from any possible ambush, but both had eyes on the two women and the group of men. I drummed my fingers against my thigh. "You answer my question, and I'll answer yours. Seems like a fair trade."

"We were here all night. You can ask Cybil and Addie," Ian gritted out.

I looked to the women. "They were both here? All night? You know for sure?"

Neither woman said a word, but Addie's eyes shifted to the side as if she didn't want to respond.

"Answer the man," Allen barked.

"They were here," Cybil said.

Addie nodded. "I went to bed early, but I didn't see anyone leave."

That was an interesting way to put it. "Did you hear anything out of the ordinary?"

Addie blanched, and Allen stepped between his daughter and me. "That's enough. We've answered your questions. Now, tell us your business here."

"Someone set Everly's barn on fire last night."

Allen's expression was carefully blank, but Ian took a few steps forward, his knuckles bleaching white. "That's *my* land. So, it's my barn. If we had burned it down, it would've been within our rights to do so."

"So, you *did* burn it down?" My fingers itched to reach for the butt of my gun, but I forced them to remain at my side.

"I said *if*. But, apparently, they don't teach you the English language at pig school. If I burned it down, I wouldn't be able to sell it for as good of a price now, would I? Everly will turn it over to me eventually."

Allen clamped a hand on Ian's shoulder. "We've given you what you asked for. Now, leave."

I tipped my head to the women on the porch. "If you ever need anything, the department is always open to you."

Allen stepped into my line of sight again as if he could block my words from reaching their target. "They don't need anything from you. We provide for them. Protect them. And they know that."

Cybil wore outrage carved into the lines of her face. But Addie? She had bone-deep sorrow in her eyes. I forced my hands to stay relaxed, but I clocked every movement around me. "That offer isn't just for them. It's for any of you. If you need help, my door is always open."

One of the men who'd been hanging back scoffed. "Don't need no pig-help. Rather be set on fire."

"That's your choice." I inclined my head to the SUV, and Young and I headed back to it. It was a conscious decision to turn my back to the men. It could've been a costly one. I counted that four of the six were armed. But I also couldn't show weakness. Instead, I watched the shadows on the ground, watching for even minor movement. But there was none.

I started the engine and headed down the drive. It wasn't

until we hit the pavement that Young let out a whoosh of air. "That was…"

"Messed the hell up?"

"I was going to use even stronger language, but that works, too." Young glanced over her shoulder at the disappearing ranch. "Addie might break rank. She sometimes has a stall at the farmer's market in town. Sells jams and stuff. She's kind and seems interested in the world around her, not full of hate like the rest of them."

I knew Addie could be the one to turn. But what would it cost her if she did?

Chapter Seventeen

Everly

I KICKED AT A CHARRED PIECE OF WOOD. EVERYTHING smelled as if I'd been living in a large bonfire—I guessed I was. And it wasn't only the barn. Three trees had to come down, as well. Thankfully, the cabin hadn't gone up, but I kind of wished the main house had. I still hadn't been able to venture inside. My gaze traveled back to the destruction. I'd need to order a dumpster and buy a chainsaw.

I didn't want to even think about how long it would take me to clear away all of the debris. Since I only had nights and week-ends, it would likely take me at least a month. That put me even more behind schedule. Not to mention that I had no idea how to cover the cost of building a brand-new barn. And I needed one to house some of the animals I wanted to give homes to.

Tears stung the corners of my eyes. And the fact that they did only made me angrier. Angry that my family hated me this much. Angry that I cared. So damn rageful that it still ate me up inside.

I wanted to let it all go but I couldn't even do that. I was back here on the land I grew up on, trying to make it right again. To somehow find some peace. But it was nowhere to be found.

Someone let out a low whistle behind me, and I whirled, my hand going to my waistband where my holster usually sat. I hadn't even armed myself before coming out here, that's how messed-up my mind was. But instead of my brother or Allen, I found Shiloh.

Her gaze traveled over the destruction before landing on my face. "Shit. You're crying. I-I'm not good with tears."

Her panic matched mine, and I couldn't help but laugh. "I'm not good with them either—having them, anyway."

She nodded, shifting on her feet.

"I didn't hear you come up."

Shiloh inclined her head to the tree line where a horse was tied off. "I took Trick. Needed a good ride."

It was more than good. It would've taken her hours to make it over here. "I think we'll be on hold for a bit when it comes to work. I need to order a dumpster and get all of this debris cleaned up."

"Do you know who did it?"

"The fire investigator and your brother haven't said anything, but I think it's still pretty early."

"Do *you* know?" Her gaze bored into mine, cutting through all the noise and carefully couched statements.

I backed out of the rubble and sat on a stump. "Probably my brother. If my uncle did it, he would've gone for the building I was sleeping in. Ian is more of a reactor. He probably got pissed off and decided to do something to soothe that anger."

Shiloh leaned against the fence. "He could've killed you."

"That would've been a bonus for him." But as I thought about it in the silence that Shiloh let linger, I knew that wasn't true. Ian would want me to hurt. To fear. And if I were dead, he wouldn't get that pleasure.

The sound of an engine working a bit harder than normal cut through the air. I pushed to my feet, stepping between Shiloh and whoever was coming up that hill. A hand landed on my shoulder, giving an awkward pat. "It's just Dad."

Gabe's truck appeared, along with the reason for the extra noise—a massive dumpster towed behind him. My nose began to sting. "What's he doing here?"

"You needed help. We're good with help."

She said it so simply. As if it were the easiest thing in the world. And maybe for the Easton family, it was. Gabe pulled alongside the burned remains of the barn, lining the dumpster up perfectly. Julia waved from the truck's cab, but they weren't alone.

Hayes' SUV appeared next, followed by another, and a truck I didn't recognize. I turned to Shiloh. "Why?"

She shrugged. "You need us."

Julia appeared with another wave and moved to wrap an arm around Shiloh, which she quickly ducked out of. "How are you holding up?"

"I, uh, I'm okay."

"Sorry for just barging in without calling, but I had a feeling you'd only blow us off if we did."

The corners of my mouth curved up. "You might be right."

"Gabe was able to get this bad boy today, so why not get a jump start?"

I glanced at my watch. "It's after four."

"Good thing we've got that late light. We'll work until the sun starts to set, and then I brought sandwiches for everyone. It's not fancy, but it'll fill your belly."

Those tears burned my eyes again, trying to break free. "Thank you."

She patted my shoulder in a move that came easily, as opposed to Shiloh's awkward one. "This community comes together when the chips are down."

I'd never experienced that before. My family had been too

busy looking at everyone in Wolf Gap with suspicion as if they were out to get them. I'd missed out on this experience. Emotions warred and flooded. Anger that I'd never had this before, and gratitude that I was receiving it now—all of it tossed in with a heavy dose of awkwardness. "I don't know what to say."

Julia turned me to face the approaching crowd. "Just say 'Thank you' and meet the rest of our ragtag crew."

I recognized the firefighter from two nights ago, Calder. He held the hand of a little girl, one who looked to be about eight or nine, and gave me a shy smile. Another woman followed him with a little girl on her back who had to be the first girl's twin.

And behind them, Hayes. My throat went dry as our gazes met. He was out of uniform, clad in dark-washed denim and a t-shirt that might as well have been made for him. I forced my eyes away and back to the first group. "Hi," I croaked.

"Hey," Calder greeted. "It's good to see you again."

"You, too." I looked at the little girl holding his hand. She ducked her head slightly. "And who's this?"

She didn't answer, but the little girl on the woman's back did. "She's Sage, and I'm Birdie. You're Everly, right? Dad said you're going to build a home for animals here. That's cool."

The smile that came was as natural as breathing. Something about the excitement of little ones. "I am. Think you'll come visit when I'm done?"

"Duh."

"Birdie…" Calder warned.

"I mean, yes. I'm definitely coming."

I chuckled and extended a hand to the woman as Birdie slid off her back. "I'm Everly. You must be Calder's wife."

She barked out a laugh. "Oh, God, no. We'd murder each other. I'm Hadley, Hayes and Shy's sister."

My cheeks heated. "Sorry, I just—"

She waved me off. "No big. Birds and Sage are just my best pals. It's really nice to finally meet you."

"You, too."

Hayes came to a stop in front of me. "Hey, Ev."

Ev. It wasn't a nickname anyone had ever called me before, yet it fell from his lips as if he'd been using it all his life. I couldn't stop looking at his mouth, wanting him to form the single syllable again. "Hi."

I couldn't come up with anything else to say. I was on people and emotion overload. Hadley seemed to sense this and hooked her arm through mine. "Come on, show me where we're getting this party started."

I could've kissed her. She got me moving and gave me direction. Soon, we were all piling the debris into the dumpster. Even the girls helped by putting smaller pieces into a wheelbarrow. As we worked, I could see the dynamics of the family come into play. The way Shiloh worked away from everyone else. How Hadley and Julia butted heads more times than I could count. The way Hayes or his father always stepped in to play peacekeeper in any sort of dustup.

It wasn't perfect, but it was more than I'd ever had. Love and care poured out of all of them—even when they fought.

Hadley climbed up the ladder on the side of the dumpster. "Here, I can take the end of that board."

"Hads, get down. Let me do that," Calder said as he crossed to the dumpster.

"I'm fine, Officer Safety. Just help Dad hand me that piece. I'll tip it in."

"You could fall."

"So could you."

Calder swiped his hat off his head. "I have training for this kind of thing."

"I had ten years of gymnastics. I think my balance is better."

A shadow moved across the ground, and I looked up to see Hayes. "Are they always like this?"

He rolled his eyes heavenward. "They fight like cats and dogs. I mean, don't get me wrong, they would do anything for each other, but it's a battle of wills every time they're in the same room."

"Hadley," Calder growled as she did some sort of pirouette thing on the lip of the dumpster.

"Don't mess around up there. You could hurt yourself," Julia called.

Hadley's expression tightened. "I guess I'll just get down, then." Instead of heading back for the ladder, she moved to the far end of the dumpster.

"What the hell—?"

Calder's words cut off as Hadley hurled herself into the air, tucking neatly into a backflip. The air froze in my lungs as she rotated. She landed with a thud. But it wasn't exactly clean, and she went from feet to butt pretty quickly, laughing.

"Are you kidding me right now?" Calder hurried over to her, but she waved him off.

"I'm fine. But I gotta work on that landing."

Birdie rushed over. "I wanna try."

Calder sent a look in Hadley's direction that could've melted ice in Antarctica. But she wasn't cowed. She simply got to her feet and took Birdie's hand. "Why don't we start with cartwheels?"

Calder's glare didn't leave Hadley's back as he watched her walk away with his daughter in tow. Julia squeezed his shoulder. "I'm sorry. I'll have a word. She really shouldn't be doing that kind of thing in front of the girls. Or at all."

"Mom," Hayes warned, "leave it."

I watched as Hadley led Birdie over to a patch of grass that looked a little worse for wear. She demonstrated a cartwheel and then walked Birdie through it, spotting her as she went.

The sound of the girl's giggle, carefree and light on the air, took me back.

"*I can balance longer,*" *Addie said, her hair flipping upside down as she balanced on her hands.*

"*Nuh-uh. I can.*" *I kicked up into a handstand but wobbled until I fell over.*

Addie collapsed next to me in a fit of giggles. "Told you."

"*I'm going again.*" *I kicked up harder this time, but my force was too great, and I went cascading into the fence. I cried out in pain as I crashed.*

Addie rushed over. "What is it? What'd you hurt?"

I gripped my forearm. Pain sliced through it in hot waves as tears filled my eyes. "My arm."

Mom appeared on the porch. "What's going on, girls?"

"*Evie hurt her arm,*" *Addie called, louder than she would've normally.*

Mom started down the steps, hurrying across the drive. "Oh, baby girl. Show me where."

I held up my arm, but as I lifted it, I cried out in pain.

"*That's okay. Try not to move it too much. I'm going to help you up, all right?"*

I nodded, tears streaming down my face.

On the count of three, Mom helped me to my feet. The tears came faster and harder as we walked to the house. The steps groaned as we walked up them, and my mom hurried to hold the door.

"*Howard,*" *she called as she moved inside.*

"*Kitchen,*" *my dad called back.*

He turned as we made our way towards the space. "Now what's with all the tears?" He crouched to make it to my level.

"*I-I hurt my arm.*"

"*Let me see.*"

I held out my arm for his inspection. His finger moved lightly over a scrape, but when his hand wrapped around the limb to feel for injury, I howled in pain.

Mom moved in, sweeping a hand over my head. "I think I need to take her to the emergency room."

Dad stood instantly, his eyes flashing. "We don't need any doctors. That's why you have your medical training."

"Midwife training and basic first-aid. I don't have an x-ray machine or know how to set a broken bone."

"No doctors. We've been over this, Carly. Treat her here. You have your tinctures. Wrap it and put it in a sling."

"Howard," she said softly. "Let me take—"

"I said, no! Do you want her to be poisoned by their drugs? Maybe they'll decide to take her away from us altogether. Is that what you want?!" Each word built on the last until he was screaming.

Mom pulled me against her as Addie backed away. "Of course, not. I'll treat her here."

He eyed her as if my mother had suddenly become the enemy. "Good."

"Come on, Evie. Let's get you patched up."

"Ev."

My mother's voice melded with Hayes'. I blinked a few times as I came back to myself. "Sorry, what?"

He moved closer. "Are you okay?"

I nodded quickly. "Fine. I just need some water."

I hurried away from Hayes' prying eyes, ones that asked too many questions. I moved towards the little cabin, the spot that had always made for a good hiding place. One that didn't hold nearly as many memories as the main house.

Jogging up the steps, I pulled open the screen door. It slammed with a bang behind me. I moved to the small kitchen and pulled out a glass. As I went for the pitcher of water in the fridge, my wrist twinged. It, along with so many other injuries, had never healed exactly right.

I had to use my other hand to balance the carafe. It wasn't even that heavy, but the weight was enough that my arm trembled. Tears blurred my vision as I poured, then set the pitcher down with a thud. The tears came faster. I rubbed at my wrist and forearm as if I could erase it all—every single memory carved into my bones. But I couldn't. And maybe coming back here wouldn't heal them, after all. Perhaps it would only reopen old wounds.

Chapter Eighteen

Hayes

I STOOD FROZEN TO THE SPOT; MY FEET GLUED TO THE threshold. My back to the world outside, my family; my front facing the woman who pulled at me more and more. I couldn't have moved if a herd of wild mustangs was headed in my direction.

She was weeping. I'd never heard a more beautiful sob—or a quieter one. Yet it tore at my insides just the same. Her body shook as she cradled her arm to her chest.

There was so much grief there. Bone-deep sorrow. And pain. It was the pain that unglued my feet. I moved before I could even think about the wisdom of it, letting the door slap closed behind me.

Everly jolted at the sound. She made a valiant effort to pull it together, straightening and dropping her hold on her wrist. She wiped at her face. But whatever she battled in the tiny kitchen was too much to hold back.

By the time I reached her, she was shaking again, tears flowing down her cheeks. Instead of saying a single word or going for my mom or Hadley like I should have, I wrapped Everly in my arms.

She seemed stunned for a moment, her body locking, but

instead of pushing me away, she collapsed against my chest, the sobs coming louder. The force of them ripped through her and seeped into me, and each one spilled a little more of her pain.

In that moment, I would've done anything to stop it. Because this woman didn't deserve whatever had caused it. I knew that like I knew the sun rose in the east every morning.

I held her tightly, not saying a word. I simply let her release some of whatever she had been holding on to for too long. If the dam needed to break, I could catch the overflow.

Slowly, the sobs quieted, and her shaking softened. The haphazard bun her hair had been wrapped in had fallen free, and I ran a hand over the strands. Her hair often looked a little wild, but the strands felt like silk. "You're okay."

"I'm not. I snotted all over someone who doesn't even like me."

"We've been over this. I like you," I grunted. I liked her *too* much.

"I'm surprised you didn't start yelling at me because my tears surprised you."

I barked out a laugh. "That's always a risk."

Everly tipped back her head, and I saw that her eyes were swollen, and her face was red. But she was still so damn beautiful. The raw truth in her was undeniable. A fierceness only matched by her tightly guarded vulnerability.

She patted at my chest. "I'm sorry. I just—"

"Don't apologize," I gritted out.

She straightened in my hold. "Don't growl at me."

"I'm not growling."

"You are—"

I put a finger to her lips. It was a mistake. They were plump and so damn soft. I dropped my hand immediately.

Everly's mouth opened, closed, and then opened again. "Did you just physically shush me?"

"Sorry. I just—you don't have to apologize. Sometimes, you just need to let things out. I'm glad I was here."

She took a step back, moving out of my hold. My fingers twitched as my arms fell to my sides. I wanted to pull her back. Everly looked down at her boots. "Thank you."

"What brought this on?"

Her gaze lifted, those blue eyes punching right through the walls of my chest. "It…nothing, I—" She stopped herself mid-sentence and shook her head. "I guess you deserve that much for letting me destroy one of your t-shirts."

I glanced down at my tee. There was a wet patch, and the cotton was stretched in places where her hands had fisted the material. "It's an old shirt. And it's hardly ruined." I lifted my gaze to hers. "Tell me."

It was a gentle demand, but a mandate, nonetheless. Something inside me clawed to get out. Some need to know what had hurt this woman so deeply. To understand the wounds so I could tread just a bit more carefully, unlike the bull-in-a-China-shop scene I'd pulled in our early meetings.

Everly leaned back against the counter, her fingers curling around the lip of the sink, knuckles bleaching white. "Hadley and Birdie doing cartwheels. It just reminded me of something."

"Cartwheels?" It was the only thing I managed to get out. Because how in the world did cartwheels lead to pain that I could feel across a room?

"It reminded me of the good and bad. Addie and I used to have handstand contests to see who could balance the longest."

My sisters had done the same thing. And whoever had won got bragging rights for the rest of the day. "You guys were close growing up?"

"The closest. More like sisters than cousins. Her mom left when she was young, so mine looked after her a lot."

"Okay…" I let the word hang in the air, a silent request for more.

"One time, I got a little carried away and sent myself flying into one of the fences."

"Ouch."

Everly's mouth curved the barest amount. "It wasn't pleasant."

I'd pulled more than one boneheaded move in my childhood. I'd broken a collarbone, my wrist, and sprained my ankle at least three times. I'd lost track of the number of stitches I'd received over the years. "Did you break anything?"

She held out her arm and traced an invisible line along her forearm. "Right here."

"How long were you in a cast?"

Her jaw worked back and forth as she searched for the words. "I wasn't."

"You didn't have to get a cast?" I was pretty sure every broken bone required one.

"My father wouldn't let me go to the hospital."

Everything in me stilled. It was the first time she'd brought him up in front of me. She hadn't even said his name, and my blood still went cold. "Why not?" I could barely get the words out.

She stared down at her arm as if she could see where the bone had been torn apart. "He didn't trust doctors. Thought conventional medicine was poison. That they gave you things you didn't need. Sometimes, he thought it was one of the ways the government tracked people."

"Did your mom take you?"

Everly's chin lifted, her eyes so bleak. "No. She couldn't go against him. Not like that."

"Fuck that." I started pacing back and forth across the kitchen, needing to move or I'd explode. "She should've left and taken you and your brother with her. What kind of messed-up person stays and puts her children through that?"

"A weak one."

I stopped and turned slowly back to Everly.

"She was weak. Fallible. Human. She'd used all of her courage to go against her parents' wishes and marry my father. When it wasn't what she thought it would be, she had nowhere to go. No one to turn to. She met him when she was nineteen. Barely had a high school diploma. She had Ian when she was only twenty-one—still a baby herself."

"Calder was only a little older when his twins were born, and he'd do anything for them. How can you just excuse her like that?"

Everly released her hold on the sink. "I'm not excusing it. I'm still furious with her. You don't think I am? I live with hundreds of memories just like that one. But I choose to try and understand her. Otherwise, all of that anger will eat me alive."

"That's why you're here." It suddenly made all the sense in the world.

"I have to find a way to make peace with it. With her. With the rest of my family. With this place. This land was in her family for generations. Her grandmother left it to my mom in her will. There was so much good in this place for so long. And I have a chance to make it that again."

I could practically feel the need clawing at her. "That's a heavy weight to put on your shoulders."

Everly looked up, meeting my stare dead-on. "I've never fit anywhere. But these mountains? They always accepted me, grounded me. They were my touchstone when I didn't have anything else."

Her gaze drifted away from me, moving toward the window and the sprawling landscape outside. "I thought maybe I could find my place in them. Heal some of those hurts—for others and myself. All I know is, I have to try."

Chapter Nineteen

Everly

I TOOK A DEEP BREATH OF THE PINE-SCENTED AIR AS I stepped out into the sunshine, the door to the vet's office closing with a snick behind me. I closed my eyes and tipped my face up to the light. Maybe the rays would infuse some energy into my body.

I was wrung out. Physically. Emotionally. Yesterday had drained every drop. Because after my emotional unburdening with Hayes, we'd had to go back to work. He'd offered to make up an excuse for me, say that I wasn't feeling well, and it would've been true enough. But I wasn't going to let his family clean up my mess alone.

So, back out I'd gone. I'd received some concerned looks, and Hayes some stern ones, but I'd simply ducked my head and started hauling debris. The physical labor had helped, but my body was paying for it today. I would try to cram myself into the minuscule bathtub the cabin had. Or maybe I'd drive out to the hot springs. Either way, I needed a soak.

I started down the path towards the sidewalk and came up short. Addie was walking next to Ben. My heart clenched. Something about seeing the two of them together got to me—the friends I'd spent so much of my childhood with. And their lives had simply gone on. They'd stayed friends, and had left me behind. Or had I gone on ahead? I wasn't sure anymore.

Ben smiled. "Hey, Evie."

"Hi." My voice came out on a croak. "How are you guys?"

Addie looked around before answering. "Good."

"I heard about what happened up at your place. Are you okay?" Ben asked.

"Fine. Just dealing with the cleanup."

"I can come up and help this evening if you need it."

God, he still had that kindness I'd always basked in growing up. "Thanks, but I had some people helping out yesterday, and it's mostly done."

His gaze hardened a fraction. "Who? You need to be careful who you tell that you're living up there alone."

My lips twitched. Ben had always been overprotective. "It was the sheriff and his family, so I think I'm safe."

Ben didn't look quite as convinced. "Okay. Just be cautious— you know you can come stay with my folks and me at the ranch if you need."

"Thanks, but I'm good."

He turned to Addie and squeezed her elbow. "Why don't you catch up with Evie? I'll take the jams to the bakery and go to the store."

"What about—?"

Ben cut her off. "Allen's moving the cattle today. He and the guys won't venture into town."

I sent Ben a grateful look before turning back to Addie. "Let me treat you to lunch. Have you ever been to Spoons?"

She shook her head. "That would be nice."

"I'll meet you back here in an hour?" Ben asked.

I adjusted my purse on my shoulder. "An hour would be perfect. Do you want me to bring you a sandwich or anything?"

His mouth quirked. "Still trying to feed me?"

"Some things will never change."

"It's nice to have things you can count on. But I already ate."

Ben's words twisted something in my stomach. How many times had I snuck him a cookie or an extra sandwich because he had the appetite of someone five times his size? And now he was this weird mix of stranger and brother of my heart. "All right. I'll bring you a cookie, then."

"That, I'll never say no to." With a wave, he was off.

Addie and I were silent for a moment, not moving at all. She spoke first. "He always was half in love with you."

I snorted. "More like he was half in love with all of the treats I snuck him."

"He missed you. So did I."

"I tried to write, Addie."

"I know," she whispered. "I couldn't risk writing back. Dad was so mad at you."

I knew that, too. And now there was this chasm between us that I wasn't sure we'd ever be able to close. But I had to try. "Let's get some lunch."

I started down the street, and it only took a moment for Addie to follow. She fell into step beside me, and it was like an awkward version of the old times. I couldn't help but wonder what it would've been like if I'd stayed. A mix of images flitted through my mind. I wouldn't have lost Addie or Ben. We would've been just as close. But I knew without a shadow of a doubt that I would've slowly ceased to exist.

I stole a quick glance at the person I'd loved most in the world. The same had happened to Addie. The eyes that had once held a bright twinkle were dull, searching the street for signs of an attack. I swallowed against the burn in my throat.

I'd chosen myself over everyone else when I left. It wasn't that I hadn't thought about Addie—I thought of her all the time. But I'd picked myself over staying to help her. It wasn't right or wrong, it was simply survival. It ate away at me, nonetheless.

Choices. An infinite number of them. Big and small. And together, they made up a life. One that made Addie and I strangers now.

I pulled open the door to the small café, motioning Addie inside. Jill looked up from behind the counter. "I think we've got a new regular. I love it."

"I'm having a hard time staying away."

"I'll let you in on a little secret. That was our plan all along."

I chuckled. "Jill, this is my cousin, Addie."

"Nice to meet you, Addie."

"You, too," Addie answered softly.

Jill picked up two menus. "What do you think, outside in the sun or inside in the air conditioning?"

I looked at Addie in question.

"Let's do inside."

I should've guessed. Inside meant less chance someone might see her with me and accidentally drop that into casual conversation with Allen. Not that Allen had a whole lot of casual-conversation kind of friendships. But better to be cautious.

Jill led us to a table against the wall. "How's this?"

"Perfect," I said, sliding into one of the chairs. "Thanks."

"Just wave me over when you're ready to order."

She disappeared back behind the counter, and Addie and I were alone again. Addie studied the menu meticulously. "What do you like here?"

"The egg salad is my favorite, but the soups are good too if you want something lighter."

"Egg salad sounds good." She kept her eyes glued to the laminated paper as if it held all the answers in the world.

"How are you, Addie?"

It was both the simplest question and the most complicated. But it was everything I wanted to know.

She carefully set the menu down on the table and looked up. "I'm fine."

Nothing about her was fine. She was too skinny. Dark circles rimmed her eyes. And her fingernails had been bitten down to the quick.

"Please, don't lie."

A flash of heat filled her dull eyes. "And what makes you deserve the truth? My truth. You left."

God, it was good to see a bit of life in those eyes, even if it was from anger directed at me. But the words burned, as intended. "I had to go. You know, I did. But I'm so sorry that it meant I had to leave you, too."

Tears filled her eyes, and she quickly wiped them away. "It's been lonely without you."

I could only imagine. After everything that had happened with my father, Allen had tightened the reins on Addie even more. She'd been cut off from the world. "You had Ben, though, right?"

"He tries to stop by as often as he can. But he had his wife, and…" Her words trailed off.

I'd almost forgotten what Ian had said about Ben's wife. "What happened?"

Addie straightened the silverware on the napkin. "I'm not sure, exactly. There was a lot of bleeding, and no one could stop it. By the time he got her to the hospital, it was too late for her and the baby."

My chest constricted as the scene played out in my imagination. "He took her to the hospital?"

"They didn't want him to, but Ben did it anyway." Darkness flitted over her features. "Dad blames the doctors."

Of course, he did. Allen and my father stirred each other up with their conspiracies. Allen knew that my dad was taking it too far, and he didn't care. None of them had.

"How is Ben doing now?" Guilt for how I'd pushed Ben away when he'd first appeared at the cabin ate at me. He'd learned to stand up to his parents and Allen at too high a cost.

Addie adjusted her silverware yet again. "A little better, I think. But he blames himself for not taking her sooner."

That kind of weight could drown a man. "He'll have to find a way to release some of it."

"Have you?"

I picked up my water glass and took a sip before setting it down. "I'm trying. That's part of why I'm here. To finally make peace with it all. To try and let it go."

"You've seen the Eastons?"

"They're…amazing. It's so different from how we grew up. The way they help and support each other."

Addie's gaze drifted out the window. "You and I helped and supported each other."

I reached out and laid a hand over hers. Addie jolted, but I didn't let her hand go. "We did. And I want that again. You're another reason I came back. I missed you so damn much."

"Pebble for the swear jar."

Her words startled a laugh out of me. My mother had been appalled when Ian had picked up some foul language, and that had trickled down to me. The first time I'd said the word *shit*, she'd dropped a glass of lemonade, shattering it on the floor. Mom had instantly instituted a swear jar. Every time we messed up, we had to get a piece of gravel or small rock from outside and place it in the jar, along with doing an extra chore. When the jar filled to the top, Ian and I would have to do some monumental task that neither of us wanted to do. I was forever having to pick up a pebble.

"I'm afraid the jar never really did its job."

Addie's mouth curved. "I can tell." She was quiet for a moment. "You work at the vet's office?"

The curiosity in her tone only lit more anger at my uncle, but I kept my voice even. "Yeah. I went to college first, but then I did an accelerated vet tech program."

"You always did want to work with animals. And now, you are."

"I'm still going to build the sanctuary. I'm doing it on Mom's land. You could help, Addie. Come live with me. We could do it together."

Her eyes widened. "I-I can't. You know that, Evie."

"You're twenty-four, Addie. You can leave. There's nothing he can do to stop you."

"It's not that simple. I have nothing. No one."

"You have *me*."

A war of emotions played over Addie's expression. "But who knows when you'll leave again. Just like everyone else." She pushed jerkily to her feet. "This was a bad idea. I need to go."

"Addie, wait—"

"I hope you find what you're looking for."

Chapter Twenty

MY FEET HIT THE DIRT WITH MORE FORCE THAN necessary, but I welcomed the jar to my bones. That little bite of pain, along with the burn in my lungs, was my release. One I'd needed after the longest week in history.

Between the evenings I'd been pulling with my family at Everly's and the hours I'd been logging on both Cammie's case and the fire, I needed this outlet. The only thing I'd seen progress on was cleaning up the barn. The rubble was gone, and the ground leveled, ready for whatever structure Ev wanted to put in its place.

We'd hit a dead stop on Cammie's case. No one had seen a man who fit the description we had. And I wouldn't deny that a large part of me hoped it was someone passing through. That we wouldn't have to deal with any other calls like hers.

We'd come to the same crossroads on Everly's fire. Only this time, I had a real guess as to who was responsible. I'd asked Ev if I could put up a couple of game cameras on her drive to give her some additional security. She'd reluctantly agreed, and I'd made sure that word of cameras going up got around. In truth, they wouldn't do much—there was simply too much land to

But I hoped that they would make someone who wanted to stir up trouble think twice.

Koda bounded across the trail we both knew by heart, and I couldn't hold in my chuckle. It was the sheer joy on his face. Apparently, we'd both needed the run.

He took off into the trees, while I stayed on the path. These summer evenings that allowed for post-work runs were some of my favorite things about the season—that and time at the lake, which I'd had far too little of this year.

A howl split the air, and I almost tripped over my feet. It wasn't the sound of one animal calling to another. It was one of pain, and it was coming from my dog.

I ran off the path towards the sound. "Koda! Where are you?"

He let out another pained cry, and I picked up my pace. I didn't hear sounds from another creature, so I hoped it wasn't anything bad. I called his name again and picked up the sound of a whine.

I caught sight of his crumpled form, my chest wheezing. "Koda. What is it, boy?"

He tried to move towards me and then cried out. I sank to my knees. "Stay still. You're okay."

I froze. He sure as hell wasn't okay. My dog's hind leg was caught firmly between the jaws of a trap. I let a slew of curses fly as I took in the blood oozing from his leg.

Koda whined and pressed his body against my leg. I sank my hands into his fur, scratching behind his ears to try and calm him. "We'll get you out of this. It's gonna hurt more before it gets better, though. Can you stick with me?"

Koda licked the side of my face. "Okay. I'm taking that as a yes."

I did my best to examine the trap without jostling Koda. As I did, anger slid through my veins. No trap like this was humane, but this kind was the worst of the worst. I wouldn't be surprised if the force had broken Koda's leg.

"Here we go, buddy." With one swift move, I pressed down on the levers on the sides of the trap. Koda howled in pain but pulled his leg free. Once he was clear, I released my hold, and the jaws clanged closed.

I wrapped my arms around my dog as he whimpered. "All right now. I got you." I slowly ran my hands down his body to his leg, but Koda wouldn't let me near the wound. "Okay. I won't touch it."

I pushed to my feet. "You think you can stand?" Koda tried to follow but cried out, holding his leg off the ground.

I ran a hand over my head, thinking about my options. Pulling out my phone, I held it up. One bar. I tried Hadley first, knowing she had the day off. The call wouldn't connect.

"We're gonna have to get creative, buddy."

Koda looked up at me with sorrowful eyes.

"I know. I'm gonna get whoever did this." With that promise, I noted in my phone where we were on the trail so I could come back to investigate. Then I slid my phone back into my pocket. "I hope Hads and Shy haven't been giving you extra treats."

I groaned as I lifted Koda into my arms. "They definitely have." It was going to be a long five miles to the trailhead.

"It's all right, buddy. We're here." I pulled to a stop in one of the parking spots in front of the vet. Koda let out a whine from the backseat.

I'd oscillated between pissed and worried the entire drive to the vet. Thankfully, my adrenaline had carried me most of the hike back to my SUV at the trailhead. But that had melted away as soon as I started driving, replaced by anger and fear.

Pushing my door open, I jumped out of my vehicle and

rounded to the backseat so I could get Koda. My arms shook just a bit with his weight. "I'm telling you. It's diet time once you're all fixed up."

The only noise Koda made was a groan of pain. I hurried up the walkway, and just before I reached the front porch, the door swung open. Everly's eyes widened as she took us in. "What happened?"

"A hunting trap off Bear Creek trail."

A blue heat, the sharpest of flames, filled those wide eyes. "Anyone who uses those traps deserves to get stuck in one. Come on inside. I was just locking up. Miles is gone, but I'm sure he'll come back."

I hadn't even considered that it was already after five. I'd only been thinking about getting here as quickly as possible. Everly ushered us into an exam room, and I carefully laid Koda on the table. She stroked his face with one hand while pulling out her cell phone with the other.

"Hi, Miles. I've got Hayes Easton here with Koda." Her hand moved gently but efficiently down Koda's side to his injured leg. She barely grazed the limb, but he still let out a whimper. "He got his leg stuck in a trap, and I'm worried it might be broken."

She made some sounds of agreement as she listened to whatever Miles had to say and answered with succinct responses. At one point, she pulled a stethoscope from her purse and listened to Koda's heart. "Nice and strong."

I felt such relief at those words, I nearly had to take a seat in one of the empty chairs. Everly wrapped the stethoscope around her neck and then went back to passing soothing strokes along Koda's side. "No problem. I can do that now. We'll see you when you get here."

She tapped end on the screen and slid her phone into her purse. "He'll be here as soon as he can. He drove out to the Callahans' to check on a horse who's due any day, so it'll take him a bit to get back. I'm going to administer a painkiller in the meantime so we can get Koda a little more comfortable. Is that all right with you?"

"Of course. Anything you can do to help."

"I'll be right back." She hurried into the back.

I took her place at Koda's head and stroked his face. "You're going to be okay."

The back door slid open, and Everly appeared with a syringe. "If you want to stay at his head, that would be great. Most dogs aren't fans of needles, but I'm pretty good with doing injections as painlessly as possible. They usually give me the tough cases."

"Sure." I stroked the side of Koda's face. "Show Ev what a tough pup you are, okay?"

The heat from Everly's body seeped into mine as she moved in close and positioned the needle near the scruff of his neck. She bunched the skin with one hand and wielded the syringe deftly with the other. Koda didn't flinch.

"I don't think he even felt it."

She soothed any possibility of a sting with strokes along his side. "Let's hope it gets him feeling better. It should only take a few minutes to kick in."

I scratched in the spot that Koda loved behind his ears, moving in a rhythmic motion over and over until his eyes drooped and his breathing grew deep. I slowly removed my hand and took a step back. "I think he's asleep."

Everly gave my dog a gentle smile, one I wished was pointed in my direction. "He's been through the wringer. Sleep is the best thing for him right now."

I reached out and took hold of her hand, squeezing and releasing it before she had a chance to possibly pull away. "Thank you."

"It's my job."

"I know. But I'm still grateful."

She moved to a drawer, examining its contents and doing some sort of unnecessary organization.

"Don't like people thanking you?"

A flush of pink brushed her cheeks. "I don't need it. I love what I do."

"And you're good at it. You've got a way with animals. They're lucky to have you."

That pink deepened. "Thanks."

I chuckled. "I'll let you off the hook now, promise."

"Did you call in the location of the trap to the Forest Service?"

My hint of amusement fled in a flash. "Not yet. I've got a contact over there that I'll call when I leave. Hopefully, he'll sign on to letting me be involved in the case. I'd like to be there when whoever set those traps is arrested."

"I'd like to put his leg in one."

"I don't disagree with you there. You usually a fan of bloody revenge?"

She looked up and met my gaze. "Sometimes, violence is the only thing a person understands. I'd never make the first move, but I won't hesitate to fight back."

A chill skittered across my spine. Everly spoke as if she'd experienced that kind of violence firsthand. "You should always defend yourself by any means necessary."

She turned away. "I will. But not everyone has the skills to do that."

The sadness in her voice ripped at something in me. I took a stab in the dark. "Addie?"

Everly didn't turn back around, but the tightness in her shoulders told me I'd hit the nail on the head.

"I'd like to help her if I can."

After a moment, she turned. "You really are just the little helper, aren't you?"

The corner of my mouth kicked up. "Little feels like a bit of an insult…"

She snorted. "Fine, big helper."

"That's better." I took her in for a second, my gaze traveling across her face, looking for any piece of insight into this woman I could find. "If I can make someone's life better, I want to try."

Everly leaned back against the counter. "I might have ruined our chances there."

"How?"

"I pushed. Tried to get Addie to come live with me. But it was too soon. She doesn't trust me, and she has a reason not to."

"Why's that?" I couldn't imagine Everly betraying her cousin in any way.

"I left her."

The sorrow and grief in Everly's words clawed at my chest. "You didn't have a choice." I didn't know what had gone down with the Kemper family after Howard went to prison, but I knew it wasn't good. And I also knew that Ev wouldn't have left her cousin just for the hell of it.

"You don't know that."

"I do. I might not know the details, but I know that you wouldn't leave without reason. And maybe one day you'll trust me with what that reason was."

Chapter Twenty-One

Everly

"ARE YOU SURE YOU'RE OKAY STAYING OVERNIGHT?" Miles asked as he placed his stethoscope in his medical bag.

"More than." It wasn't like I had anyone to go home to. Not like Miles, who had his wife and daughters. "And Koda and I are good friends. I'd like to stay with him."

"He does seem to be partial to you. I think he'll feel at ease having you close by."

I glanced over at the German shepherd, curled up in his kennel. He was snoring away, his new cast in place. We'd lucked out that the break hadn't needed surgery, but Miles still wanted to keep him overnight as a precaution. I'd need to change his IV and give him another dose of pain meds during the night and first thing in the morning. Hopefully, with a good night's sleep and some heavy-duty drugs, he'd be feeling better in the morning.

"No one wants to be alone when they're feeling poorly. I've got my alarm set for his next two doses, so I think we're set."

Miles patted my shoulder. "I'll have my cell phone nearby if you run into any issues. Don't hesitate to call. My wife sleeps with earplugs now, so you won't wake her."

"She's learned the hard way, huh?"

"She was not a fan of having her sleep interrupted, and after my first year of owning my own practice, she got smart and got earplugs. We're both happier now. I hope you can get some sleep, too."

"I will." I waved him off, and Miles headed out the back door.

Surveying the room around me, I sighed. Koda was our only overnight guest but sleeping in unfamiliar places wasn't the easiest thing for me. At least, the office had a little cot in the corner, and Miles had given me a fresh set of linens and a pillow. It would be good enough. And I'd done without sleep before. I could do it again.

A knock sounded at the back door, and I moved to pull it open. "Did you forget—?"

A man who was definitely not Miles cut off my question. Hayes stood in the doorway with a bag slung over one shoulder, holding two pizza boxes. His hair was dark, still damp from a shower. "Hey."

"Hi."

"I thought you might be spending the night. Pizza?"

My mouth opened, closed, then opened again. "What kind?"

Hayes raised a brow. "Does it matter?"

"Always."

"I went straight ahead. One cheese. One pepperoni."

"You give me the cheese, and I'll let you in."

He chuckled and handed me a box. "It's all yours."

My stomach rumbled as I inhaled the cheesy goodness. "I thought I would have to settle for one of Tim's Cup Noodles."

"I'd never leave you to that fate. Especially after taking such good care of Koda." Hayes went to peek in the kennel. When he saw that his dog was fast asleep, he turned back to me. "Where do you want to eat?"

I inclined my head to the left. "Break room. We'll leave the door open so we can hear Koda if he wakes up."

I walked into the room that felt even smaller than usual. Memories of the last time we'd been in this space flooded my mind. Apparently, I had a penchant for losing it around Hayes, but I had to admit that he handled it well. I wouldn't have thought the man who'd been so callous at our first meeting could be so kind and caring.

I slid the box onto the table. "Want a soda or a water? We might have iced tea, too."

"I'll take a Coke if you've got one." Hayes moved to the cabinets, pulling out plates and napkins.

"That we have." I pulled two from the fridge and settled back at the table, sliding one across to Hayes.

We were quiet for a moment as we pulled slices out of our respective boxes. He glanced at mine. "So, you don't like pepperoni?"

"I don't eat meat."

"At all?"

I barked out a laugh. "You sound like I just told you that Santa isn't real."

Hayes gave a mock gasp, his hand flying to his chest. "He's not?"

"I'm just breaking hearts all over the place."

"It really is cruel. I don't know how you live without cheeseburgers."

I shrugged. "I don't begrudge anyone their cheeseburgers, but the longer I worked with animals, the harder it was to eat them." Hayes' expression soured. "Sorry."

"No, I get it. I think growing up on a cattle ranch gave me a different outlook. Mom and Dad have always been sticklers for ethical ranching. No crazy hormones to beef up the stock. Ending life as humanely as possible."

"That's good. Most large-scale operations aren't that way. I just... my heart can't handle it, I guess."

The gentle smile that Hayes gave me, hit somewhere in the vicinity of my chest. I dropped my gaze, but he didn't look away. "You guard that sensitive heart pretty well."

Heat rose to my cheeks. "Some people take it as a weakness."

"I don't. I think letting things affect you deeply means you're stronger than the rest of the world."

I broke off a piece of crust and tore it into little pieces. I needed a subject change, something that wouldn't feel as if Hayes was peering inside my mind and soul and seeing all the things I hid away. "How'd you end up with Koda?"

"He was a K-9 dropout, and I fell in love."

"Really?"

He took a sip of his Coke and nodded. "He flunked out for being too friendly."

"My kind of dropout."

"Mine, too. The program was going to put him up for adoption, but I'd already grown attached, so I took him home."

"It looks like you guys were meant for each other."

Hayes took a bite of pizza and then swallowed. "I think so. And my family loves him. They spoil him rotten. Which is why it nearly killed me to carry him the five miles back to my SUV today."

I dropped the piece of crust I was toying with back to my plate. "You carried him five miles? He weighs over eighty pounds."

"Believe me, I know. I told him he'd be going on a diet as soon as he's better. My sisters and parents give him too many treats."

"They love him."

"That they do. I swear he'd abandon me for Shiloh if he could."

I cracked open my soda and took a sip. "It seems like she has a way with animals, too."

"She does. Horses, especially. I think she likes the idea of your sanctuary."

"She seems to. She's been helping out a lot. Says she'd like to help me get it up and running."

Hayes slowly set his slice of pizza down. "I didn't know she'd come by before we had to help with the barn."

I'd realized that about Shiloh as I'd gotten to know her a little better—she kept things close to the vest. Especially around her family. "She showed up the day after your mom did and said she wanted to help. It must run in the family."

Hayes' jaw worked back and forth, and I could almost hear his back teeth grinding together. "I don't think it's a good idea. Helping out once or twice is one thing, but being there all the time...? It's not healthy."

I was quiet for a moment, trying to choose my words carefully. "Shouldn't she be the one to decide that?"

"You think you know my sister better than I do?"

"Not at all. But I think she knows herself best."

Hayes flexed his fingers against the lip of the table. "She can get triggered easily. I just don't want that to happen more than it already does."

"I get that." Oh boy, did I ever. More than Hayes would ever know. "But, sometimes, we have to confront the ghosts. I think that's what she's doing in a way. Proving to herself there's no reason to be scared anymore."

"I need you to keep a close eye on her. And tell me if she seems to be having a hard time."

I didn't think Shiloh would let me in on that sort of thing. "Hayes, if she talks to me about anything...I'm not going to betray that confidence and come running to you." He started to speak, but I held up a hand. "It's not like we've become bosom buddies or anything."

"Bosom buddies?"

"Haven't you ever read *Anne of Green Gables*?"

"I can't say that I have. But if there were boob friends, maybe I was missing out."

I choked on the sip of Coke I'd just taken and nearly sprayed it across the table. "Don't say something like that while I'm drinking."

"Good to know you think I'm funny."

"You're denigrating my favorite Anne. You probably deserve a little backwash spray."

Hayes pushed back from the table a bit. "I'll keep my distance, then."

"Wise."

He looked up and met my gaze dead-on. "I love my sister. She's different because of what happened to her, and I'd give anything to change that for her. I'd do anything to keep her from hurting now."

His words sliced and clawed. Each one cutting deeper than the last. "You're a good brother."

"I try."

I took a deep breath. "But different isn't always bad. Sometimes it's a superpower. Make sure you're not overlooking what's so special about Shiloh in search of things that are *wrong*."

Hayes was quiet for a moment, but he didn't look away. "I don't. I…hell."

I reached across the table and laid my hand over his. "There's only one thing you need to do."

"And what's that?"

"Love her for who she is now, no matter the whys of it."

"I can do that." Hayes turned his hand over so we were palm-to-palm. And, for some reason, I kept mine there.

We stayed like that as the seconds drifted into a minute, and still, I didn't pull away. Not until a whine sounded from the back room and broke the moment. But I felt the heat of that hand for the rest of the night.

Chapter Twenty-Two

Everly

I SWUNG MY KEYS AROUND MY POINTER FINGER AS I LEANED against the hood of my SUV. I'd begun to notice a pattern over the past few weeks. Every Monday, someone brought Addie into town. Sometimes, it was Allen. Other times, Ian. But every once in a while, I got lucky and it was Ben. And it was always during my lunch hour that she walked past.

Today, I wasn't taking a chance. I'd overheard some guys at the hardware store saying they were working a fencing job at the Kemper ranch. Allen would never let workers be at his home unsupervised. I had to hope that meant Ben would be the one bringing Addie today.

I looked up as two figures rounded the corner—Addie with a bag slung over her shoulder, and Ben beside her. I straightened from my spot and started towards them. "Addie, can I talk to you for a minute?"

She ignored me and kept walking past.

"Addie, please."

Ben moved in closer. "Give her some time. She needs to trust that you're back for good. And you know Addie. She doesn't trust easily."

I muttered a curse under my breath. Addie's mother leaving her with her asshole of a father had done a number on her. And I'd repeated the cycle. "I don't know if she'll ever forgive me."

He reached out and squeezed my shoulder. "She will. I promise."

"I wish I had your confidence."

"I know Addie, and I know you. Evie, you've never given up on something you truly wanted. And Addie has high walls, but you've always been able to scale them."

That was before. When Addie thought I was on her team. Now, I was pretty sure she only saw me as the enemy.

Ben raised his chin to point down the block. "Walk with me? I need to pick up a few things for my mom at the quilt store. Unless you have plans?"

I looked down at the little lunchbox cooler in my hand. I'd made enough food for two, hoping I'd convince Addie to eat with me. I lifted the insulated bag. "Hungry? I was planning on having lunch in the park. Unless you're in a hurry?"

"Fabric and thread can wait."

We started towards the little park a few blocks from the vet's office. It was impeccably kept. The grass the perfect height, and the picnic tables were refinished each year over the winter months. It looked as if they'd gotten new playground equipment since I'd been here last. There was even a splash pad now. A handful of children squealed with delight as they ran through the dancing water.

Ben led us to a table under the shade of an Aspen. I unzipped the bag, pulling out two sandwiches, a bag of chips, and two sodas. His expression gentled as he sat. "You were hoping Addie would join you."

"Hope springs eternal."

"She will, eventually. Just—"

"Give her time. I know."

Ben unwrapped his sandwich in the same methodical way he always had. "This looks delicious."

"I have to warn you, it's veggie. But I promise it's good."

He raised a brow. "A vegetarian now?"

"I think it's a hazard of the job."

"Understandable. You always did have a soft spot for critters."

I unwrapped my sandwich and popped the tab on my Coke. "How are you doing?"

Ben washed down a bite of his sandwich with a sip of his drink. "It's been a tough year, but I'm hanging in."

"I heard that your wife passed away. I'm so sorry."

His Adam's apple bobbed as he swallowed. "She was amazing, my Liza. You would've really liked her. Knew just how much to push. Could go against the grain without even Allen realizing it."

"If she could pull one over on Allen, we definitely would've been friends."

"I think so. I miss her every day."

"That's a measure of how much you loved her." I'd never known that kind of love. I tried to imagine what it would feel like to have someone talk about me in the same reverent tone Ben had slipped into for his late wife. But I couldn't picture it.

"You're right there. But it's hard to live with guilt. The millions of what-ifs. Mom says, sometimes, we can't know God's plan for us. But this feels like a really shitty road to put me on."

My heart seized at his words, its rhythm tripping and stuttering. I didn't have words of comfort for something like this. I wished I could think of something that might ease him just a little, but I kept coming up empty. "Seems to me that if God is who they say He is, He can take our anger and grief. He can take our rage. It's when we stuff it down that we get into trouble."

Ben's gaze lifted to mine. "You get into trouble?"

"Maybe *trouble* isn't the right word. But I've struggled to find my peace. To hold my anger and love at the same time." It often felt as if there was only room enough for one of them at any given moment. That I could rage about all the ways my mother had let me down or remember the tender moments we shared in the garden or out on a hike, where she showed me which plants were edible. But I couldn't hold both.

"She loved you. You know that, right? I know she wasn't perfect. Far from it. Just like I know she regretted not doing more to protect you. We both carried that burden."

That war was lighting inside me again. Wanting to reach for forgiveness and, at the same time, feeling like nothing would ever be enough. "I'm trying to find my way to understanding her more. I think that's part of why I needed to come back here."

I picked at a piece of my sandwich's crust. "I've found empathy for her. Especially the girl who got married so young. Who really didn't know what she was getting into. She was barely past her teenage years when she had Ian. Few would be equipped to handle that at her age."

"But she did her best."

"I'm sure she did. But she got so wrapped up in my father's conspiracy theories. Fell down that rabbit hole. She constantly moved in response to whatever he did or didn't do." I tore the piece of crust into bits. "Looking back, I realize that he manipulated her with his emotions. Dad never raised a hand to her in anger. But if she displeased him, he ignored or berated her. That happens enough, you begin to toe the line."

Ben's brows pulled together as he studied his lunch. "I think she slipped into the same pattern with Allen. After you left, she did whatever he asked, but it was almost robotic."

"She'd given up any fight left in her."

"I guess you're right," he agreed. "I hate that he leads that way. There's so much more power when you gain your devotion through respect."

I took a sip of soda. "That's how your parents work." While

Ben's folks had different beliefs than most, they never forced them on others. They worked hard and led by example, instead of force.

"I can only hope to be half the man my father is one day."

"I'm sure you will be."

Ben flicked at the tab on his can, twisting it in some sort of rhythmic pattern. "You know you'd be welcome to come stay with them. Or me. Whenever you want. I hate the idea of you up at that cabin all alone."

"I can't, Ben." It was too close. Too much in that world I'd done everything to escape. "I want to be where I am." It felt like I was making a true home for myself. Maybe it was having the Eastons' help these past few weeks, or perhaps seeing the paddocks start to take shape as Shiloh and I put up fencing. I was beginning to see what the property could be.

Ben's mouth pressed into a firm line, but he nodded. "That invitation doesn't have an expiration date."

I reached across and patted his arm. "Thank you." I wanted to find a way to meld the good parts of my past like Ben and Addie with the future I was building. That was what had always been at the heart of this journey. Melding the old with the new and forming it into something good.

Because as much as I tried to simply ignore the past, to build myself into an entirely new person who didn't have a father in prison or a brother who never resisted using his fists, or a mother who had simply faded away, that wasn't me. And who I was had strength and empathy because of where I'd come from.

"Well, isn't this cozy?"

I lifted my head to see Ian strolling across the grass. I didn't stand or let any glimmer of alarm rise to my face. I simply picked up my Coke and took a sip. "Hello, Ian."

He ignored me and turned to Ben. "Allen needs you at the ranch. There's an issue with the water pump, and no one can figure out how to fix it."

Ben had always been gifted with machinery and mechanisms. He'd constantly taken apart old appliances to see if he could figure out how to fix them. Apparently, that hadn't changed.

"I'll head over as soon as I've finished up lunch."

Ian swiped his hat off his head. "You'd side with *her* over the people who have had your back your entire life?"

Ben rolled his eyes heavenward. "It has nothing to do with sides. I'm hungry, and I'd like to finish eating. I need to wait for Addie anyway."

"I'll wait for Addie," Ian gritted out.

Ben opened his mouth to argue, but I waved him off. "Take your sandwich to go. We can catch up another time."

Ben met my stare as if checking to see if I really meant what I said. The tiny action made my chest tighten. It was a silent promise that he had my back against Ian this time. I gave him a small nod, and he rose, picking up his lunch.

"Does this mean you're finally learning your place?" Ian asked.

"My place is wherever I want it to be."

My brother scoffed, turning to Ben. "She always did have grand ideas about what she thought she could be. You might want to keep your distance from that one. She was willing to throw anyone under the bus to get what she wanted. It's why she's alone now. Burned every bridge she ever had."

"I don't know," Ben said, "I think a few grand ideas is a good thing."

He sent me a wink as they took off across the park, and I let out a slow breath. This was what the new normal would likely be. It seemed my brother might be settling, and I could only hope Allen did the same. They would never be friendly, but maybe over time, they would be content with snide jabs and rude comments.

I only hoped that Ben and Addie would be able to withstand them, too. Then maybe I could have both of my worlds and wouldn't be so alone anymore. Maybe I'd build that rich life I'd always wanted. If I could just hold onto all of the pieces.

"You okay to lock up?" Tim asked as he gathered up his water bottle, phone, and keys.

"No problem. I want to finish up these chart notes so they're not hanging over my head."

"Paperwork is everyone's least favorite thing."

"And I wouldn't want you coming after me if I don't get it finished on time."

Tim chuckled. "I am pretty terrifying."

"You've got us all quaking in our boots."

"Right where I want you."

He waved as he headed out the front door, and I turned back to the file in front of me. Miles had let me take point on Koda's two-week follow-up today. The pup was healing well and surprisingly spry while lugging around his cast.

I grinned down at the desk. The shepherd was giving Hayes at least a dozen heart attacks a day. He'd been taking Koda to work with him so he could keep an eye on the canine, but Koda wanted to be in everyone's business and explore every nook and cranny. He was jumping on and off of furniture, but Hayes didn't have the heart to crate him all day.

Hopefully, in another few weeks, they'd both be free. But I had a feeling Koda was already used to going into the office with Hayes, and Hayes would have trouble keeping him at home now. Maybe Koda could become the Sheriff's Department mascot.

I moved through my stack of charts as quickly as possible while double-checking my work. Being the new person on the roster meant I wanted to make sure I was pulling my weight and not making more work that others would have to clean up. After scanning the last page one more time, I shut the folder and stood. I raised my hands over my head for a stretch.

The darkness outside the window took me by surprise, and I glanced at my watch. It was after nine. We stayed open late on Thursdays so people who worked could bring in their pets after the close of business, but it made for a late day. My stomach growled as if to punctuate the point.

I had a feeling it was a frozen-pizza kind of night. I quickly filed the charts and moved to pick up my purse. Double-checking that the correct lights were off, I headed for the door.

I made quick work of the alarm and lock and started for my SUV. The moon was almost full, and the sky not quite black yet. It was more of a dark twilight—one of my favorite times of day. Enough light to see by, but it had an almost magical glow to it.

I'd eat my pizza on the back deck tonight. Maybe even make use of the outdoor shower back there. It was certainly warm enough. I beeped the locks on my vehicle, but as I did, a hand curved around my middle, and another around my mouth, jerking me back.

The shock stole the air from my lungs and froze my muscles. Those first few seconds seemed to last a lifetime. Everything tunneled as I realized a cloth covered my mouth. The taste of the cotton and something sweet jerked me out of my frozen state.

I bit down, hard. The man behind me howled in pain, and the cloth fell away. I was hazy and sluggish. Whatever had been on the fabric was already working its way into my system. But I still managed an elbow into my assailant's ribs.

"Hey, what are you doing? Let her go!"

The voice came from down the street but it sounded so very far away. The arm around me released, and then I was falling. There was blinding pain, and then nothing at all.

Chapter Twenty-Three

"HERE'S A REFILL, SHERIFF."
I looked up as Cammie slid a Coke across the table. "Thanks, Cam. Just holler at me if I'm keeping you from closing up."

I'd turned the booth at the bar and grill into my office for the evening. Koda was spending the night with Shiloh, and I hadn't wanted to go home to an empty house. So, instead, I'd holed up here and worked as I ate.

"You're fine. We don't close until eleven."

I glanced towards the bar end of the space. They were doing steady business, but the restaurant half was pretty much empty. Collecting my papers, I inclined my head to the bench opposite me. "Why don't you sit for a minute?"

Cammie glanced around to see if anyone needed her, but clearly they didn't. "Okay."

I studied the girl across from me. Dark circles rimmed her eyes, and her hands couldn't seem to keep still. "How are you holding up?"

"I'm doing okay."

I arched a brow in question, and Cam blew out a breath, sending her bangs fluttering.

"All right. I've been better. I've had a hard time sleeping."

"Nightmares?"

She nodded. "And once I have one, I don't want to go back to sleep."

"I get that. I've been there. After we got Shy back, I had 'em for almost a year."

The fluttering of Cammie's fingers stopped for a moment. "You did?"

"It's normal. Did the ER doc talk to you about seeing a therapist?"

Her cheeks heated. "Yeah, but I don't know if that's for me. I'm not that bad."

"Cam, there's nothing to be embarrassed about. Talking to someone about what happened will help you heal. My whole family went for a long time."

"But nothing actually happened to me. I'm fine. I fought him off."

"And that's damn admirable, but it was still a trauma. You don't want to let something like that fester. Do me a favor and call someone. If you want a rec, I think Dr. Kensington is amazing." I pulled my wallet out of my pocket and riffled through it to find her card. I always kept a few on hand.

Cammie took it hesitantly. "Thank you."

"Are you going to call?"

Cam rolled her eyes. "*Yes.*"

I chuckled at the action, but it lightened a little of the worry sitting on my shoulders. "Good."

My phone buzzed on the table, and Cammie stood. "You take that. I need to clean some tables."

I hit accept on the screen and put the phone to my ear. "Easton."

"Sheriff, we've got another attempted abduction."

"Where?"

"Wolf Gap Veterinary."

My blood turned to ice, and everything around me seemed to slow and fade. The noise from the bar, the bright overhead lights, the country music drifting through the speakers. "Who?"

"Everly Kemper."

I stood, tossing a twenty on the table and gathering up my pile of papers. "She okay?"

"Not sure. EMTs were called. Ruiz and Williams are headed over there now."

"On my way."

All sorts of scenarios, each one worse than the last, filled my mind as I made my way to my SUV and climbed inside. The steering wheel creaked as I adjusted my hold. What the hell had she been doing at the vet's office so late? Why had she been walking to her car alone?

I took a deep breath, the air whistling through my clenched teeth. It took less than two minutes to get to the vet's, but it felt like two decades. Lights from an ambulance and a cruiser painted the streets and buildings in a red and blue staccato rhythm.

I pulled my SUV to the side of the road and added my lights to the symphony. Something in me released at the sight of Everly on a gurney, awake and talking. But my rib cage gave a painful squeeze at the sight of my sister holding a compress to Ev's head.

My boots hit the cement with a thud, my pace picking up with each step. Hadley's gaze met mine. "Hayes, dial it back a notch."

I glared at my sister. "What happened?"

"Everly was attacked, but she's going to be fine."

"I'm okay, really. Just feeling a little woozy." Everly tried to smile, but it was wobbly, and her skin was so damn pale.

I didn't think, I simply moved, slipping my hand into hers and squeezing gently. "Tell me what happened." I pulled my phone out of my pocket with my free hand and hit my recorder app. I didn't want Ev to have to recount this over and over.

"I stayed late to finish up some paperwork so it wasn't hanging over my head this weekend. I locked up and was walking to my SUV when someone grabbed me. I didn't even hear him coming. I'm usually really good about being aware of my surroundings, but I was looking at the sky. The moon and the stars aren't nearly as clear in Seattle. I missed them. So dumb."

I squeezed her hand again. "It's not dumb, and it's not your fault."

Everly's hand twitched in mine, but I held firm. "I should've been paying better attention. But I wasn't, and it felt like he came out of nowhere. He yanked me hard and covered my mouth with a cloth."

My gaze met Hadley's over Ev's head. Hadley's normally relaxed expression had hardened to granite. "I'd guess chloroform or something similar. Her vitals are still a little sluggish."

"Then what happened?" I asked.

"I bit him. Hard."

I swept my thumb across the back of her hand. "That's my girl."

Her fingers gave another twitch, but she didn't let go. "I was losing my balance, and everything was fuzzy, but I got him with an elbow to the ribs. Then someone yelled from down the street."

I glanced over to where Sergeant Ruiz was interviewing a couple—I guessed the people who had interrupted the crime.

"I don't really know what happened next. I guess I fell…"

Hadley removed the gauze pad, and it was soaked in blood. She quickly replaced it with another one, even though Everly winced as she did. "Everly knocked her head pretty good on the pavement. It's going to need stitches, and she might have a concussion. Whenever you're done, we're going to take her to Forest Lake to get checked out."

One of the few downsides of living where we did was that

there wasn't a hospital close by. We had a good Urgent Care, but we were forty-five minutes away from treatment for true emergencies.

Everly tried to sit up on the gurney but winced. "Hadley, I don't think I need the Emergency Room. Can't someone give me stitches here?"

"You're getting checked out," I barked.

"Bedside manner, Hayes," my sister warned.

My back teeth ground together. "You need a doctor to look at you, and probably some x-rays or a CT scan."

Everly slumped back against the gurney.

"They'll get you in and out as fast as they can," Hadley assured her. "You done?" she asked me.

"Just one more question. Did you see the attacker? Anything about him or her at all?"

"Based on size, it was a man. He was behind me the whole time. I never got a look at him."

"What about his voice? Did he say anything?"

"Nothing—" Her words cut off.

"What?"

"He made a noise when I bit him…but nothing about it was familiar."

It was all just a little too similar to Cammie's attempted abduction—and easily could've been a crime of opportunity. "Do you usually work this late on Thursdays?"

"No. I normally leave with everyone else."

One more point in the opportunity column. But I had to ask one more thing. "Do you think this could've been Ian?" I wasn't sure Allen had the strength to overpower Everly. She was much stronger than her size suggested.

Pain danced across Everly's eyes, and this time, it wasn't from the gash on her head. "I don't think so. It's not his style. Attack me? Sure. But try to kidnap me? That's not him."

"Okay. I'll need to talk to him anyway. I'll tell him to keep his distance, but you may get blowback." I hated that there was almost nothing I could do to shield her from it. Nothing legally, anyway.

"I'll be prepared."

"I really need to take her in, Hayes."

"Go." I forced myself to release Ev's hand, but it hurt like hell. She looked so damn small and alone on that gurney. "Take care of her."

"You know I will."

I looked at Everly. "Text me and let me know what the doctor says. Or if you remember anything else."

"Okay."

The single word was soft—quieter than I'd ever heard Ev before. And I had to fight the instinct to climb into the back of the ambulance they were loading her into. Instead, I turned to my officers. The way I could help was to find whoever had done this.

Chapter Twenty-Four

Everly

"I'D STAY, BUT I HAVE TO HEAD BACK FOR THE REST OF my shift. You going to be okay? Is there anyone you want me to call?"

There was no one. I fought back the rush of tears that wanted to surface with that knowledge. "I'll be fine. Thanks for every-thing, Hadley."

She moved to my purse on the hospital gurney in my ER bay. Riffling through it, she pulled out my phone and handed it to me. "Add me to your contacts." She rattled off her number, and I plugged it in, even though my vision was still a little blurry. "Call me if you need anything."

"I appreciate that."

"No problem." She patted my leg. "Take care of yourself."

I nodded and immediately regretted the action. My head thrummed as if a full marching band was practicing inside my skull. I closed my eyes against the light, trying to block out the brightness and the incessant beeping and chatter around me. It helped a little, but it only made me feel more alone.

But that's what I was, wasn't I? No one would come running when I called. Maybe Ben, but he didn't have a cell phone. And asking for help from him would only give him another reason to believe that I couldn't handle things myself.

I fisted and flexed the hand free of an IV—the one Hayes had held for what seemed like hours. I hadn't felt alone then. Not with his rough palm pressed against mine, his thumb sweeping back and forth across my skin. I'd felt warm for the first time in forever.

But that warmth didn't belong to me. Not really. It would belong to some other woman someday—someone who would share his bed and his life. Become a member of his family. It was ridiculous how much that felt like a stab to the heart.

The familiar burn climbed up my throat, but I swallowed it down. I couldn't break. Not here, and not now.

"Everly Kemper?"

My eyes opened at the feminine voice, and I blinked a few times before taking in the woman at the foot of my bed. She was petite with jet-black hair and golden skin. "I'm Dr. Balicanta."

"Hi."

She gave me a kind smile. "You've been through the wringer tonight, haven't you?"

"It hasn't been one of my favorite evenings."

She chuckled and moved to the side of my bed. "Well, let's see if we can get you feeling better." A man in scrubs stepped through the curtains. "This is Nurse Joe. He'll be helping me out. Is that okay with you?"

I realized she was asking because I'd been attacked, and the knowledge of what could've happened tonight made me shudder. "It's fine. As long as he has access to the good drugs."

Nurse Joe chuckled. "Honey, I've got you covered."

"I'm glad to hear it."

Dr. Balicanta slipped on gloves and carefully peeled back the gauze near my temple. "Joe, can you get me a suture kit? I'm afraid this is going to need a few stitches. Luckily, I aced my plastic surgery rotation, so I think I can get you through it without a scar."

A scar was the least of my worries. "Whatever gets it to stop bleeding."

"I'm agreed with you there." She probed the wound a bit, and I winced. "Pain on a scale of one to ten?"

"I don't know…seven?"

"Okay. I'm going to shine a light in your eyes, and it might not feel fun." She plucked a penlight from her coat and aimed it at me. I squinted but did my best not to let out a moan. "Painful?"

"Not a trip to Disneyland."

"I like her," Joe said as he set something on a tray next to Dr. Balicanta.

"If you've won Joe over, that means you're a good egg," she said. "You've got a mild concussion. I'm going to send you for a CT scan, just to be safe, but I think you'll be feeling better in a few days. Do you have pain anywhere but your head?"

I did a mental inventory. "My side."

"Let's have a look." Dr. Balicanta pulled down the blanket. "Just roll onto your side." I did as she asked, and she lifted my scrub top. "Ouch."

Angry scrapes and blooming bruises looked back at me. "Not exactly pretty."

"Joe, can I get antiseptic, ointment, and some bandages?"

"You got it, boss."

She ripped open a gauze pad and poured something onto it. "This is going to sting, but I'll be as gentle as I can."

"I can handle it." Pain was something I'd learned to live with as a child, and that had stuck with me—a handy by-product.

The doctor moved swiftly, and I simply focused on my breathing. The ointment soothed away the sting the antiseptic left behind, and soon, Dr. Balicanta was taping off a large bandage. "All done with that portion of events."

I rolled to my back. "Thank you."

"Let's see if you're still thanking me when I do these stitches." She moved with practiced ease as she readied her tools. "Ready for a little pinch?"

"Sure." Pain was one thing, but I'd never been a fan of needles. What other choice did I have, though?

Joe moved to the other side of the bed. "Here. Squeeze my hand. It helps."

I took his offered hand. It wasn't as rough or warm as Hayes', but it was comforting. And the kindness of the gesture had that burn returning to my throat. "Thank you."

"Anytime."

Dr. Balicanta readied the syringe. "Here we go."

I kept my eyes closed as she worked. I mentally reviewed all the bones in a cat. The symptoms of diabetes in a dog. Anything I could think of to keep my mind off the needle in my flesh.

"We're all done. I just need to cover the sutures. And Joe will print out aftercare instructions while you're getting your scans."

I slowly released Joe's hand, heat rising to my cheeks. "Thanks for that."

He sent me a wink. "Any excuse to hold a pretty girl's hand."

Dr. Balicanta chuckled. "I'll be back as soon as we get your results, and then we can get you some painkillers."

Anything to dull the pounding in my head would be a miracle at this point. I didn't have to wait as long as expected. An orderly came in moments later, and the scan itself went quickly. I guessed that was the benefit of coming in after ten on a weeknight.

"Knock, knock," Dr. Balicanta said as she pulled back the curtain. "Everything looks good. Since you have a concussion, we can keep you overnight, or you can go home if you have someone who can stay with you and wake you up every three hours."

The burn was back, and it was fiercer than before. The last thing I wanted to do was stay here tonight. I wanted real sleep.

"I guess I'll have to stay. I don't have anyone to come get me—" The curtain being pulled back cut off my words, and then Hayes appeared. "W-what are you doing here?"

He rubbed at the back of his neck. "I figured you'd need someone to take you home."

Dr. Balicanta's eyes held a twinkle when she spoke. "Can you stay with her tonight? Everly will need to be woken up every three hours and asked simple questions since she has a concussion. If she seems confused or her pain worsens, you'll need to bring her back. But I'm about to give her a painkiller and a prescription that should help."

"It's okay. I can just stay here."

"No. You'll stay with me."

I couldn't help the scowl that rose to my lips. "Will I now?"

He took the papers the doctor handed him and turned to me. "Do you really want to stay here and be woken up every hour to have your vitals taken? Or would you rather suck it up and sleep in my guest room for the night?"

I really didn't want to stay here. "Fine."

"Or, you could say 'Thank you.'"

"Thank you," I gritted out.

Joe peeked his head in. "I couldn't help but overhear. You two are like a soap opera." Hayes glared at Joe, but he simply ignored it and handed me a bag. "Had this filled at the pharmacy for you. Take care of yourself, doll."

"I'll try. Thanks for holding my hand."

"Anything for you," he said with a wink and bustled out. Hayes' glare intensified.

Dr. Balicanta cleared her throat, but it sounded more like she was trying to cover a laugh. "Well, now that that's settled, all I need is for you to sign these discharge papers while I give you a dose of these meds through the IV."

I signed while Dr. Balicanta gave me the drugs. After a couple of minutes, she took out my IV, giving me another of her kind smiles. "Take care of yourself and come back if you have any concerns."

"Thanks again. For everything."

She patted my leg through the blanket. "Thanks for being a trooper."

The drugs were already making their way through my system, and I started to feel as if I were floating just a bit. Hayes moved to my side. "Think you can sit up?"

"I might need a little help there."

"I got ya." He moved smoothly and gently, one hand going behind my shoulders and the other taking my hand. He guided me to a sitting position. "Think you need a wheelchair?"

"No. Maybe just an arm to lean on."

Hayes' gaze met mine. "I won't let you fall."

"Okay." The single word came out as a whisper, and I forced myself to look away.

We moved slowly through the halls and then out into the night. That first hit of mountain air soothed my fraying nerves—a balm to all the pieces that felt just a bit ragged at the moment. As I stepped off the curb, my entire body twinged.

"What is it? Is something wrong? Should we go back?"

The panic in Hayes' voice had the corners of my mouth tipping up. For a man who dealt with emergencies every day at his job, it was amusing to see one little grimace send him running. "Nothing a few soaks in the hot springs won't cure."

He stayed still for a few more moments, studying my face as if to assess if I was being honest with him. "More than just your head hurting?"

"I landed pretty hard on my side. I'll be tender for a week or so."

"Shit. I'm so sorry this happened."

"Me, too." I started moving towards the parking lot,

scanning the vehicles for that familiar Sheriff's SUV. "Did you find anything?"

Hayes took my arm again. "This way. And not much. We've still got officers looking, and we got a bit of a description from the couple who came along, but it was dark, and he was wearing a hat. All we've got is a better idea of height and build."

"Better than nothing, I guess."

He beeped the locks on his SUV and opened the passenger door. "We won't stop searching."

"I know you won't." I looked at the seat I needed to climb into. "This might be tricky."

"Trust me?"

I turned back to face Hayes. That question held so much more than this moment. It held baggage and forgiveness and a million other things. I searched his face, looking for all the answers I needed in those dark eyes. I didn't see all of them, but I saw enough. "Yes."

He moved in, swift and smooth. One arm went under my legs, and the other behind my back. He lifted me as if I weighed no more than a sack of flour and deposited me carefully in the seat.

I let out a whoosh of air. "Well, that's one way to do it."

Hayes chuckled. "Easier than anything else. Do you want me to buckle you in?"

"I think I can handle that."

"All right, then."

He closed the door softly and rounded the front of the SUV. Climbing behind the wheel, he turned over the engine and started us back towards Wolf Gap. We were quiet on the ride, both of us lost in our thoughts.

I turned my gaze to the sky, searching for the constellations my father had taught me. It was one of the good memories I had of him. And I tried to hold on to the good bits. To remind myself that no one was all good or all bad. But, sometimes, the good pieces held more pain than the bad ones, as if the stars themselves became tattered remnants of what they once were.

Instead of thinking of that, I let my vision blur with the landscape, allowing it to become a beautifully dark impressionist painting in my mind. By the time we pulled up to a house on the outskirts of town, my eyes were drooping, but I was in a lot less pain.

"Here we are."

I forced my eyes open and did my best to take in the place in front of me. It wasn't what I'd expected, but it somehow fit. *Classic* was the word that came to mind. A historic white farmhouse with black shutters and a wraparound porch. There was even a porch swing. He probably had a full acre of land yet could walk to town if he needed to.

"I love a porch swing."

Hayes grinned. "That one's solid. A great place to drink a beer and let the day go."

"I think I need one at my place."

"Sounds like a good plan to me. But why don't I get you inside first so you can get some rest?"

I yawned. "I think that's smart."

Hayes hopped out of the vehicle and came around to open my door. "I'm gonna lift you again. I think it'll be easier on your body."

"Okay." This time, it didn't hurt nearly enough. Instead, I felt the planes of muscle as Hayes leaned me into his body. I smelled the hint of something that wasn't pine but similar.

He eased my feet to the ground. "You okay to walk?"

I nodded, unable to find words at the moment. He led me up the path. The front yard was simple, grass and some basic shrubbery in front of the porch. But it worked. A few pots of flowers with gorgeous blooms sat on the porch steps.

Hayes followed my line of sight. "That's all my mom. Every time she comes over, she moans about how boring my yard is. Then, a few days later, another pot appears. I had to hire a neighbor girl to water them because I forget and then break my mother's heart when my black thumb kills something else."

I could see the interaction in my mind as clear as day. Julia harping on Hayes and fussing with plants. And him simply letting her. Not only that, he'd made it so the plants grew and prospered. "I think they're beautiful."

"I don't hate looking at them." He put his key in the lock and opened the front door.

I couldn't help my intake of breath. Hayes was just full of surprises. Instead of the tight corridors and small enclosed rooms I expected from a historic home, it was open and airy. "This is gorgeous."

"We gutted it pretty much down to the studs. I loved the exterior, but the interior was a mess. But that meant I got her for a song. I had a friend who was just starting up his contracting business, so I let him use my place to prove what he could do—and I got a steal on the labor."

"I'd say it paid off." I moved into the space, walking by a small study with its glass doors and floor-to-ceiling bookshelves, past a wall filled with a scattering of black and white prints of Hayes with his family and friends, and into the kitchen. It was a showpiece somehow managing to be both light and masculine with unique light fixtures and creative drawer pulls.

"Glad you like it. Do you want water? A soda? Maybe something to eat?"

"Honestly, I just want a shower and bed, if that's okay."

"Of course."

He led me around the kitchen, through a living space with deep couches and a massive TV, and to the back stairs. "You go first in case you get a little wobbly."

My hand went to the railing, a rustic but smooth wood, and I made my way up without any dizziness.

"Second door on your left."

I stopped just inside the space. It was that same mix here—a dark wood headboard but white duvet and pillows. The bedding resembled a cloud, and I couldn't wait to fall into it. "This is gorgeous."

"Glad you approve. My sisters left some sweats in the dresser in case they come over for a movie night and want to be comfortable. Those should fit you."

"Are you sure that's okay?"

"Don't be dumb."

I scowled at Hayes. "I'm not dumb. But I also don't want to be presumptuous."

He rolled his eyes heavenward. "They're just clothes. It's not the family jewels."

"Do you have family jewels?" I asked with a smirk.

"I think we might've misplaced the crowns somewhere along the line."

"Such a shame."

Hayes shook his head and moved in close. He paused for a moment and then wrapped his arms around me in a hug that managed to be both gentle and all-consuming. "I'm glad you're okay. Scared the life out of me when I got the call."

My eyes burned as I pressed my cheek against his chest. "Thanks for coming back for me."

"I'll come back for you anytime you ask, Ev. Or even if you don't."

Chapter Twenty-Five

Hayes

I EASED DOWN INTO THE CHAIR IN MY STUDY, HITTING THE timer on my phone for three hours. I scrubbed a hand over my face as I watched the seconds tick by. Sleep wouldn't be happening tonight.

Everything in me felt like it was going haywire. Short-circuiting and sending jolts of electricity through me. Like when Everly had pressed her cheek harder against my chest as if I were her only source of comfort. Or looking at her asleep in my guest bed just now. She'd curled herself into a position that didn't seem at all comfortable, as if she were shielding herself from potential attack, yet her face was completely relaxed.

"Get a grip, Easton." I tapped a recent call on my phone.

"Sheriff's department."

"Hey, Williams, it's Easton."

"Hey, Sheriff. How's Ms. Kemper doing?"

The kid had a good heart on him, and I hoped he kept it as he worked the job longer. It was tough not to let this line of work harden you a bit, make you more skeptical. But if you logged the moments where you saw the best in humanity, you could hold onto that optimism. "She's going to be fine.

Got a concussion and some stitches, but it could've been a lot worse."

"Who's doing this, boss?"

"I wish I had a clue. Has anything turned up tonight?"

"You know I would've called you if it had."

I leaned back in my chair, my muscles protesting the movement. "I had to check."

"I know it. Ruiz and I logged the evidence, and the techs should get to it first thing."

"Thanks. Call me if anything else pops up."

"Will do. Get some sleep if you can."

I hung up without agreeing. I didn't lie to the people who worked for me, and I wasn't going to start now over something as stupid as sleep. Instead, I lifted the screen to my laptop and tapped a key, waking it up. Keying in a couple of passwords, I logged into our department's system.

I needed to read over Cammie's statement again. Maybe that would knock something loose. Any clue that might send me in a new direction. I read everything we had four times before my eyes started to cross.

I pushed to my feet and paced the wide-planked boards of my floor. Maybe I needed to cast a wider net. These were the only incidents in our county, but that didn't mean there weren't more elsewhere.

I turned back to my computer and sat, typing in a few search terms. The number of cases that lined my screen had a wave of nausea sweeping through me—too much darkness in this world. But I'd have to start somewhere, and that meant combing through each individual case.

I slid a cup of coffee across the counter to Hadley. "Thanks for coming over, even though you worked last night."

"No problem. I actually got five hours of sleep after we took Everly in. Looks like it was a hell of a lot more than you."

I knew I looked like death warmed over. My eyes felt like someone had poured acid in them, and my head was giving a steady thrum. "Nothing a few gallons of coffee won't fix."

"You could take a day off and catch up on some sleep."

"Not with everything going on right now. I've got a slew of cases I need to sift through and see if any of them match what's going on here."

Hadley straightened on her stool. "You're thinking serial?"

"It has to be the same person who tried to grab Cammie. That's two attempts. He has most likely done this before. But not around here. We don't have any unsolveds with the same MO." I bent forward to meet my little sister's gaze. "That means you need to be careful. No going off on your own for a hike or mountain biking. Take a buddy. No walking to your car alone at night, either."

"Hayes. I carry bear spray and a keychain with spikes. I'll be fine."

"Hadley… This isn't me being overprotective. Someone's trying to take women in your age range. It would kill me if something happened to you. Please. Until we catch this guy, just cut me a break."

She was silent for a moment as she scanned my face. "Okay. But you know the whole world doesn't rest on your shoulders, right? It's impossible to keep every single person in this county safe at all times. Bad things happen."

"I'm well aware that bad things happen. And I'll just start with keeping my family safe. Dad's having the same talk with Shiloh this morning. Everyone is on the buddy system for now."

"Even you?"

I sighed and leaned a hip against the counter. "Even me. I'm taking Young with me to interview some suspects now."

Everly appeared at the edge of the kitchen. I hadn't even heard her silent feet on the steps. "Ian?"

She looked so damn adorable, her hair a rat's nest from sleep, her feet bare. "I need to have a word with him and Allen. I know I won't get far, but at least I can read their reaction."

"I really don't think it was him. Like I said, it's not his style."

"What *is* his style?"

Everly visibly swallowed. "Brute force attack. He would've done whatever he intended to right there."

Heat rose through my body, filling muscle and sinew, pouring into my blood. What the hell had Ian done to Everly?

Hadley cleared her throat. "You're sure he doesn't want you back home with the rest of your family? Maybe he decided to force that. You and Cammie look a little bit alike. Maybe he thought she was you."

Everly let out a chuckle, but it had a bitter air to it. "Trust me, the last thing Ian wants is for me to be home with him."

I hadn't thought about it until now, but Cammie and Everly *did* look alike. Same hair color, similar builds. Whoever this was, obviously had a type. "For now, everyone just needs to be careful."

Hadley set her coffee down on the counter. "Yeah, yeah, buddy system at all times."

I sent a pointed stare in my sister's direction. "If I find out you're not holding to that, I'll tell Mom about the time you snuck liquor out of the cabinet for that bonfire and were sick for days."

Her mouth fell open. "You wouldn't."

"Test me."

"I know a few things about you, too, Bubby. Careful before you start a war."

I slid my phone into my pocket and palmed my keys. "You know I have far more ammunition on you."

She looked to Everly for help. "He's right, dammit."

Ev pressed her lips into a firm line to keep from laughing. "Better wave the white flag now."

"Listen to her, little sister." I moved through the space and acted on instinct, dropping a kiss to the top of Everly's head. "Call if you start feeling worse. Your pain meds are on the counter."

Her eyes widened a fraction. "O-okay. Thanks."

I nodded and ignored the mischievous grin on Hadley's face, heading for the door. As I drove to the station, I swore I could still feel the silk of Everly's hair and smell the hint of jasmine that always seemed to float around her. I was screwed. And not in a good way.

As I passed the hardware store, a familiar truck caught my eye, and I hung a quick right. I parked a few spaces down from the older vehicle, turned off my engine, and stayed seated, waiting. It didn't take long for him to appear. I breathed a sigh of relief when I saw that Ian was alone. Maybe without Allen whispering in his ear, I'd finally get the truth.

I slid out of my SUV and started towards him. Ian caught sight of me in seconds and scowled. "I'm starting to think you're stalking me."

"Was just driving by and saw your truck. It saves me from having to drive out to the ranch later this morning."

He balanced a bag in one arm. "What now?"

"Where were you between nine and ten last night?"

Ian stiffened. "You've got no right to ask me that. I don't buy into your authority. I don't answer to—"

I held up a hand. "Save me the spiel. I've heard it all before. Just tell me where you were, and I'll leave you alone."

"No."

"I'll take that to mean you don't have an alibi."

"It means I don't tell pigs shit."

I dialed in to everything about Ian at that moment. His fingers wrapped tightly around his keys. The set of his jaw. Anything that might give me any sort of clue when I relayed the next bit of information. "Someone attempted to abduct your sister last night."

His eyes shifted to the right, his hold on the keys tightening. "What are you talking about?"

"Someone tried to grab her outside the vet's office a little after nine."

A muscle in Ian's jaw ticked. "That's what happens when women go out on their own, unprotected. Maybe a little scare will finally show Everly her place."

"You think it's your job to give her that scare?"

Ian's eyes narrowed on me. "I do whatever I want, whenever I want. I only report to God and my family."

"Somehow, I don't think God would be too pleased with some of the things you've done, Ian."

He set his bag on the hood of his truck. "What did Evie tell you? Whatever it was, she lies. Invents all sorts of stories."

There was a slight edge of panic to his tone. That simple fact had ice sliding through my veins. "Everly hasn't told me anything. But why don't you share what would have you running scared, all of a sudden?"

"I'm not scared of anything. Not her. Not you. No one. Fuck off, pig." He grabbed his bag and jumped into his truck, the tires squealing as he pulled away.

Everly had something on Ian. And the fact that she was back scared him. I just needed her to trust me enough to tell me what it was.

Chapter Twenty-Six

Everly

"I'M NOT GOING TO LIE. I'M RELIEVED TO HAVE YOU back, and not just because it means you're feeling better."

I winced as I watched Miles rise from our break room table and throw away what remained of his lunch. "I'm sorry I left you in the lurch for a few days."

"It wasn't your fault. I'm just so sorry this happened. And right outside, too. I had some new floodlights installed. That should help discourage any lurkers. And you and Kelly aren't to lock up alone anymore."

"I hate that you had to go to all of this extra trouble."

Miles met my gaze. "It's not trouble when it comes to keeping you and the rest of my staff safe. You're an asset to this team, Everly, and I'm lucky to have you."

"Thank you. I love working here."

There wasn't a dishonest word in my statement. Even two days away had left me twitchy. But the way Hayes had set Hadley and Shiloh on me, I hadn't had a chance to do anything but watch movies or play cards. When my forty-eight-hour prison sentence was up, I'd practically run back to work.

Miles gave me one of his warm smiles. "I'm so glad you do because we've been a little lost without you. And I think Kelly was ready to throttle Tim and me."

A small laugh escaped. The other vet tech and I had really found our stride and made a great team. "I owe her a cup of coffee, at least, for covering for me."

"I'm sure she wouldn't mind that. I'm going to get a jump on paperwork before our next patient. Enjoy the rest of your lunch."

"Thanks, Miles."

I turned back to the salad and chips I'd packed this morning. It wasn't an egg salad from Spoons, but it did the trick. I reached into my bag and pulled out my small bottle of Tylenol. I had the stronger prescription but didn't want to take that while working. Acetaminophen would have to cut it. Swallowing two pills down, I rubbed at the back of my neck.

Dr. Balicanta had told me that, even though my concussion was mild, it could take weeks for the symptoms to go away completely. It was mostly a dull ache running through my skull, but I sometimes got dizzy if I moved too quickly. And I didn't have weeks for that. I needed to be back to helping Shiloh build some shelters for different animals.

A knock sounded on the door. "Come in." It slowly swung open, and a familiar face peeked in. "Addie?"

She hesitated in the doorway. "Hi, Evie."

"Come in. I'm just having lunch. You can sit if you want." I was doing everything in my power to keep from pushing. The last thing I wanted was to scare her away again.

She stepped inside but didn't take a seat. Instead, she stood twisting her fingers into intricate knots, then untwisting and starting the process all over again. "Are you okay? I heard someone attacked you."

"I'm fine. Just a bump on the head."

Addie studied the bandage near my temple. "That doesn't look like a bump."

"A few stitches."

Her fingers bleached white as she knit them tighter together. "You hurting?"

"Not bad. Just a headache. That should go away in a week or so. How are you? Everything okay?"

She ignored my question. "Ian's really mad that the sheriff talked to him again. You need to be careful."

As much as I didn't think the attack was my brother, I had to ask… "Was he around the night it happened?"

Addie stiffened, the manic acrobatics of her hands stilling. "I don't know. I go straight to my room after dinner. I don't want to be around if they're drinking."

"Addie…"

"I'm fine. I know how to take care of myself."

Taking care of herself was one thing. Having to play a constant guessing game for when your father or one of his ranch hands might lose his temper was another thing altogether. I would've given anything for Addie to trust me in that moment. For her to come stay with me. I wanted to protect my baby cousin how I'd failed to all of those years ago.

"I know you can, Addie. I just wish you didn't have to."

The look in her eyes was so bleak—exhaustion and something that appeared as if she'd given up. "Me, too."

Before I could say another word, the door opened again. This time, broad shoulders filled the space, and dark eyes cut to me. Hayes' gaze stayed on me a beat longer than normal as if surveying to make sure I was still in one piece, before moving to Addie. "Afternoon, Adaline. Ev."

Addie winced at the use of her full name. Her father was the only one who always called her by the moniker. Everyone else called her by the shortened version.

"Call her Addie. Everyone does. Have you met Hayes officially?" I asked my cousin.

She had shied back a few steps. "No. It's nice to meet you."

"You, too, Addie. I'd like to give you my card if you don't mind. That way, you can call if you ever need anything."

She moved farther away, shaking her head. "I can't. If he finds out I have it—I just…can't."

"All right, then. You need me, just come to my office." His gaze locked with hers. "There's always a way out. And I'd be happy to help you find that path."

"Not always," she whispered. "Not for me."

And with that, she bolted around Hayes and headed straight for the door. I didn't call out this time. Didn't try to stop her. I needed to give her some room. Space to bolt when she needed to, and a place to come back to when she was ready. But that didn't mean it didn't hurt. My headache pulsed behind my eyes as I tried to hold back tears.

Hayes slipped into the empty chair next to me. "Hell. I'm sorry. I had to try."

"I know. And I think it's good that you keep telling her she has you to run to if she needs it. She came here on her own today. I think that's progress." My breath hitched. "I hurt her so bad. Pretty much everyone who was supposed to love her has let her down in one way or another."

Hayes set a small paper bag on the table and curved his hand around mine, that now-familiar sweep of his thumb picking up across my skin. "You're here now. That's what counts."

"Does it?" A single tear slipped out of the corner of my eye, and Hayes wiped it away. "Those hurts may run too deep. It's all she's known for so long. I'm scared she'll stay in that familiar place forever."

"I don't think she will. The more Addie sees you living your life, free with a job you love and chasing a dream…I think that will make her want to reach for more. What was it that you told me? She only needs twenty breaths of bravery."

His finger ghosted along the tattoo behind my ear, sending a pleasant shiver down my spine.

"I hope you're right."

"Let's hold on to hope right now."

I took a long inhale, letting the air out slowly again. I could hold on to hope for Addie. It might be one of the most dangerous emotions there was, but right now, I needed it. I looked up at Hayes. "What are you doing here, anyway?"

He raised a single brow. "Not happy to see me?"

I was happy to see him anytime he popped up. But that wasn't something I was ready to admit yet. "Depends why you're here."

He chuckled and released my hand. "I came to check on the patient and bring you a little something. Hadley said you were a fan of the whoopie pies at Spoons."

I straightened instantly. I'd discovered the perfect little confections last week, and Hadley and I had consumed half a dozen on her babysitting day. "What's in the bag?"

He held it close to his chest. "Gonna change your tune about being happy to see me?"

"I'm the happiest person you'll ever meet if you've got whoopie pies in there."

Hayes carefully unrolled the bag and handed over a chocolate cookie sandwich with thick vanilla buttercream frosting in the middle. "Now, I get one, too." He set the other on a napkin he stole from the center of the table.

"I think one might be my limit. I had three with your sister and felt a little sick."

Hayes shook his head. "Hadley's not real good with limits."

"I'm starting to learn that. I think she was going more stir-crazy than I was being cooped up."

"She always wants to be moving. It's why being an EMT works

so well for her. She'd hate being cooped up in an office or having to do the same thing day after day."

I broke off a piece of cookie and popped it into my mouth. "I like her. She's hilarious and has a really good heart."

"That's for sure."

I paused for a moment, wondering if I had any right to ask what I wanted to. "I get the sense she and your mom struggle."

Hayes leaned back in his chair. "You're not wrong there."

"Why? I can tell they love each other."

He broke off a piece of his cookie and dipped it into the frosting. "Mom held the reins pretty tight after we got Shiloh back. A lot of folks would say *too* tight. Everyone else understood why, but Hadley…she was so young. When she got old enough, they battled. Mom was used to me and Beckett, who simply let her have her way. Or Shiloh, who would just disappear into the barn or the fields when she didn't want to talk about something. But Hadley…she's always had a firecracker of a temper on her. And she doesn't back down from anything."

"I can see both sides."

"So can the rest of us. It's why Dad and I are always trying to run interference. To get them both to see the other's perspective. But a lot of hurt has built up over the years."

Fire lit along my throat, and I did my best to swallow it down. "I'm so sorry, Hayes. One action and so many lives were affected." It wasn't just Shiloh. It was every member of the Easton family. Mine, too. Even Addie was paying the price.

Hayes leaned in and grabbed the seat of my chair with both hands, pulling me close. "Don't you dare take that on. It's not yours. You did everything you could to right that wrong, even though it wasn't on you."

"Sounds like someone else I know."

The corner of his mouth kicked up. "I guess we're more alike than I ever knew."

"Careful, Hayes, I might start to think you like me a little bit."

"Heaven forbid."

"You really didn't have to walk me to my car."

Stubbornness flitted across Tim's features. "Yes, I did. And you're just going to have to get used to it because I'm doing it from now on."

Warmth spread through me at his words. Somewhere over the past couple of months, I'd started to develop a little community of people who genuinely cared. "I appreciate it. But I don't think anyone's going to jump out of the bushes in broad daylight." I gestured around at more than a few people walking down the streets, locals and tourists alike.

"Don't care." Tim came to a stop in front of my SUV. "I felt like the lowest of the low after I heard what'd happened. I left you here alone, and—"

"Oh, Tim. No." I reached out, grabbing his arm. "What happened wasn't your fault."

His face hardened. "Maybe not, but I could've stopped it."

"You're going to have to let that go," I said softly.

"I'll try to if you'll let me walk you to your car at the end of the day."

"I think I can live with that." I went on impulse and threw my arms around him for a quick hug. It was so fast, he barely had time to react before I let him go again. "You're a good man."

Pink hit his cheeks. "I'm working on it."

"You're doing a good job."

"Get in that SUV before this ground swallows me whole."

I laughed and climbed behind the wheel, giving Tim a wave and starting the engine. He headed down the block towards his apartment over one of the shops in town. As I went to set my phone in the cupholder, it dinged.

Shay: *How's your week going?*

I winced. I hadn't exactly filled my best friend in on all that had gone down lately. Not the fire or my attack. But there wasn't anything she could do. I typed out a quick response.

Me: *Good. We're about to start on shelters for the critters. Once we actually have some animals, maybe you can come to visit.*

Shay: *You say the word, and we'll be on our way.*

That might take a little longer than she thought, but that would give me time to get my stitches out, and hopefully for the scar to fade. I set the phone back in my cupholder and moved my hand to the gearshift, but a flicker of movement caught my eye. Someone had shoved a folded piece of paper under my windshield wiper.

I opened my door and stood to pull it free. Settling back in my seat, I shut the door and opened what I was sure was a flyer. Only, it wasn't. The pulse behind my eyes intensified as I took in the sloppy scrawl.

Next time, you won't be so lucky. Just remember, I'm watching.

Chapter Twenty-Seven

Hayes

THE MUFFLED SOUND OF MY CELL PHONE RINGING CAME from somewhere on my desk. "Crap." I patted the stacks of paper and the map I had spread out across the surface. When I couldn't find it, I finally sent the map flying to the floor.

I grabbed up the tiny device and hit accept without checking the caller ID. "Easton."

"Hayes? It's Everly."

It was the first time she'd called me, and that alone had the hair rising on the back of my neck. The hesitancy in her voice only put me more on edge. "What's wrong?" I was already pulling open my desk drawer and going for my keys.

"I'm fine."

"You don't sound fine," I growled.

"I'm in my SUV outside the vet. Someone left a note on my windshield."

My steps faltered as I pulled my door open. "What kind of note?"

"Not the kind asking me to a friendly tea."

I muttered a slew of curses and picked up my pace, winding

my way through desks and past reception. "I'm leaving the station now. Are your doors locked?"

A click sounded in the background. "They are now."

"Stay on the phone with me."

"I'll be fine. You shouldn't drive and talk on the phone."

I hit a button on my screen as I climbed behind the wheel of my SUV. "You're on speaker, happy?"

"So grouchy."

"Damn straight, I'm grouchy. And you should be, too."

Everly sighed. "I'm too tired to be grouchy."

Hell. She'd been through the wringer since she'd been back in Wolf Gap, and these last few days had been the worst of it. She needed a break, and I was going to do everything in my power to get her one. "Just hold on, Ev."

"I'm holding. Think we should play a game while I wait?" Her voice trembled slightly as she asked.

"What kind of game?"

"How about *would you rather*?"

I pulled out of the department parking lot. "Isn't that something teenagers play?"

"Humor me. We're gonna play the PG version."

"All right."

She cleared her throat as if getting ready to give an important speech. "Cookies or cake?"

"Cookies. Easier to bring with you wherever you go."

Everly made a *hmm* noise in the back of her throat. "Lemonade or iced tea?"

"Depends on who's making it."

"Fair enough. I'll always go for lemonade."

"My mom makes the best there is. I'll have to bring you some." I pulled into a spot two down from Everly's SUV. "I'm here."

"Okay."

Her voice was so damn soft, I wanted to hit something. That

wasn't the Everly I knew, the one I was falling for. Her voice was strong, never wavered. I slid out of my SUV, scanning the area. Nothing seemed out of place—the usual mix of tourists and locals peppering the streets, taking advantage of the late-summer light. I couldn't pick out a single person who was focused on Ev's vehicle.

I pulled a kit out of the cargo area of my SUV and started for Everly. She'd already climbed out and waited for me as I approached. She pointed to her passenger seat. "I put it down so I wouldn't get a bunch of prints on it."

"Smart." I hadn't even told her to do as much because the moment I'd heard her voice, that little hint of fear, I hadn't been thinking straight.

I set my kit on the hood of the SUV and, instead of going for the note, I went for her. I pulled Ev into my arms and held on tight. The small hitch in her breath echoed around my rib cage like a cannon, pinging off my heart. "You're okay."

"I know."

"Give me a sec to reassure myself of that."

Her hands fisted in the sides of my uniform shirt. "I really am all right. It just spooked me, is all."

I took a deep breath, filling my lungs with fresh air and that hint of jasmine that was all Everly. "Let's see what we've got."

Everly hovered behind me as I pulled on gloves and opened an evidence bag. I opened the passenger door and picked up the paper by one corner. As I took in the angry slashes on the page, everything in me slowed to a crawl. My heart rate. My breathing. Even my blood seemed to halt.

I slid the note into the evidence bag and sealed it, placing it in my kit. I didn't want Everly to even have to see it. Snapping off my gloves, I pulled out my phone and hit Young's contact. She answered on the second ring. "Sheriff."

"I need you to go by the Bar & Grill."

"Got trouble?"

"Not there, I don't think. But I need you to ask Cammie Sweeney if she received any notes. Make a drive-by at her parents', too. See if they've gotten anything."

The squeak of a chair in the background told me that Young was already moving. "What's going on?"

"Everly got a threatening note on her SUV."

"Shit. Is she okay?"

I looked up at Ev. "She's hanging tough. Call me once you've talked to them."

"Will do."

I hit end and shoved my phone back into my pocket. "We're going to figure this out."

"I know you will."

Something about the casual certainty in Ev's words twisted everything inside me. "I need you to do me a favor."

Wariness filled her features. "And what's that?"

I picked up my keys and worked one off the ring. "Run by my house and pick up Koda. He'll at least be an early warning system until I get off work."

"Until you get off work?"

"I'll be a couple of hours, but Koda and Shiloh will keep you company in the meantime."

"You're coming over?"

"You've got a guest room, right?"

She nodded slowly.

"I'm going to stay with you until we've got this sorted." There was no way I was going to leave Everly alone when this asshole was clearly watching.

She tipped her face up to the heavens as if praying for patience. "It's normal to *ask*, Hayes. '*Hey, would it be all right if I stayed with you for a few days? It would make me feel a lot better.*' Something like that."

I shrugged. "Normal's overrated."

Everly let out a sort of growl of frustration and threw up her hands. "I give up. Give me the damn key."

I grinned as I placed it on her palm. "See you tonight."

"You'll be lucky if I don't short-sheet your bed."

I chuckled. But the humor didn't quite reach the depths it usually did. I was too damn worried. I hated that I had to watch her drive away right now. But she'd have others looking out for her until I could return. I pulled out my phone to text Shy and my dad to tell them to do just that.

I pulled up to the tiny cabin. As I climbed out of my SUV, I caught movement in one of the paddocks. I moved towards it, leaving everything I'd hauled over in my vehicle. As I approached, Koda lifted his head from the blanket bed someone had made for him. He thumped his tail but didn't bother getting up to greet me. He was too enthralled with the scene in front of him.

Shy and my dad braced a two-by-four on the inside of the metal animal shelter while Everly hit it with a nail gun. They moved in a silent rhythm that spoke of all the time they'd spent working together over the past couple of months. I cleared my throat. "Aren't you supposed to be resting? You do have a concussion."

Everly glared at me. "I'm fine."

Shy snickered. "We're almost done."

They fit two more boards into place, and then the interior walls were done. As Everly straightened, she wobbled just a bit. I pushed off the fence and strode to her side. "You're pushing it too much. If you don't rest, you're going to end up back in the hospital."

Dad wiped his brow. "He's annoying and interfering, but in this case, he's also right. Don't push it. We can pick back up in a couple of days."

Everly handed the nail gun to my dad. "You guys are ganging up on me."

"Or we just don't want you to keel over."

She rolled her eyes, but I didn't miss the slight wince afterward. "I'm fine."

I resisted the urge to throw something. "A couple of days isn't going to make a difference. Give yourself a break."

Everly opened her mouth to say something and then promptly shut it when Shiloh sent her a look. She turned her annoyed glare to me. "Then you're giving me work hours this weekend."

I held up both hands. "I'm happy to help."

She traced a design I couldn't make out in the dirt with the toe of her boot. "Any leads on the note?"

"Not yet." It was amazing to me that in a town so busy with local foot traffic, no one had seen anyone hovering by Everly's SUV. "I've still got officers asking around and looking at camera feeds from nearby stores. And the lab will process the note first thing tomorrow."

"Maybe they'll find some prints."

She didn't sound especially optimistic, and neither was I given what we had right now. "I won't stop until we find him, Ev."

"I know." She gave herself a little shake. "I think we're done here for the day."

Everly gave my dad a quick hug and then moved to give one to my sister, but Shiloh stiffened. Ev didn't miss a beat, simply gave her a light shoulder bump instead. I could've kissed her in that moment. She seemed to be so in tune with Shy and didn't make her feel out of place. Shy wasn't one for casual affection. It was as if she needed space in all things. And Everly gave her that.

"How about Friday?" Ev glanced at me. "Will I be free by then, warden?"

"Depends if you're on your best behavior."

She looked at Shy. "I'm going to short-sheet his bed, I swear."

"You could always put pink dye in his shampoo," my sister offered.

"Traitor. My own flesh and blood, stabbing me in the back."

Shiloh shrugged. "You're bossy. It gets annoying. I'm team Everly on this one."

Ev crossed her arms over her chest, the action causing my focus to zero in on the swells peeking out from her tank top. "Face it, you're done for, Easton."

I forced my gaze up to her face. "I guess I'll just have to watch my back."

"Sleep with one eye open," Shy warned as she headed towards her truck with Dad.

"Come on, Mr. Bossypants. I'll show you to the guest room."

"I'm not sure I'm a fan of that nickname."

Koda lumbered to his feet, and I picked up the blanket he'd been resting on. Everly gave him a scratch behind his ears. "And what nickname would you like?"

"Oh, I don't know…ruggedly handsome. Ruthlessly charming."

"Those aren't nicknames."

"But they work."

Everly shook her head. "I think I'll stick with Hayes."

"That works, too."

We headed up the steps to the small front porch, and Everly pulled open the screen door. "Welcome to Chez Kemper."

I'd been inside once or twice before, but this time, I took a few moments to really study the space. It was small but homey. The cabin's rustic history somehow worked with the slightly feminine décor—an overstuffed, light gray sofa scattered with pink and cream pillows, two chairs, and a coffee table. A small TV on a console against the wall—though I doubted she got cable up here since I hadn't seen a dish on her roof.

"Worrying about how you're going to watch the ballgame?" she asked.

"It might have crossed my mind."

"You might be able to pick it up on the radio."

I scrubbed a hand over my jaw. "You know how to wound me."

The corners of her mouth tipped up. "You're the one who wanted to stay here."

A flash of fur flew across the room, making me stumble back again. "Shit. Let me get a shovel. I think I can get it." Apparently, with the rustic history of this place came rodents.

"Don't you dare." Everly moved to the kitchen and pulled out a bag of nuts. Crouching down, she made a clicking noise behind her teeth. A small chipmunk appeared from around the corner.

I took hold of Koda's collar, so he didn't get any ideas about chasing down a snack. Everly held out an almond, and I watched in fascination as the little guy took it right from her fingers. Then he darted back across the room into a small hole in a cabinet. "What was that?"

"That's Chip. He lives here, too, so you have to be friendly."

I blinked a few times, looking from the cabinet to Everly and back again. "Whatever floats your boat. Chip just better not try to snuggle with me."

Ev shook her head. "He's very happy in his home in the cabinet there." She pointed to an open door on the opposite side of the living space. "That's your room. We'll have to share the bathroom here." She inclined her head to another door off a small hallway. "And my room is next to it. I'm going to hop in the shower and get cleaned up. You can start one of the frozen pizzas if you want. I'll make a salad."

I was lost as soon as she said the word shower. All sorts of images that I didn't need, roamed through my head. I cleared my throat. "Pizza. I can handle that."

Who was I kidding? Nothing about being in such close proximity to Everly for who knew how long was something I could handle. But I'd have to figure out how to keep my thoughts in check and my hands to myself.

Chapter Twenty-Eight

Everly

MY FINGERS CLAWED AT THE ARM DRAGGING ME BY the hair. "Ian, please." But he didn't seem to hear me at all. He simply kept pulling as I tried to gain my footing in the dirt, my bare feet scrabbling for any sort of purchase.

"Mom!" I yelled, but she was in the greenhouse, far from where my shouts could reach her. And Ian knew that.

His hand slapped out with such force that I barely saw it coming. And there was no way I could escape. The blow hit me across the mouth. For a moment, I didn't feel anything at all. Then pain bloomed, along with the taste of blood.

"Don't you dare cry for her. You're a fucking traitor." He threw me to the dirt.

"Ian, no!" Addie wailed, but her father held her back.

I could just make out Allen's cold gaze. "She's earned this punishment. If she doesn't want to be cast out, she'll take it, and she won't say a word to her mother."

Spit hit my face as Ian's boot collided with my stomach. All the air was forced out of me. "Stop. Please."

"You took him from us. You deserve worse than I could ever give you."

The next blow hit my ribs with a sickening crack, and I couldn't hold in my scream.

I shot up in bed, barely holding back the scream that had escaped in my dreams. My chest heaved, and my t-shirt and sleep shorts clung to my body with sweat. "Just a nightmare." I said the words over and over as I climbed out of bed.

It was my mantra as I stripped the sheets off the mattress and put on fresh ones. I'd learned long ago to have a spare set ready to go. "Just a nightmare," I whispered one more time. Only that wasn't entirely true. It was a memory. The images and pain carved so deeply into my body that I knew I'd never get them out.

"You're safe." I mouthed the words to an empty room. But I wasn't sure how true they were, either. The angry note flashed in my mind. The feel of that hand covering my mouth.

My fingers dug into my comforter as I pulled it up. "I'm safe." Hayes was just down the hall. There was a tug along my sternum. A pull to go to him and ask him to chase all of the bad dreams away.

I pushed the thought out of my brain as quickly as it appeared. Now wasn't the time to be reckless. Instead, I pulled a fresh set of PJs out of my drawer and went to the bathroom. I turned on the shower as cold as I could stand it—I needed the shock to my system. Anything to clear out those last haunting memories.

The blast of water did the trick. I rinsed the sweat from my body and lifted my face to the spray as if that pounding force could erase whatever lurked in my brain.

I dried off quickly, reapplying my favorite lotion and letting the fresh scent soothe me. Tossing my old PJs into my laundry basket, I moved down the hall as quietly as possible. I listened for a moment, but only the familiar sound of crickets greeted me.

I heated a mug of water in the small microwave I'd purchased, pulling it out before the beeping could wake Hayes. I went for chamomile tonight, with just a touch of honey. The simple process of preparing the tea was a comfort. Soothing before I'd even had my first sip.

I grabbed a throw from the basket at the end of the couch and moved to the back deck. The night was cold, but I welcomed that, too. The stars were clear as diamonds against black velvet. I eased into one of the two chairs I'd picked up at a secondhand shop in town. They were the Adirondack kind with wide arms and reclined backs. They almost felt like a warm hug.

I wasn't sure why I'd gotten two. It wasn't as if I expected anyone to use the other one. But it felt depressing to buy only one.

I tipped my face to the sky and began looking for constellations, but the tears blurring my vision hampered my quest. How had a father who'd taught his daughter to trace the stars had such cruelty and sickness in him? How had that grown ten-fold in his son?

I didn't think I'd ever find the answers, no matter how hard I looked. I wanted to find a way to be at peace with it all. But how did you find that with violence?

I wasn't sure I could get my way there. Ian didn't want my forgiveness. And he certainly hadn't changed. So, what did it mean to let go of it all?

Footsteps sounded on the boards of the back deck, but I didn't look up. I kept my gaze focused on the forest behind the cabin as Hayes lowered himself into the chair next to me. The one I thought might never be filled.

"Couldn't sleep?"

"Bad dream."

There was no point in lying. Hayes saw too much. In everyone, but especially in me.

"About the note?"

I wrapped my hands around my mug of tea, staring down into its swirling depths. "Something else."

"Your brother?"

My head snapped up. "What are you talking about?"

I saw a gentleness in Hayes I'd never seen before. As if he were approaching an injured, wild animal. "It doesn't take a genius to figure out there's something there."

I turned my focus back to my drink. I ran my thumb up and down the handle of the cup, unsure of what to say.

"Let me in, Ev."

Hayes didn't realize how much he was asking with that single request. And yet, I wanted to tell him. To unburden myself of something I'd carried with me for years. I hadn't ever spoken of it. Not even to Jacey when I went to live with her. My mom had tended to my wounds, stitching my lip and wrapping my ribs, but only after my bruises had faded and the stitches had been removed did she take me to my sister's.

"After my father's sentencing, Ian was angry. He took it out on me."

Hayes' eyes hardened. "He hit you? You were only eleven. He was a teenager."

I remembered how big Ian had seemed at the time, towering over me as his boot made contact with my ribs.

"How bad?"

The two words were rough, grating over my skin. "Split lip. Broken ribs. Probably a concussion."

Hayes' fingers dug into the arms of the chair, his knuckles bleaching white. "No one called the goddamned sheriff?"

"That's not how my family operates. It's why they were so angry with me. They didn't think that what my father had done was right, but they thought I should've waited until my mom came home so she could've talked Dad down or gone to get Allen."

"If you had waited another couple of days, Shiloh could've died."

"I know," I whispered. "The only thing I regret is not going sooner. I'd take the beating again if it meant she was okay."

"Fuck." Hayes pushed to his feet and began pacing. The back deck wasn't large, but he used every inch.

I rose slowly, setting my tea on the chair. I moved into his path, stopping Hayes in his tracks. "I'm okay."

His rough hands came up to frame my face as he bent down and got close. "You're not okay. How could you be? All I can think about is what you've had to endure. And the words I threw at you the first day I came up here. I'm so fucking sorry, Ev."

I tipped my face forward so our foreheads touched, then just rested there and circled his wrists with my hands. "I am okay. Or I will be. I stuffed a lot of this down. Haven't dealt with it the way I should have. But I'm facing it now. It's not easy, but it's good for me to be back here."

Hayes was silent for a moment, the only sound that of his ragged breathing. "You're the bravest person I've ever met."

"It's just twenty breaths—"

"It's not only twenty damn breaths. It's *you*. Whatever's running through those veins that makes you stronger than everyone else." Hayes tipped up my face so that our lips were only a breath apart. "Ev?"

"Yes?"

"I need to kiss you."

I wanted it so badly. The feel of his mouth on mine. To know that I wasn't alone in that moment. I was the one who closed the distance. His lips were softer than expected, the pressure so gentle, it was as if he worried that I might break.

But the moment his tongue slipped into my mouth, everything changed. Hunger and need took over. We were both searching for something, yet not quite sure what that was. My fingers fisted in his t-shirt, and I pulled Hayes closer until I wasn't sure where he ended, and I began.

An owl cried out in the night, likely swooping down in search of a snack. It was a bucket of cold water dumped right over my head. I jumped back, my hand going to my mouth. My lips tingled as I took in the man before me. I waited for him to say something about this being a mistake. He didn't. He simply stood there with a grin curving his mouth.

"That—that—we shouldn't have done that."

Hayes moved in closer. "Why not? You hiding a husband here somewhere?"

"No…I just…it's too complicated. There's too much water under too many bridges."

His hands came back to my face, his thumbs sweeping across my cheeks. "I don't give a damn about any water. You and me, that's what matters."

I would've given anything to believe that. But I knew it couldn't be. Whenever something reminded him of who my father was and what he had stolen from Hayes' family, it would kill something inside of him. And I couldn't stand around and watch that happen. So, I did the only thing I could. I ran.

Chapter Twenty-Nine

Hayes

"**Y**OU'RE WHISTLING."

I stole a glance at Young in my passenger seat. "So?"

"You never whistle."

I turned my focus back to the road, but my neck felt hot. "Guess I have a tune stuck in my head."

I could feel her gaze on my face, studying me. "Something's different."

"Is this your weird mom radar going off?"

Young chuckled. "Raising two little hooligans definitely helps the spidey senses. What gives, boss?"

I shifted in my seat. What gave was that I could still taste Everly. The tea and the hint of mint from her toothpaste. She might have hightailed it back to her room and left before I'd gotten up, but that didn't change anything. There was something between us. "Guess I'm just in a good mood this morning."

"Fine. Keep your secrets."

I would. This wasn't something I was ready to share with anyone. And I knew moving forward would be more akin to dismantling a bomb than pursuing a woman. Everly was right. It wouldn't be easy. More than a few moments would be complicated. But I couldn't walk away, either. She seemed to pull me in. And each layer she revealed tethered me to her. Amazed me and sliced at any sort of defenses I'd built up.

The wheel creaked as I adjusted my grip, Everly's pale face flashing in my mind. She'd given me a gift last night. The most precious thing she had—her truth. But that had me resisting the urge to betray the oaths I'd taken and search out Ian Kemper for myself.

"How's Everly doing?"

Young's voice cut through my spiraling thoughts. "What?"

"How is Everly after what happened? She hanging in there okay?"

"I think she's doing as well as she can be." But I knew that what had happened—the attack and the note—had brought on those nightmares last night. "I'm hoping there's something on the note. I asked them to bump it to the front of the line."

Young raised a brow. "Calling in favors?"

"We have to figure out who's behind this." We hadn't had a case this serious in years. Certainly never a serial offender stalking our county.

"I know. I'm just giving you a hard time because I know you like her."

"What?" I almost drove off the road.

Young gripped the handle above her head. "Hell. Please don't kill us because I know you have a crush."

"I do not."

"You sound like my five-year-old."

I clamped my mouth shut. Anything that came out now would sound like an idiotic denial.

Young grinned. "Now you're giving me the silent treatment, huh?"

"She's a good woman. And I'm going to leave it at that."

"Fine. I'll let you off the hook for now. Give me the rundown on what we're driving up on."

I rolled my shoulders back. "Samuel Miller. We've gotten a few calls on him now for animal abuse and neglect. He's had animals removed from his care before. He's on parole. If we've got enough evidence this time, he'll see the inside of a prison."

Young tightened her grip on the handle above her head. "God, I hope so. There's a special place in hell for people who hurt animals and children."

"I agree with you there."

The drive out to Miller's place wasn't a quick one. He lived thirty miles outside of town on a five-acre plot. When we drove up, a number of sheriff's department vehicles were already on scene, and I recognized Miles Taylor's truck. I nodded in the vehicle's direction. "Vet's here, so that's good."

"At least, there's that."

I pulled into a makeshift spot next to a cruiser and hopped out of my SUV. My gaze immediately went to the scrawny man sitting on a stump with his arms behind his back. He might have been restrained, but he was still cursing up a storm.

Sergeant Ruiz met my gaze. "Well, he took a swing at me, so we can arrest him for assaulting a law enforcement officer, at least."

"Small mercies," I muttered. My entire team was beyond frustrated that we were still dealing with this asshole. But animal abuse cases were hard to prove and even harder to get a decent sentence for. I strode forward, meeting Samuel's angry gaze. "You're on probation, Mr. Miller."

"Trumped-up charges. I ain't did nothing wrong."

My gaze traveled to the paddock behind him. A paint mare who would've been gorgeous if she wasn't skin and bones was behind the fence, along with a miniature donkey who limped away from Miles. Then I caught sight of another figure. This one moved with practiced ease, her hair piled up in a messy bun. Everly looked my way for just a moment before turning her attention back to the horse. And I turned my focus back to the man in front of me.

He didn't even deserve to be called a man. He was the lowest of the low. I took a step closer. "Praying on innocent animals doesn't make you strong. It makes you lower than dirt."

"Hey! You heard that. He insulted me. Told lies. I'm gonna sue."

Ruiz let out a low whistle. "You know, I didn't hear a thing. Did you, Young?"

"Just the wind. And maybe the phantom sound of a jail cell locking."

"I'm not going to fucking jail," Samuel blustered. "They're my animals. I can do whatever I want with them."

"That's where you're wrong. And I'm going to make sure the judge throws the book at you this time."

His eyes narrowed on me. "You already told a bunch of lies about me. Said I was an animal beater. I had to go to Idaho to get those two useless fucks."

I'd done everything I could to keep Samuel from hurting another creature. But apparently, not even spreading the word around the county had been enough. "Good thing you won't be able to buy any more while you're sitting in a cell." I looked at Ruiz. "Keep an eye on him. I need to talk to Miles."

"Happy to, boss."

I left Young with Ruiz and moved towards the paddock. My steps were slow and measured, not wanting to spook the paint. Everly's were the same as she spoke to and stroked the horse. "You're okay now. No one's going to hurt you ever again. Hayes will make it so. He might be overbearing, but he's a great defender."

"Is that so?"

Everly didn't jump, but when she turned to glance at me, it was with a scowl on her face. "You might have a few redeemable qualities."

I couldn't help the fact that my mouth started to kick up at the corners. But that smile died when I took in the wound on the mare's neck. "What the hell happened?"

"Keep your voice easy, Hayes. This beautiful girl doesn't like the sound of anger. I'm not sure how it happened, but it was never treated, and now it's infected." Everly moved a gauze pad with some sort of antiseptic gently over the wound. "That's it, girl. We're going to get you fixed up."

The mare rested her head on Everly's shoulder as if exhausted to the bone. Everly used her free hand to rub soothing circles on the unmarred side of the horse's neck. "We'll have to get her on antibiotics and a high-calorie diet so she can get back some of the weight she needs. Miles said he'd take them both to his barn for a while."

"That's good. It'll be a lot calmer there than at the county shelter." They always lacked space at the shelter and needed more hands on top of it.

"She can't go to a shelter, Hayes. It took me an hour just to get her to let me touch her. Another hour to look at her wound. She'll freak in a place like that."

"Maybe you should take her, then."

Everly's eyes swiveled in my direction. "Me?"

"You've got one paddock done, another almost there. That's enough space for these two." I inclined my head towards the tiny donkey Miles had managed to catch. He was now examining it while the animal chowed down on some grain.

"I don't know…I wanted to get a barn up before I took on any animals. Have some storage sheds built. A few other things."

I leaned against the fence. "You'll never be completely ready. But you have to start somewhere."

Her fingers ran along the paint's coat. "You have a point there."

"I know my family can pitch in this weekend and get you as set up as possible."

Everly tipped her head back to look the horse in her eyes. "What do you say, beauty? Want to come live with me after you're all healed up?"

The mare blew air out through her lips, making Everly laugh. The sound was light and free as if all the things that weighed on her shoulders had been lifted in that one moment. I wanted more of those laughs. I could drown in the sound and be a happy man.

I cleared my throat. "I think that's a yes."

Everly pressed her forehead to the horse's cheek. "I think so, too. I'll take good care of you, girl. And I promise you'll never have to be scared again."

Chapter Thirty

Everly

I'D MADE AN ART OUT OF AVOIDING HAYES FOR THE PAST FEW days—at least when other people weren't going to be around. I didn't trust myself. That kiss had been too much. And now it haunted me. It had been the perfect mix of heat and comfort, a feeling I could sink into, get lost in, and never return from.

So, I'd stayed busy. So busy that I'd poured myself two cups of coffee this morning. I listened for sounds of Hayes stirring but only heard Koda's soft snores from his dog bed. Chip was perched on the edge of the pillow, looking at the dog with fascination.

"Careful, buddy. He could eat you in one bite."

Chip's head jerked in my direction, and then he ran back into his hidey-hole. I wanted to do the same thing. But the entire Easton clan would be here in less than an hour. I'd opted to hold off on the barn and focus on the paddocks and a couple of storage sheds instead. I could make do with that for a year or two and let my savings grow.

I had the exact plans I wanted. Gabe had been kind enough to go over them with me, suggesting a few tweaks or places I could save money, so I was ready to go when the time was right.

What could only be a large truck sounded from the gravel

road leading up to the property. I set down my coffee and headed for the front porch. My eyes nearly bugged out of my head when I saw the eighteen-wheeler coming over the ridge. I had no idea how it had even made some of the turns on this road, let alone how it would turn around to get back.

Gabe hopped out of his truck and directed the massive vehicle towards the area where the barn had once stood. The trailer carried a huge load of lumber and other materials. I moved down the steps like a robot, not even noticing when Hayes came up alongside me, and an array of different vehicles parked in open spots.

"Morning. You sleep okay?"

Hayes' voice was full of concern as he took in my face. I blinked up at him. "What is happening right now?"

"Don't be mad."

"That is never a good start to any statement."

Hayes' expression seemed to battle between amusement and worry. "Dad wanted you to have your barn now."

"What?"

"He said your plans were sound and simple. His buddy who runs a construction crew heard what you were doing, and he and his crew said they'd love to help. They're between jobs right now and can give this project a week of dedicated work."

"What?" It was the only word I seemed capable of saying. My head turned as people began spilling out of trucks, SUVs, and cars. They laughed and chatted—faces I knew and ones I didn't recognize. "Why?"

"You want to do some good here, and people want to help with that."

Tears stung the corners of my eyes. "Even though they know who I am?"

"Ev." Hayes took my face in his hands, turning me towards him. "Who you are is an amazing, brave, selfless woman. Why wouldn't they want to help someone like that?"

A few tears slipped free, and Hayes wiped them away with his thumbs. I grabbed hold of his arms, worried if I didn't, I might lose my stance. "I can't afford to pay all of them."

"It's a gift. And we got the materials at cost. Those are a gift from my family."

My head shook between his hands. "No. I can't accept that. It's too much."

"They've wanted to do something. Needed to. Let them."

"I can't—"

He silenced me with a swift kiss. That mix of heat and comfort I'd felt before nearly brought me to my knees. "Please, let them do this."

The pleading in his tone had me giving in. "Okay. But there's something I want to give them, too."

Hayes released his hold on my face and straightened. "What's that?"

"I'll show you."

Hayes called his dad over, and I motioned to Shiloh and Julia. Hadley had to untangle herself from a Birdie piggyback ride, but she came, too. I took in the family. One mine had stolen so much from, who still gave to me freely anyway. "I can't thank you enough for all you've done for me. I wanted to do something for you. And I couldn't think of what that might be."

Julia reached out and squeezed my shoulder. "You don't need to give us anything." Her eyes darted towards Shiloh. "You've already given us everything."

A burn lit in the back of my throat. "I think this is something we can do together."

I moved to a crate I'd set at the foot of the porch steps. Lifting the lid, I looked up. "There's one for each of you."

Hadley bent down and picked up one of the items in the crate. "A sledgehammer?"

I met Shy's gaze and then looked behind her to the shed in

the distance. We'd kept our distance from the space every time we'd worked together. Consciously or subconsciously, I'd woven the paddocks we'd created away from that area. But if any of us had a prayer of moving past what had happened here, we needed to face it.

"The shed." The structure Shiloh had been kept in for five days all those years ago still stood strong. While the main house was barely habitable, and the barn was gone, that damn shed was still there. "It's time to tear it down. I thought it might be a good place to put a garden. Pour some life into the space."

I looked around at the faces, seeing a mixture of reactions. And for a heartbreaking moment, I wasn't sure if I'd overstepped my bounds. But then Shiloh stepped forward and picked up a sledgehammer. "I think that's a great plan."

She started walking without waiting for the rest of us, but we followed. Julia first, giving me a tight hug and whispering, "Thank you." Then Gabe, who seemed to be wrestling with tears. Hadley simply shot me a grin. "Let's beat the hell out of some wood."

Hayes bent, picking up the last two sledgehammers. "How do you always seem to know what Shy needs?"

I took one of the hammers from him and started walking. "I don't know that I do. I just know that ignoring what happened here hasn't been good for any of us. I hid from it for so long, and it chased me, haunted my nightmares, influenced everything. It has to give us a better shot to actually face it."

Hayes wrapped an arm around my shoulders. "I wanted to burn this place to the ground so many times I lost count."

I stiffened in his hold. "Hayes—"

"But I was wrong. I'm ashamed that was my reaction."

"You're allowed to feel whatever you need to."

He tipped his face down to look at me. "It's so much better to create good here. To make new life where one was almost cut short." His voice hitched on the words. "Doing what I do, you'd have thought I'd have learned this by now. More destruction won't heal or cast out that darkness."

"We're about to do a little destruction right now."

"This is different. It's clearing the way to create something new."

"I like looking at it that way."

"Me, too."

He bent to press a kiss to the corner of my mouth, but I stepped out of his hold. "Hayes," I hissed. "Your family."

He grinned. "I think I'm going to try making a habit of kissing you wherever I can and as often as possible."

My cheeks heated. "I can't talk about this right now."

"But we are going to talk about it sometime. And that means you're going to have to stop running away from me."

"I'm not running."

He arched a brow.

I picked up my pace. "I've just been busy."

"Suuuure."

"Later," I hissed as we came to a stop where his family gathered.

He moved in close to me. "That's a promise."

I tried to ignore the heat coming off him in waves, the promise of safety and comfort I wanted to lean into so badly that it hurt. Instead, I focused on the faces around me. "Shiloh, you get the first blow."

She didn't say a word, simply stared at the structure that had taken so much from her. It seemed so small now, yet it had been a prison. She arced her hammer back and swung. As the first plank splintered, it sounded like freedom.

Chapter Thirty-One

Hayes

I LEANED BACK ON THE COUCH, KICKING MY SOCKED FEET UP on the coffee table. Koda's exhausted snores sounded from the dog bed in the corner. All of the excitement today had worn him out, but we'd made more than a little progress. More paddocks were finished, and the barn might even be done by the time the mare and donkey were well enough to come to their new home.

The door to the bathroom squeaked, and I glanced over my shoulder to see Everly appear. Steam billowed out of the bathroom, and I instinctively reached for my beer. Her hair fell in loose waves around her shoulders, her tank top hugged each dip and curve, and those damned shorts she wore to bed... They had my mind delving into places that she wasn't ready for.

Her cheeks pinked. "Bathroom's free if you need it. Or there's an outdoor shower on the back deck."

An outdoor shower. My brain went in all sorts of new and unhelpful directions. "Sounds like a storm's coming. I don't think an outdoor shower is a good idea right now." A crack of thunder sounded as if to punctuate my point. "Come here."

She stayed put. "Why?"

"Please?"

Everly rolled her eyes. "Because you asked so nicely." She paused in the kitchen to pull a beer out of the fridge and pop the top. Then she made her way over to the couch, settling herself on the opposite side as me.

"How does your head feel?"

"Fine."

I arched a brow.

"All right. It's hurting a little, but nothing a good night's sleep won't fix."

I reached out and tugged one of her bare feet onto my lap and then the other. As my thumbs dug into her arches, Everly let out a moan. The sound shot straight to my bloodstream, making my entire body stand at attention. I ignored it and kept up the ministrations.

"I'll pay you a million dollars if you never stop."

I chuckled. "You pushed yourself today."

"So did you."

"I'm not recovering from a concussion."

Everly stared out the window at the dark sky with stars dotting the black. "Think Shiloh's okay?"

My sister had more than pushed herself today, and she'd kept her distance from everyone while she did it, opting to run fencing alone instead of helping in any group project. "She's processing."

"I really like her. She's not afraid of what anyone thinks about her. Just does what she needs to. And she's kind."

I switched my attention to Everly's other foot. "Do you worry about what other people think about you?"

"I wish I didn't. But I think it's inescapable with my history."

My movements stilled for a moment as I took her in, studying the shadows behind her eyes. "Was Seattle not a fresh start for you?"

"It was, eventually. But the few times Ian and Allen showed

up…they made a scene. At Jacey's house. At my school. The school was the worst. The cops were called. But I was young enough that kids were jerks about it. I already struggled to fit in, and there was so much I'd never experienced. I didn't know the tv shows, the video games, popular music. It was all out of my reach. So, I was the oddball."

A thick coating of shame swept over me as I realized this woman had dealt with even more than I knew, things I hadn't given the first thought to. "I can't imagine how hard that must've been."

She shrugged and took a sip of her beer. "A lot of kids were worse off. I was safe and cared for. Once we moved to the new place, I never had to look over my shoulder."

Even though Everly hadn't needed to be on alert, I had a feeling she remained that way. That kind of thing was burned into you and was hard to let go of. "So why come back?" She stiffened a bit, but I kept digging my thumbs into the arch of her foot. "If you finally broke free, why come back here?"

"Because I wasn't free. Not really. I…" Her gaze drifted out the window. "I was hiding. Doing everything I could to keep my family from knowing where I was, even though I don't think they ever looked after those first few visits. I just needed to face it. To prove that I could. If I did, I thought maybe I wouldn't be so scared all the damn time."

"I think if you look at something dead-on, it takes some of its power away."

"Exactly. So that's what I'm doing."

I leaned forward, tucking a strand of hair behind her ear. "I think you're damn brave for it."

Everly laid a hand flat against my chest. "I can't. Not right now. And not because I don't want to. I just need to wrap my head around all of this. Make sure it's wise for me."

I leaned back in my spot on the couch and picked up her foot again. "I can give you time. Just make sure you're not taking that time to talk yourself out of something you want."

Everly blew out a breath, sending wisps of hair flying around her face. "You sure don't lack any confidence, do you?"

"Not when it comes to this. Because I've lived some years, and I know one thing for sure: I've never felt how I did when I kissed you, Ev. I've never been so drawn in by someone."

Her fingers drifted to her lips, and I couldn't help the grin that spread over my face. She'd felt it, too. I just had to trust that the pull between us would be enough to make her take that leap.

"You're up early," Everly mumbled as she walked into the kitchen in bare feet, her hair a mess.

"Sorry if I woke you. I wanted to get a run in before work started today and see if there was any damage from the storm." The wind had howled like crazy last night, thunder sounding like it had been right on top of us.

Everly bent to scratch behind Koda's ears as he leaned against her legs. "You're going on a run before we spend all day hauling, lifting, and hammering? Do you have some weird obsession I should know about?"

"Gotta make sure I can chase down the bad guys." And I needed to burn off some of the fire running through my veins. I'd tossed and turned for hours before finally finding sleep, my mind unable to let go of the temptation down the hall. Then I'd been awoken from a dream so real it had required a cold shower.

"Whatever floats your boat, I guess. I haven't ventured on any of the old trails around here yet, so I have no idea what kind of shape they're in. Be careful you don't get lost."

"I was thinking I'd just stick to the roads today."

"Probably smart." Everly moved towards the front door. "Looks like the skies cleared. It's the perfect morning for it." She pulled open the door, leaving only the screen in place. "What in the world?"

She stepped out onto the front porch and gasped, looking across the way to where my truck was parked.

I was by her side in a flash, letting a slew of curses fly. "Stay back."

My hand went to the holster at the small of my back, the one I wore for running because you never knew when you might run into wildlife that was less than pleased with your appearance. I slid my gun out and held it at my side, peering around the door.

Someone had smashed every single window on my SUV. The side mirrors, too. Tires slashed. This wasn't simply anger. It was rage.

But I didn't see any signs of life other than the trees moving in the breeze. "Stay here. Lock the door."

I slipped out the screen door, holding it so it didn't slam. I systematically made my way around the cabin, then the dilapidated house next door and the two new storage sheds that had gone up yesterday. I checked paddocks and piles of lumber to make sure no one lurked there. Whoever this was seemed to be long gone.

I started back towards the cabin, my steps faltering as I took in Everly. She stood in muck boots and those tiny-ass sleep shorts, a shotgun resting under one arm, surveying the damage to my vehicle. "I thought I told you to stay inside and lock the door?"

She didn't jolt or startle, which told me she'd known where I was at all times. "I'm not hiding away when someone's messing with things on my property. When they still might be around, and you could need backup."

My back teeth ground together. "I have training. You don't."

Her eyes narrowed on me. "I have more training than you could ever dream of. I started shooting when I was five—every weapon my father could get his hands on. I've run drills in the blistering heat, waist-deep snow, and the pouring rain. I've learned to fight off an attacker blindfolded. Been woken up from a dead sleep and taken through simulations that would never actually happen.

"And when that was all over? When I could finally walk away? I had to keep it up because I was so damn scared my brother might show up. And I refused to be surprised again. So, don't you tell me I don't have training."

I moved fast, pulling her against me and wrapping my arms around her. "I'm sorry. I just don't want anything to happen to you."

"If it does, I'll be ready."

But the last thing I wanted was for Everly to have to face whoever had enough rage pulsing through them to do this to my vehicle.

Chapter Thirty-Two

Everly

"**H**EY, ARE YOU OKAY?" Tim looked down at me as my head rested on the break room table. "Long weekend."

He shuffled his feet, sneakers squeaking on the linoleum. "I heard what happened to Hayes' SUV. But you guys were okay, right? You weren't hurt?"

Normally, I would've blushed over the fact that everyone in this town likely knew that Hayes had been spending nights at my cabin. But I was too tired to care at the moment. After a crime scene tech and a couple of officers had come out to process the scene, we'd cleaned everything up and had Hayes' SUV towed to a body shop a county over. Work had started again, but I hadn't been able to rustle up the positive glow I'd had the day before.

I let out a long breath and sat up. "No. No one was hurt." My stomach twisted at the thought of what might have happened if Hayes had heard the destruction. It was only the fact that he'd parked farther away to leave room for those helping out yesterday, combined with the noise from the storm, that had kept us from hearing the destruction.

Tim looked down at the tips of his sneakers. "You know, you're welcome to stay with me if you need. I don't have a ton of space, but you can have the bedroom, and I'll sleep on the couch."

"Thank you. That's so kind, but I think I'm going to stick it out at the cabin. Hayes is staying in my guest room until they figure out what's going on."

"Okay. But if you change your mind, you have my cell. You can call anytime."

I couldn't help but smile at the tall but somewhat gangly boy-man in front of me. His kindness was more of a balm to the wounds of the past twenty-four hours than he would ever know.

"I want to talk to my fucking sister. I don't care if she's on her lunch break."

I stiffened at the sound of Ian's voice coming from the waiting room. I pushed to my feet and hurried out there. Kelly was scowling at my brother from behind the counter. "I'll call the sheriff if you don't back off, buddy."

"You think I give a damn about some pig? I don't."

"Ian," I clipped. "I'm right here. Why don't we go outside and talk?"

Tim stepped up to my side. "I don't think that's such a good idea, Everly."

I laid a hand on Tim's shoulder. "I'm fine. Promise."

Ian sneered at the action. "Just how many men are you spreading your legs for, Evie? There's the cop who won't get off my case thanks to you, this joker, and given the way Ben jumped to your defense, I'd guess him, too. I shouldn't be surprised you turned into a slut. Mom would be ashamed."

The room around us went deathly silent. That heat I couldn't find earlier rose to my cheeks now. The shame that this was who I shared blood with, that my *brother* would speak to me this way. But I didn't duck my head or hunch my shoulders. I wouldn't let Ian see that making a scene at my workplace was a direct hit to everything I was building here. "Leave."

"You're not the boss of me."

Tim took a step forward. "This is a private business, and we have the right to refuse service to anyone. We're doing that now. Leave, or we'll call the sheriff's department."

"I already have," Kelly said from behind the counter. "Deputies are on the way."

Ian spat on the floor. "Your little lap dog coming in handy yet again. Hope you're sucking his dick good. I'm gonna sue both of you for harassment."

The heat in my cheeks burned, but it wasn't just there. It was in my blood, too. The shared blood that flowed through my veins. "You're the one who showed up here. Somehow, I don't think that makes for a very strong case."

Sirens sounded, and Ian's eyes flashed. "I should've killed you that night. Finished you off instead of settling for broken bones."

And with that, he turned on his heel and jogged off. My ears buzzed. Kind of how a fluorescent light sounded, only amplified. I was only partly aware of Tim ushering me over to a seat in the waiting room and easing me down into it. I thought he might've asked something, but my brain couldn't seem to comprehend the words.

I could feel the burn in my scalp. The crack of my ribs. I could taste the blood filling my mouth. All of it. And he wanted to hurt me more.

Hands gripped my calves, and I blinked as the face in front of me came into focus. Hayes. Somewhere in my jumbled mind, I put together that those dark eyes and the sharp, angular jaw belonged to Hayes.

"He wishes he'd killed me." My voice broke on the words, but the tears didn't come. I was simply empty. Too many tears cried over the brother who was supposed to love me. The family who had never stepped up for me when I needed them.

For some naïve reason, I'd thought my brother could have

outgrown this hatred. That he would never be a fan of mine but wouldn't wish me ill, either. That he might be mad that Mom had left the property to me but would get over it. That he would've grown up. Matured. But he hadn't gotten over anything.

Hayes' jaw ticked as he framed my face with those rough hands. Hands I was beginning to know by touch alone. The pads of his fingertips. The raised scar on his palm. "I'm so sorry, Ev. I had to send a deputy out to talk to him and Allen since we've had a few run-ins lately. It's just procedure."

"I know." This was why Hayes and I would never be. Because my family would destroy it. Just like they ate away at any other good thing in my life. I'd been so stupid to think that all I had to do was face them again to put this haunting anger to rest. They'd never be done with me.

I blinked around the room, a worried Kelly and Tim filling Miles in on what'd happened. I loved working here. And I truly believed I could create a sanctuary at home that was so needed in our community. But maybe I'd have to give that up, too.

"I don't like where your head's at right now."

I focused back on Hayes. "It's not anywhere."

"Bullshit." His thumbs sweeping back and forth across my cheeks took away some of the sting of the word. "You're thinking about running. Don't."

I clamped my mouth closed. How was it that in a matter of months, Hayes could read my mind and decipher my tells better than anyone ever had before?

"You run, I'll chase you."

"I shouldn't have come back," I whispered. "I knew they wouldn't be happy to see me, but I thought…sixteen years. That's more than enough time to take away some of the sting. Figured they'd have moved on, and I could do what I needed to."

"They don't get to stop you from finding your peace."

"What peace?" I waved my hand around the waiting room, now teeming with officers. "There is none."

He gripped my face more firmly, making me meet his gaze. "You have to fight for it."

I let my head tip forward to rest on his. "I'm too tired to fight."

"Then you rest for a little while and pick up the sword again when you're ready. There are other people who can hold it for you in the meantime."

Other people, who would quickly grow tired of its heavy weight. And then they would walk away, too.

Hayes pressed a soft kiss to my temple. "Just rest."

"Okay."

It didn't matter either way. I would just have to hold on until everyone walked away. Then I could leave on my terms.

"Why the hell haven't you arrested him?"

My head snapped up at Tim's biting words. Hayes stood, his hand going to my shoulder. "Careful, Tim."

He waved an arm towards the door. "He just barged in here. He could've had a weapon. Could've hurt her or worse."

I struggled to my feet, my legs still feeling a bit wobbly. "He's doing everything he can, Tim."

"There's an all-points bulletin out on him now. We're going to bring him in."

"And then what?" Tim demanded.

"Then, Everly is going to file a restraining order."

I opened my mouth to argue and then shut it again. I'd have to file the papers, if only in hopes of protecting my employer's business. That was if I even still had a job. Maybe my time in Wolf Gap would be coming to a close sooner than expected. My chest constricted with the thought that, one day, I wouldn't feel those familiar hands cupping my face anymore. Would never push into that touch. And that was enough to break my heart, more than a little.

Chapter Thirty-Three

Hayes

"STOP HOVERING. IT'S ANNOYING, AND IT'S STARTING to piss me off."

My father covered his chuckle with a cough at Everly's words. I sent a scowl in his direction before stopping my pacing to rub Ev's shoulders. She, Dad, and Shiloh were poring over some plans for the rest of the paddocks, including some sort of weird play equipment for the goats that would one day be housed in one of them.

I pressed into the knots along her shoulder blades. "I'm not hovering."

"You are," Shiloh muttered.

"Traitor."

Everly turned in her seat, shaking my hands free. "Go have a beer with Calder."

"He said he was fine coming here."

"And I said you're driving me crazy. *Go*. We're not going to be invaded by zombies, and my brother is locked up at the station."

It had taken us all day to track Ian down, and I'd chosen to hold him. I hoped a night sleeping next to whatever intoxicated individual my deputies brought in might loosen his tongue. And in the meantime, Everly had signed the papers we'd put before a judge. She now had an emergency restraining order in place. She'd have to go back for a permanent one in a few weeks, but at least we had something.

I just wasn't overly convinced that Ian would take it seriously or that her uncle wouldn't retaliate in some way. I'd been on edge all afternoon and had a deputy sitting outside the vet's office just in case. "I just want to make sure you're safe."

She motioned around the room. "I've got company with cell phones if there's an emergency. I've got Koda. And I've got Betty."

My brows pulled together. "Betty?"

"My shotgun."

Shiloh snorted a laugh and leaned back in her chair. "Get lost, brother. You're cramping our style."

I'd noticed that Shiloh was talking a little more since she'd built a sort of friendship with Everly. Not epic, heartfelt confessions or anything but simply joining in a little more—even if it was at my expense.

"Go on, Hayes. We won't leave until you're back," my father said.

Everly stiffened. "I appreciate the gesture, Gabe, but I'm perfectly capable of watching my own back. I've been doing it a long time."

He eyed Everly carefully. "I know you're more than capable, but that doesn't mean you shouldn't ever have help."

"And you've helped more than enough. You don't need to be locked up in this cabin with me because my brother said something stupid. He has always had a big mouth."

One that spewed threats I knew he'd made good on.

Everly sighed when no one said anything. "It's important to me that I have control of my own life. I don't want to feel like I'm being herded or cornered. And they don't get to influence my life. Not anymore."

"She's right," Shy agreed. "Ev can take care of herself. She's not stupid. She's letting Hayes stay here nights, even though he's annoying as all get out. Let that be enough."

Ev reached under the table and squeezed Shy's knee, mouthing, "*Thank you.*" Shiloh moved away from the touch but nodded in acceptance of the gratitude.

"Okay. I'm gonna go meet Calder for an hour or two—"

"Two," Everly interjected.

"All right, two." I bent and pressed a kiss to her temple. "I'm not trying to control you," I whispered. "And I know you can take care of yourself. But anyone can be taken by surprise. It's the same reason I take backup to question a suspect."

She relaxed a fraction. "Have fun with Calder."

I started for the door. "I will. I left you whoopie pies on the counter."

"Well, why didn't you say that sooner? I probably would've been a hell of a lot less cranky if I'd known."

I chuckled as I headed out, locking the door behind me. Everly had given me an extra key, but that didn't mean she fully trusted me—to stay, to stand by her when her family pulled their crap. I'd seen the look of panic on her face earlier in the day. I'd seen the look of defeat. I could see the fight in her literally draining out.

Everly wanted to bolt. But I wasn't sure I could watch her go. We weren't even together, and I could already see myself following her wherever she went. Because, all of a sudden, I couldn't imagine my life without her.

And I wasn't sure my family could, either. They'd folded her into the fabric that was us. She'd become a support to Shiloh, showed my mom incredible kindness, gave Dad purpose with all of the projects they worked on, and she made Hadley feel at ease when Mom had her on edge. She was everything we hadn't known we needed. And I was going to make sure we gave all of that back to her and more.

"I still can't believe she kicked you out," Calder said as he chuckled into his beer.

"Yeah, yeah, yuck it up."

"Come on. It is pretty funny. Usually, it's you trying to sneak away from some woman you've decided isn't the right fit. And now, one's booting you to the curb. Some of your exes would say it's poetic justice."

I rubbed at the back of my neck. "So I'm not great with confrontation."

Calder blinked at me a few times. "Hayes. You're the sheriff. Ninety percent of your job is confrontation."

"Okay, I'm not great with confrontation when it comes to the women in my life."

"That is more like it. You're the peacekeeper and protector. You want everyone you care about to be safe and happy. Especially your mom and sisters."

I picked at the label on my beer. "I'm not so sure Everly's thrilled with that role. The protector part, anyway."

"She's pretty much been on her own a long time, hasn't she?"

"She had her sister and her sister's family, but I get the sense they aren't especially close. I've never heard her on the phone with her, and she doesn't talk about her much."

Calder rubbed his thumb against his glass, clearing a path of condensation. "The little time I've spent with her, she seems to value her autonomy and her ability to take care of herself. Given the way she grew up, I'm guessing she didn't have a lot of control there."

"I'm not trying to control. I just want to make sure she's safe." I felt like a broken record.

"But you usually do that by controlling every factor you can. Let me guess, you didn't want her to be alone tonight?"

"Wouldn't you feel the same?"

"I sure would. I'd just hide it better."

I let out a snort of laughter. "You always did have more tact than I did."

"Damn straight."

My phone buzzed on the table, and Hadley's name flashed across the screen. I hit accept. "Hey, Hads. What's up?"

"I might have a problem."

I straightened on my stool. "What's going on?"

"I'm pretty sure someone's following me."

"Following you where?"

Calder was on his feet in a flash, pulling some bills out of his wallet and tossing them on the table. He motioned for me to follow him towards the door.

Hadley muttered a curse across the line. "I thought he was just riding my ass at first, but he's following every turn I make."

I pushed open the door. "Where are you?"

"On my way home."

"Turn back towards town."

Hadley had taken her inheritance from our grandparents and bought a gorgeous piece of property fifteen minutes outside Wolf Gap. But the price for that beauty was isolation. None of us had been crazy about her living by herself, but she'd been determined.

"I'd turn around if there was a place to do it, but I don't want to get boxed in."

I beeped the locks on my department loner vehicle and climbed behind the wheel, Calder jumping into the passenger seat. "Calder and I are on our way. You're going to be okay."

I glanced at Calder as I hit the lights. "Hold this and put Hads on speaker."

He did as I instructed as I radioed for backup. "We'll be there in a few minutes. Just hold on," he assured her.

"Shit," she cried out.

"What the hell was that?" Calder barked.

"He rammed my bumper."

I pushed down on the accelerator. "Can you make out anything about the vehicle or the person in it?"

"Not really. A truck or SUV. Big grill." Another crash sounded across the line.

Calder gripped the phone tighter. "Hadley!"

"I'm okay," she said through gritted teeth. "You want to play, asshole? Hold on."

"What are you doing, Hads?" God, I hoped it wasn't something completely insane.

Tires squealed in the background, and then a loud thump sounded. I held my breath, waiting. The sound of what could only be gravel and rock spitting out from under tires came through the phone speaker. "Got it."

I gripped the wheel harder. "What exactly did you get?"

"I turned off my headlights and pulled a U-turn around that old pine a mile from the turnoff to my place."

Calder let out a whoosh of air. "You could've gotten yourself killed."

"Better than whoever's behind the wheel of that truck killing me."

I turned onto the road that led towards Hadley's place. "Are they following you?"

There was silence for a moment and then the release of an audible breath. "No. I don't think so. I think whoever it was kept going."

There was a whole network of roads out there that led to a million different places. Whoever it was could hide anywhere. And, at any point, they could turn back around. I accelerated yet again and didn't take a breath until I saw my sister's truck in the distance. "Pull over. This is us."

For once in her life, Hadley did what I asked the first time I asked it. She slid the truck over and shut off the engine, and I did the same but left my lights flashing. As Hadley climbed out of the vehicle her legs trembled.

Calder moved before I had a chance to round the SUV, pulling her into his arms. "You're okay. I've got you."

For the first time in years, my sister burst into tears. The sound startled the hell out of me. Hadley held her emotions close to the vest, rarely letting me or anyone else in our family in on what was going on in that head of hers unless she was pissed off. To see her break like this, shaking in Calder's arms, made me want to rip whoever had done this limb from limb.

"You're safe, Hads," Calder whispered into her hair. "No one's going to hurt you."

"I know," she choked out. Hadley let him hold her for another few seconds and then straightened. "Sorry. I guess it scared me more than I realized."

Calder gave her a gentle smile. "Adrenaline dump. You know how those can be."

"I'm not usually such a sissy about them."

I pulled her in for a hard hug. "You're not a sissy. You're damn brave—if a little foolish."

Calder's face hardened. "You never should've made that turn. It was crazy."

"And it worked," she said, pulling out of my hold. "It saved my butt, so don't give me a hard time."

He opened his mouth to say something, but I shot him a look, and he closed it. A squad car came screeching up, and Young and Williams were out in a flash. Young looked Hadley up and down. "You okay?"

"Fine."

I looked at my two officers. "See if you can find any sign of him. SUV or truck, large grill."

Williams winced. "That could be half the county."

"The grill will have paint from Hadley's bumper, so if you pull someone over, look for that."

Young nodded, waving Williams back to the car. "We'll let you know what we find."

Hadley let out a shaky breath and leaned against the side of her truck. "Can one of you drive me to my place? I don't think I'm quite ready to get back behind the wheel."

Calder scowled in her direction. "You're not staying at your place alone. He could be waiting there for all you know."

"It was probably just someone with a severe case of road rage. They have no idea who I am or where I live."

"Hads…" I began. "Calder's right. You shouldn't stay there tonight. Especially when you're on edge."

"You can stay at my place. Or your mom and dad's," Calder offered.

Hadley crossed her arms under her chest. "I'll stay with Hayes."

"I'm staying at Everly's, remember?"

"Well, then I'll stay there. I can sleep on the couch."

I knew that tone. Stubbornness coming through. She'd never spend the night at Mom and Dad's by choice, and Calder had stepped on her toes. I wrapped an arm around her shoulders. "Come on. Let's get you to Ev's. I bet you could use a drink."

"Try ten."

I forced out a chuckle but didn't feel it at all. Because all I could wonder was whether whoever had tried to run Hadley off the road was the same man who'd tried to take Everly. And I still had no idea who he was.

Chapter Thirty-Four

Everly

I CLOSED THE DOOR TO THE GUEST ROOM SOFTLY, MY SOCKED feet padding along the floor. Hayes looked up from his spot on the couch. "She okay?"

I eased down onto the couch next to him. I didn't opt for the other end like I should've. I went for close—I wanted to feel Hayes' warmth and safety. I wanted to hook into that phantom pull that always dared me to lean just a little bit closer. "She will be."

He wrapped an arm around my shoulders, pulling me into him. "She still pissed at me?"

The corners of my mouth tipped up. "She might have been talking about interfering, overprotective asses, but I think that was mostly about Calder."

"At least, I can always count on her to be more annoyed with him than me."

I traced an invisible design on Hayes' chest. "We've given you a hard time today, haven't we?"

"Nothing a beer or two won't fix."

I still felt guilty. Seeing how Hadley reacted to her brother's overprotective ways had put things in perspective for me a bit. "I need to know I'm in charge of my life. That I'm the one who gets to make decisions about how things will go."

Hayes set his beer on the side table next to the couch. "Who else would be?"

I arched a brow in his direction.

"All right. I know I tend to want to corral. To plan for all contingencies. I don't think that will ever change. But I can try to remember that it's important I don't bulldoze."

I curled my knees up to my chest, turning my body into his. "Thank you. And I'll try to keep in mind that the bulldozing comes from a good place."

Hayes brushed the hair away from my face. "I care about you, Ev. You came in like a flash flood with no warning, and now I can't imagine my life without you."

I swallowed, my throat sticking with the movement. Because I cared about him, too. More than cared. "It scares me."

"That I care about you?"

I nodded. "And what I feel for you."

"I'm not gonna lie; it's a damn relief to hear those words from your mouth. That I'm not in this alone."

My palm rested flat against his chest, his heart thumping against it. "You're not in this alone. But I'm not sure how it will ever work. How me staying here will work. There's this mountain to overcome, and I'm not sure if I'm strong enough to climb it."

One hand came up to frame my face, that rough thumb sweeping across my cheekbone. "You are. A mountain always looks terrifying from the bottom, but you just have to take it one step at a time."

"One step?" My heart rattled against my ribs. Not the quaint flutter of a crush but a violent battle cry.

"One step. Can you do that with me?"

I wanted to. So desperately. I wasn't sure when I'd last done something reckless just because I wanted to. "I can do that."

Hayes' head dipped, moving so slowly it was almost painful, giving me every chance to pull away. But I didn't. I waited with the violent beat against my ribs until those lips met mine. I sank into the kiss—the warmth and comfort and fire.

The slow pull of it turned hungry in a matter of breaths. Hayes' hands went to my hips. Soon, I was straddling him, his tongue dueling with mine as his fingers dug into my flesh. I rocked against him, feeling the hardness beneath his jeans and letting out a little mewl.

The sound only seemed to stoke Hayes higher. The kiss took on a slightly feral edge, desperate and seeking. But I still wanted more. If I were going to jump, it might as well be from the highest cliff.

"Bedroom," I said as I tore my mouth from his.

Hayes searched my face. "Are you sure?"

"Yes." I wasn't certain this wouldn't end in wreckage around us, but I was sure I wanted to feel what it was to wholly belong to this man, body and soul—even if only for one night. I wanted to give myself over to everything he could make me feel, even if I didn't think it could last. "Make me yours."

Hayes' eyes flashed, and he lifted me in one swift move. My legs encircled his waist as I simply held on. We strode towards my bedroom on the other side of the small cabin. I thanked my lucky stars for walls made of thick lumber that insulated sound.

He closed the door behind us with a foot and continued to the bed, stopping just shy of it. Hayes never once looked away from me as he lowered me to the floor. Each millimeter of movement sent sparks of sensation dancing across my skin.

As soon as my feet touched the floor, my hands were in his tee, tugging and pulling until golden skin greeted my eyes. Planes of lean muscle I couldn't resist exploring. My fingers traced a pec as his hands went to the button on his jeans. Hayes hissed out a breath as I circled a nipple. "Ev…"

I looked up at him with a wicked grin. "Yes?"

He pulled me flush against him as his jeans fell, and he stepped out of them. "You know, I've wanted those clever little fingers on me since the moment I saw you."

The knowledge of that, the power, made something stir to life inside me. "Then let's give you what you want." My hands went to his boxer briefs, sending them to the floor. My fingers curled around his shaft, stroking.

The groan he let out made everything in me tighten. Hayes traced a hand over the center of my sleep shorts and then slipped under the hem. He pulled back a fraction. "No underwear?"

"Not when I'm going to sleep."

"You mean to tell me that every time I've seen you walking around this house in those damn shorts, there's been nothing underneath?"

I shrugged.

Hayes' head dropped to my shoulder. "You're going to kill me. I'm going to die of an actual stroke."

I gave his neck a playful bite. "Let's have a little fun first."

"Damn straight."

In a flash, Hayes had me on my back on the mattress, pulling my sleep shorts from my body. He tossed them over his shoulder as he moved for my tank top next, throwing that somewhere else. "I knew you'd be beautiful." One finger circled my nipple. "But you steal my breath."

"Hayes." His name was a cross between a whimper and a plea. "Need you."

Those dark eyes caught fire, and I'd never seen anything more beautiful. "You have me." He tore open a foil packet, rolling a condom over his length as my legs encircled his waist once more, bringing him closer to me. His tip bumped against my opening. "You with me?"

"Always." It wasn't a lie. After this, a piece of me would always be with him. Buried somewhere deep, even if I had to walk away.

My eyes fluttered closed as Hayes slid inside.

"Stay with me, Ev."

My eyes flew open as he began to move. My back arched as I met him stroke for stroke. It was different. Whatever was between us made it so. That pull had rooted itself deeply now, and I didn't think it would ever break.

My fingers curled into Hayes' shoulders as he angled his hips, driving himself impossibly deeper. Sparks of light dotted my vision with each thrust. I dug in deeper, searching for that last piece.

That thumb, the same one that'd gently stroked my cheek to ease me, found that tightly wound bundle of nerves. The rough pad circled and teased, then flicked with a force that sent everything crashing down around me. And as we came apart, I knew nothing would ever be the same.

Chapter Thirty-Five

Hayes

"Y ou're whistling again," Young said as she pulled up a chair in the meeting room.

I immediately stopped. No part of me should be whistling. Not when we'd had two attempted abductions recently, and someone had nearly run my sister off the road last night. But I had been. Because amidst the storm swirling, I was the happiest I'd been in years. "I think you're hearing things, Young. No whistling over here."

She snorted and took a seat. My phone buzzed in my pocket, and I pulled it out.

Mom: *You need to talk to Hadley. Convince her to move home until whoever's doing this is caught.*

I sighed and slid the phone back into my pocket without responding. I knew this was triggering for my mother but trying to force Hadley to move home would only make things worse.

"Not whistling now. Everything okay?"

"My mom isn't dealing with all of this well."

Sympathy filled Young's face. "I can't imagine how scared she must've been. If someone took one of my babies from me..."

"I know she's hurting. But she doesn't always deal with that pain or fear well when it comes to Hadley."

Young winced. "They're still struggling, huh?"

I nodded. "And what's going on isn't making things any easier." I looked back at the whiteboard I'd moved into our meeting room. There was a scattering of facts about the case, locations, and other information. The pressure of finding whoever was behind this was only mounting.

More officers flooded the room, and I did my best to shake it off. "Grab a seat, folks." I'd called in everyone, even those currently off duty. Only those needed for active assignments weren't here, and they'd get a recount at another time.

The chatter died down as everyone found a chair and pulled out either their phones or old-school pen and paper. I surveyed the room. "As you know, we've had two attempted abductions in the past few weeks. Last night, my sister, Hadley, was almost driven off the road. We don't think it was related, but we're not ruling anything out. Because of my ties to the case, I'm handing over the reins to Sergeant Ruiz. He'll walk you through what we have so far."

Every single person in the room was laser-focused on what Ruiz had to say. We laid out a plan and asked every officer to be on alert for any suspicious activity. I'd also decided it was time to put the word out in the community, an alert that would suggest that women stick together in groups and not go anywhere alone. It burned to do it, to create panic in the community, but panic was a hell of a lot better than regret.

"I think that's everything." Ruiz looked to me for confirmation.

"That should do it. If you have questions, we'll stick around to answer them."

There were a few, but people mostly headed out for their days off or back to whatever task they'd been working on before. I gave Ruiz a fist bump. "You did good running your first rodeo."

"I hate talking in front of crowds."

"Come on. I'll get you a cup of coffee to celebrate."

We didn't even make it to the door before Williams flagged me down. "Uh, boss? Your mother's here, and she's agitated."

I sighed and glanced at Ruiz. "I guess that coffee will have to wait." I turned back to Williams. "Send her back to my office."

I wound my way through desks to get to my space. At least, I could shut the door there. I searched for the buzz of happiness I'd had this morning. The one from waking up tangled with Everly. The one that was fading far too quickly.

The door burst open just as I eased down into my chair. It didn't take an investigator to see that my mother had worked herself into a state. "You don't answer your phone anymore?"

I pulled out my cell and saw five missed calls. "I was in a meeting. You know my work schedule. If I don't call you back, there's a reason."

She paced back and forth across the small space. "You have to talk to Hadley. She's being ridiculous. She can suck it up and stay with us for a few weeks, so I don't have to worry."

My cell phone buzzed in my hand.

Shy: *You need to calm Mom down. Tell her I'm going to stay with Hads for a while.*

I kept staring at the words on the screen, trying to figure out some way to shape this into a good thing for my mom.

"What? Is that Hadley?"

I looked up from the device that wasn't giving me one lick of help. "No. It was Shy. She's going to stay with Hadley for now so neither of them will be alone."

Mom's jaw fell open. "You think *that* makes me feel better? They'll be in one spot, so whoever this madman is can just pick them off." She started pacing again. "This is Hadley's doing. She's got Shiloh all upset now, too."

"Mom…"

"Don't *Mom* me."

"You need to calm down. Just take a breath, or you're going to lose them both."

My mother looked as if I had slapped her. "How could you say something like that?"

"Because it's the truth. We can't keep avoiding what happened. Ev was right. We need to face it."

"I face it every day. Every single one since the day she went missing—was *stolen*—and I can't believe you'd think otherwise."

I let out a long breath, looking my mom directly in the eyes and seeing the panic and devastation there. "That's not what I'm talking about. I know you live with this every single day. We all do. But Hadley…she never got a chance to be free. To run wild like the rest of us did. She was too young before the kidnapping, and after…" I didn't look away, needing my mother to really hear this. "There was no normal. No sleepovers or riding bikes to the store with friends or even high school parties if an adult wasn't present. Beck and I understood why, and Shy didn't want to do any of that anyway. But Hadley, she wanted all of it. And she never got it."

My mom slid into one of the empty chairs. "I was scared."

I stood and rounded the desk, taking the seat next to her and grabbing her hand. "I know. And I hate that for you. It kills me. But if you don't give Hadley some room to be who she is, you *are* going to lose her."

Mom sniffed. "I know. But sometimes I just get so angry that she doesn't give me a little empathy."

"I think she does. She's just not willing to give up who she is so you don't worry."

My mom was quiet, clearly mulling it all over but not being willing to admit that she might be wrong.

"I'm going to have an officer stationed outside her house each night, okay? Would that make you feel better?"

"Yes. I just want her to be safe."

I pulled my mom into a hug. "I know you do." But for the first time, I could really see just how stifling that might be. And I knew I had to keep myself from doing the same to Everly.

Chapter Thirty-Six

Everly

I MOVED AROUND MY KITCHEN, FINISHING THE LAST FEW dishes from last night as Chip chowed down on a small bowl of nuts. "I hope you know how cushy your life is."

He let out a little chatter in response. It better have been in agreement. The little guy pretty much lived in the lap of luxury.

The breeze from the window picked up, swirling my hair around my face and rustling the branches of the trees outside. God, I loved the silence here. And for the first time in weeks, I was truly alone.

I might have come to appreciate how Hayes' overprotectiveness showed his care, but that didn't mean I was used to having people around all the time. I'd been on my own since I was eighteen. Never had roommates, even if it meant living in a shoebox of a studio apartment. And I valued that solitude.

Now I had to find some balance. I took a deep breath of pine air, letting it center me. I reached for that ever-elusive peace. It felt closer than it had in the past. I could grab it for brief moments; I just needed to find a way to get it to stay.

It didn't help that I knew Ian was walking the streets now, having decided to shell out bail instead of waiting out the wheels of justice. Hayes had made a trip down to the vet's office to tell me. I had my restraining order, but I knew that piece of paper was useless. It was only kindling to Ian.

The only way it would help was if he broke it and got jail time. And if that happened, it would likely be too late. The damage would already be done. A shiver snaked up my spine, even though the air was warm enough for a tank top.

Tires on gravel sounded, and I checked my watch. Just about quitting time for Hayes, but I still moved to the corner of the cabin where I'd put my gun locker and pulled out Betty. Lifting the curtains a fraction, the tension in my shoulder blades eased as I saw the lights atop his SUV.

I placed Betty back in the locker and shut the door. Taking another deep breath, I reached for that calm again. I pulled open the front door just as Hayes reached the bottom step. "Are those flowers? And takeout?"

He almost looked a little bashful. "I haven't had the chance to take you on a proper date yet. I thought I'd remedy that." He handed me the brightly colored blooms and pulled me close.

"They're beautiful."

Hayes bent his head and took my mouth in a slow kiss. "Missed you today."

"You saw me in the middle of the day."

He pulled me in closer, inhaling deeply. "Still missed you."

My arms rounded his body as I burrowed into his hold. "I missed you, too." More than I wanted to admit. Something about Hayes grounded me. The frenetic energy that normally ran through me eased just a bit around him.

"Glad to hear it. It would be a real bummer if you were fine without me."

I grinned into his chest, but at the same time, a lick of panic flitted through me. Because I would never be fine without Hayes. But I might have to learn to live that way anyway.

I released my hold on him and stepped back. "Come on in. Whatever's in there smells amazing."

"How do you feel about a Mexican feast?"

"I feel great about it. Hey, where's Koda?"

"He's with Shy today." We moved into the living area, and Chip scurried back into his hidey-hole. "I'll never get used to that dang thing."

I pulled out some plates and cutlery. "He's cute. Admit it."

"He'd be cute if he lived in the barn."

"Too late now, he's domesticated. He wouldn't survive out there with that limp. And he was my first friend."

Hayes lifted a brow. "Your first friend."

"I wasn't sure what the welcome would be like when I got here. I was bracing for a full town shunning. I thought he might be my only friend."

Hayes set the bags of food on the counter. "Come here." I walked into his open arms, and he rested his chin on the top of my head. "I'm sorry you were so scared. And even more sorry that I was such a grade-A jerk when I came up here that first time."

"That first couple of times, you mean?"

He grunted. "I was an idiot."

"It takes a real man to admit the truth," I said with a chuckle. Then I tipped my head back so my chin rested on Hayes' sternum. "But you're forgiven. You don't need to keep apologizing."

"I do when I feel like an ass."

I slipped a hand under the hem of his untucked work shirt, running my fingers along the golden skin and taut muscle. "You learned from it. That's all any of us can ask for. Hope for."

He brushed the hair away from my face. "I've learned a lot from you."

"Really?"

"Yup. Come on, I'll tell you over dinner."

"Want to eat on the back deck? I got a new table from the secondhand shop after work. It's all set up."

He frowned at me. "I would've helped you with that."

I rolled my eyes. "I can handle a table and a few chairs."

He felt my biceps. "You look so tiny, but you've got muscles."

"I have to lure my enemies into underestimating me."

Hayes chuckled. "I'd say you've got that covered. Come on, let's eat."

I put the flowers in some water and then followed Hayes out to the back deck. He'd already set up an elaborate display of food, enough to feed at least eight. "Are we celebrating something I don't know about? Having a party?"

"As a matter of fact, we are celebrating something."

I sat down in the chair catty-corner to Hayes'. "And that is?"

"I had a talk with my mom that was long overdue."

I took a sip of the Coke Hayes had brought out for me and studied his face. There was worry there but there was also relief. "About Hadley?"

"Yeah."

"How'd it go?"

Hayes picked up a chip and dunked it in some salsa. "Mom doesn't see how the tension is eating away at all of us. Not yet. Her pain and fear are still overriding everything. But I'm going to hope I planted some seeds that will grow. And, at the very least, I cut off the latest emergency."

"What was that?"

"Hadley not wanting to stay at my parents' with everything that's going on."

I broke off a piece of a chip and popped it into my mouth. "She likes her independence."

"That she does. I just hope my mom starts to see why."

"I think she will with time. The more you gently bring it to her attention, the more she'll start to see the signs on her own."

"It was you who made me realize I needed to do it."

"Why me?"

Hayes nodded. "You showed me that there is more power in facing the ghosts and tearing them down, than pretending they don't exist."

I reached over and laced my fingers with his, relishing the feel of his rough palm. "I'm glad I decided to face them." And no matter what happened, I always would be. Because I got these stolen moments with Hayes. I knew what it felt like to be cherished by him in every way imaginable.

He leaned in and brought his mouth to mine. Comfort and fire, a combination that was solely Hayes, burned through my veins. The shattering of glass had both of our heads snapping up. I gaped at the hole in my window, and the rock I could see on the floor.

"Get inside," Hayes barked as he scanned the forest.

"Hayes, don't. You don't know who's out there or if they have a gun."

He pushed me towards the back door. "Go. Call the station for backup. Tell them I'm in pursuit."

I swallowed down the bile that crawled up my throat and ran for the door as Hayes took off for the forest. I scrambled for my phone, calling nine-one-one and relaying the details. The dispatcher assured me that deputies would arrive in twenty minutes. But twenty minutes was too long.

I moved to my gun locker in the corner and went for my rifle this time—better accuracy. I closed the cabinet with a bang and locked it. Moving for the back door, everything stopped as the crack of a bullet filled the air. Then there was nothing but silence.

Chapter Thirty-Seven

Hayes

BARK FLEW AS ANOTHER BULLET HIT THE TREE NEXT TO me. I let a few choice curses fly as I ducked behind a tree for cover. "Time's running out. Reinforcements are on the way."

I just needed whoever this was to make one dumb move. To leave himself open for a shot or give me enough of a visual that I could make an ID. Something.

Another bullet flew past me, embedding itself in a downed log. "You need to work on your shooting. Why don't you come out here, and we can settle this man-to-man?"

Only silence greeted me. "Too scared? Is that why you try to get the jump on women who aren't expecting it?"

A hail of bullets peppered the tree I stood behind. Now, I was getting somewhere. I bent and picked up a good-sized rock. Pulling my arm back, I sent it flying into another tree about fifteen feet away. Bark splintered, and the unsub turned his gun in that direction. I aimed, catching sight of the movement, a hand or arm maybe. I fired, and the man hollered.

I charged forward, but before I could make even a few feet of progress, the crack of a bullet filled the air. Fiery, burning pain lanced my shoulder. The bloom so red-hot I saw stars. Another bullet whizzed past my head, and I was forced to duck behind another tree.

Footsteps pounded the forest floor, not towards me but away. Less than a minute later, that changed to hoofbeats. The force they echoed with told me he was getting away at a gallop.

I took a breath, my lungs rattling with the adrenaline dump. Looking down at my shoulder, I winced. Blood soaked through my short-sleeve uniform shirt. I carefully rolled it up. "Shit." It was only a graze, but it was deep.

I pushed to my feet and started back towards the cabin, my gait a little unsteady. My uninjured arm rose, gun centered on the figure who stepped out of the trees. "Ev, what the hell?"

She slowly lowered her rifle. "Your arm. Oh, God, your arm."

"I'm fine. It's just a graze."

"That is too much blood for a graze. We need to get you back to the cabin. Is he still out there?"

"Long gone. Horseback."

Sirens sounded as Everly led me up the stairs and towards a chair. "You sit. I'll get the reinforcements."

Within moments, Young, Ruiz, and Williams appeared on the back deck. "Shit, boss," Ruiz said. "Should we call the paramedics?"

Everly answered "Yes," at the same time I said, "No." She moved in close. "You have to be kidding me. You're bleeding all over my deck, and you don't want a medic? We need to take you to the hospital."

"Call Hadley. She can stitch me up."

Ev glared at me. "I'll call her, but only so that she can drug you so we can take you in." She pulled out her phone and walked to the other side of the deck to make her call.

"I like her," Young stated.

"Of course, you do." I winced as I tried to move my arm.

Young tracked the movement. "Are you sure you shouldn't go to the hospital? That looks rough."

Williams, looking a little green, nodded. "She has a point."

"I'll be fine. Hads will get me all patched up, she's done it before."

Everly sent me a glare as she walked inside still on the phone.

I turned back to my officers. "Call Forest Service. Unknown male subject on horseback."

"You get a look?" Ruiz asked.

"Only enough to say, 'male.' I think shorter than me, but I can't be sure. I only saw his back. I think a shot may have hit his arm."

Ruiz lifted his chin in assent and moved to make his call.

Everly came out of the back door with what looked like a first-aid kit. "Hadley and Shiloh are on their way. They were picking up pizza so it shouldn't be too long. In the meantime, I need to put pressure on the wound."

Ev opened the kit and pulled out a gauze pad. She gently pulled up my sleeve and sucked in an audible breath. "This is going to hurt, Hayes."

"I can take it."

She slipped her free hand into mine and then pressed the gauze to my wound. "I'm sorry. Just hold on."

Those same white lights danced in front of my eyes as the pain flared back to life. "I'm okay," I gritted out.

Young did her best to distract me, asking me to walk her through the night's events. By the time Hadley and Shiloh arrived, she was running out of questions. Thankfully, Williams had taken that time to bag the rock and clean up the broken glass because even on his bum leg, Koda tore through the cabin out to the deck like he knew something was wrong.

I held out my hand. "Here, boy. Everything's okay." He let out a whine as I scratched behind his ears.

Hadley appeared with her massive medic kit, Shiloh behind her with a stack of two pizzas. Calder was on their trail and seemed to be a mix of worried and exasperated. Hadley took one look at me and simply shook her head. "Really, Hayes?"

"I had to try and get him."

"Men," she huffed and squeezed Everly's shoulder. "You okay?"

"I'm not the one who got shot."

"It's just a graze," I argued.

"A *bullet wound* because you chased after God knows who *alone*. You're not getting a lot of sympathy from me," Hadley retorted.

"That much is clear, dear sister. I'm so glad you're worried about me."

Young let out a laugh. "I love your family."

"You okay, man?" Calder asked.

"Fine, really. Just pissed I didn't get to him." I'd been close but not close enough.

Calder met my gaze. "You might not have gotten him this time, but you will."

A charged silence took over the back deck. Shiloh broke it, offering, "Pizza?"

Young rubbed her hands together. "You know, I'm starving."

"Me, too," Williams agreed.

"Hunger even in the presence of blood," I said as Everly pulled back the gauze.

Hadley snapped on some exam gloves and prodded around the wound.

My head jerked in her direction. "Hey, be careful, would you?"

She ignored my complaint. "I'm going to need you to take off this shirt."

"Here. I'll get it." Everly pulled a pair of scissors from the kit and moved towards me. "This shirt is a lost cause anyway."

I looked down at the blood staining the khaki-colored fabric and knew she was right. "Do your worst."

Everly moved carefully but efficiently, cutting through my uniform and undershirt. She set the scissors down on a side table. "Stand up and let your arms hang loose."

I obeyed. "This would be a hell of a lot better if you were naked."

"Hayes," she hissed.

Hadley choked on a laugh. "If you ever want to get laid again, I'd hold your tongue."

I shut up and did what I was told, letting my arms hang at my sides. Everly moved gently, careful not to let the shirts touch my wound. When the fabric dropped to the floor, I bent forward and brushed my lips against hers. "Thank you."

Her cheeks deepened to a pretty pink color. "You're welcome."

"Enough with the lovey-dovey stuff. Let's get you stitched up so you don't bleed to death. Mom would blame me until the end of time."

I met Everly's gaze. Maybe my sister and mother had farther to go than I'd hoped.

Chapter Thirty-Eight

Everly

I couldn't take my eyes off Hayes as Hadley fixed him up. Not even when the needle pulled through his skin, creating a neat row of stitches. "You're sure you didn't get a good look at who was shooting?"

Hayes looked up from his phone where he had been texting with someone on the Forest Service team. "No, only his back for a split second."

I picked at a loose thread on my t-shirt until Hayes tugged me towards him with his free hand.

"Hey, watch it. I'm working here. Do you want me to scar you even worse?" Hadley groused.

"A scar will just make me sexier."

Hadley rolled her eyes.

Hayes laced his fingers with mine, pulling me down onto the arm of the chair. "You okay?"

No. I was not. Not in the slightest. "I'm fine."

"Liar. Talk to me."

I found that same thread and picked at it. "I just wonder if it was Ian or Allen."

"I had the same thought. And I honestly can't say one way

or the other. The guy was wearing a hat, so I didn't get hair color, just a rough idea of size that could've been any number of people."

I nodded slowly and kept tearing at that string, trying to break it off. But if I did, maybe the whole shirt would unravel. Just like my life. What would be the breaking point for Hayes? For his family? They'd brought me into their fold now, but that could change in the blink of an eye.

My stomach roiled at the thought of how this could've turned out. Hayes really hurt. Or worse. The Eastons had already almost lost one daughter because of my family. I couldn't be responsible if they lost a son.

"Ev."

Hayes' soft voice turned my focus to him. "Hmm?"

"I don't like where that beautiful head is at right now." He squeezed my hand. "No running, okay?"

I didn't look away. "I'll run if that's what keeps you safe."

His expression turned stony. "You run, and I'll just follow."

"He's right," Hadley interjected. "You can't let some crazy run you off. You shouldn't let anything scare you away from what you want." Her gaze flicked to Calder for the briefest of moments and then back to me. "You deserve to be happy."

Happy. It felt too dangerous to reach for. Yet I'd had so many bright starburst moments of it. But that only felt more reckless. Just like my hope and my peace. I wanted them but was scared to fully reach out.

Because as I looked at this man in front of me as Hadley tied off the final stitch, I knew he made me happy. Just like his family did. Spending little bits of time with Addie and Ben. My job with Miles, Kelly, and Tim. And seeing the sanctuary becoming a reality… It all made me ridiculously happy—this life I was building.

But it all felt like sand, slipping through my fingers. I was just one wrong move from it disappearing altogether. Only it wasn't my wrong move that I feared. It was my family's.

Hadley pressed a bandage over the neat row of stitches. "You need to keep that dry for two days. Take Tylenol and Motrin for pain and swelling. I'll check it in a few days."

Hayes reached out and ruffled his sister's hair. "Thanks, lil' sis."

"Yeah, yeah. Don't make a habit of it."

"I'll do my best."

Young popped the last bite of her pizza crust into her mouth. "Now that we know you're going to live, we should hit the roads with everyone else. We'll let you know if we spot anything suspicious."

I'd heard radios crackling as Hadley stitched Hayes. Squad cars relaying their positions. But no one had seen a single man on horseback.

Hayes nodded. "Give me a few to get cleaned up, and I can join—"

Ruiz held up a hand to stop him. "You know you can't work this case anymore. Advisory only. You're clearly a target."

His jaw worked back and forth as he swallowed down the words he wanted to let fly. "All right. Keep me in the loop."

"You know we will," Ruiz said.

"You put the word out to all area doctors and vets?"

Ruiz pulled his keys out of his pocket. "The phone tree has been activated. I promise, we've got it covered."

"Thanks. I'm not trying to be an asshole—"

"You just don't handle giving up control well."

"Understatement of the century," Hadley muttered.

Calder moved forward into the circle of people. "Cut your brother some slack, Hads."

"He doesn't need to be cut some slack. He needs to be more careful."

"Okay," Hayes said, holding up his good hand. "I'm fine. Let's dial it back a notch." He turned to Ruiz, Young, and Williams. "Hit the road. I'd like a brief every hour or so with any developments."

Young gave him a mock salute. "You got it." They headed through the cabin and towards their vehicles.

Hayes looked at the rest of us. "I need to get cleaned up, but it looks to me like we've got a feast to eat. Ev, you want to heat up our Mexican food?"

I forced a smile. "Mexican food and pizza. Can't think of a better combination."

Hayes' arms wrapped around my waist from behind. "Leave the rest of the dishes. We can finish them tomorrow."

"I just want to get it done tonight so it's not hanging over my head. But you should go to bed. You're probably exhausted." I certainly was. It was the kind of tired that seeped into your bones. Not one from lack of sleep but from being worn down.

"I'm not going to bed without you." He pulled back my hair so he could trail kisses along my neck.

I ducked out of his hold, moving to put two plates on a drying rack. "You can wait up if you want, but I'll be a while. I need to look over some plans before our new arrivals get here this weekend."

Hayes spun me around. "Talk to me. Don't shut me out or blow me off—or whatever else you have in your head that you think will help push me away."

"I'm not pushing you away."

"Bullshit. You might as well have been a robot tonight."

I'd thought I'd done a pretty good job of holding it together during our makeshift dinner party. Smiling and laughing when appropriate. Making polite conversation. But, apparently, that hadn't been the case.

I gripped the counter behind me. The edge of the wood bit into my palms, but the little flicker of pain kept me grounded. "I'd never be able to forgive myself if something happened to you because of me. My family has already cost yours so much."

"Enough with that already. How many times do we have to go over that the burden of that isn't on you?"

"It might not be my fault, but that doesn't mean I don't still carry it with me. That I'm not marked by it. You can't just erase it all, Hayes."

He moved in close, the heat of his body pouring into mine. "I wish I could." He placed a finger between my brows, that spot that always wrinkled when I was stressed or worried. "I wish I could take away every last bit of pain you experience. I'd give anything."

"But you can't. And you can't ask me to pretend it doesn't exist."

Hayes wrapped his arms around me, pulling me against him. "I know. I just wish you wouldn't carry everyone else's actions on your shoulders."

"If this was Allen or Ian—"

"We don't know that it was. This could be some sick stranger neither of us knows."

"Or it could be my uncle or brother."

He pressed his lips to my hair. "It wouldn't change a thing about how I feel about you. You aren't them. Just like you aren't your father or uncle or mother. You're Ev. And you make everyone's lives better. It's impossible not to fall in love with you."

My heartbeat sped up, seeming to trip over itself as it did.

"I love you, Ev. You don't have to say anything right now, but I need you to know that. And nothing your family does will ever change that."

My vision tunneled as my breaths came faster. He'd sent us careening over a cliff there was no coming back from. And even though I felt the words, I couldn't give them voice. Instead, I gave him me.

My mouth crashed down on Hayes' with a ferocity I barely recognized. His response was immediate, taking as good as he gave, meeting my tongue stroke for stroke. He lifted me in one smooth movement.

"Hayes, your arm."

"Don't give a fuck about my arm right now." His head came down, taking my mouth again. I was too lost in the kiss to argue. We fumbled down the hall, bumping into walls until we finally made it to my bedroom.

My hands were already tugging his shirt over his head, as his went to the button on his jeans. I moved to my shorts and tee, not waiting for his fingers to be free. But he caught me before I moved to my bra. "Wait." His thumbs circled my nipples through the sheer lace. "I love this on you. Just give me a minute to cement this in my memory."

"How about I give you something else to remember?" I gripped his shaft, gliding my hand, teasing and stroking.

His breath hitched as he slipped a hand under my hair to tip my head back. Hayes nipped and licked his way down the column of my throat, down my chest until he locked on to my nipple through the thin lace and sucked hard.

My body moved of its own volition, arching into him as I let out a moan.

"Like that?"

"I don't hate it."

He chuckled against my breast, and the vibrations twisted everything inside me tighter. As if there were a rope made out of my nerve endings, and he was the master weaving it all together.

Hayes unhooked my bra and let it fall to the floor. His fingers moved to the lace straps at my hips, tugging them slowly down my legs. The cord inside me turned again.

"So damn beautiful. Covered in lace or my tee, it doesn't matter. You take my breath away."

I wanted to give him those three little words. Each one clawed at my throat to get out. Yet I couldn't set them free. Instead, I gave him something else. "I'm on the pill."

His eyes met mine. "I've been checked. You sure?"

I nodded, swallowing hard. "I trust you."

He understood in that moment what I was giving him. When so many people had let me down, I was trusting that he would never lie to or hurt me.

Hayes laid me back on the bed, his movements almost reverent. He worshiped my body with his fingers, his lips, his tongue. And when he slipped inside me, it was with a whispered, "*I love you.*"

He moved with a rhythm that said he was in no hurry. Yet it made me burn for him even more as I lifted my hips to meet his thrusts. Hayes didn't need those three words to tell me what was in his heart. He showed me with every action. And as I came apart with him, I said the words silently, knowing they would always be true. Even if I never had the courage to say them out loud.

Chapter Thirty-nine

Hayes

"**H**ow's the arm feeling?" Calder asked before he took a sip of his coffee.

"It's fine." It was a little sore after last night's festivities, but a little pain was more than worth it. Being with Ev last night had been different. Almost reverent, somehow. Even if she hadn't said the words I so desperately wanted to hear from her, I'd felt them.

"No leads yet?"

"I haven't gotten the full brief yet, but my last report from Young was that there was no sign of him."

Cammie walked up to the table and winked at Calder. "You boys ready to order? The special this morning is Huevos Rancheros."

I was more than a little relieved to see the mischievous glint back in Cam's eyes. "I'll take the special."

Calder handed her his menu. "I'll do the oatmeal, and two scrambled eggs on the side."

She rolled her eyes. "Always so predictable."

I couldn't help but chuckle. Calder sent me a glare. "Don't encourage her."

"She has a point. It wouldn't hurt you to get out there and shake things up a bit."

"How is ordering a breakfast special going to shake things up?"

I took a sip of my coffee and studied my friend. "It's starting small. Then maybe you'd actually take some steps to having a life beyond your job and your girls."

"I like that life."

"I'm not saying you shouldn't. I'm just saying that there's more."

Calder met my stare. "And you've found that more?"

"I have. It wasn't where I expected to find it, and that makes it all the sweeter." Everly might as well have come along and smacked me with a two-by-four. And it was precisely what I'd needed—a wake-up call and coming home all at the same time.

"Does she feel the same?"

Calder's question brought me out of my Everly haze. "What?"

"Does she feel the same about you?"

"I think so. She's skittish. And she carries a lot of weight from things that aren't hers to carry."

"The kidnapping."

"That. And things her brother has done. Her uncle." God, I'd give anything to help her release even just a little of that. I hated that it ate at her, and I had no idea how to help her let it go. I only hoped that it would start to fade with time.

Calder ran his thumb along the rim of his coffee cup as if searching for words he didn't have. "That's rough. And I feel for her, being raised in that environment... I can't begin to imagine. But do you really think you should put all of your eggs in that one basket?"

My spine stiffened. "Is that what this breakfast was about? To tell me you think Ev isn't a fit for me?"

"It's to catch up with my closest damn friend. And to tell you to be careful."

"Everly isn't like Jackie. She doesn't have that reckless streak in her. If she has a flaw, it's that she cares too deeply."

A muscle ticked along Calder's jaw. "You've only known her a few months. You can't be sure—"

"Stop. I appreciate you looking out, but you're just pissing me off."

Calder held his tongue, but I could see every doubt in his expression.

I took another sip of coffee, trying to give myself time to choose my words carefully. Something Everly was responsible for. Knowing how I'd hurt her with carelessly dropped bombs the first time we'd talked had stayed with me. I didn't want to let my temper get the best of me with anyone I cared about.

"I love her. And that's not going to change. I also know it won't be an easy road or a simple one. But it'll be worth it. There's nothing in me that doubts that in the slightest. And we have all the time in the world."

Calder nodded, but it had a bit of a robotic quality to it. "I hope you're right."

I bit down on the inside of my cheek to keep from biting his head off. "Have you ever considered that what you went through has skewed your vision?"

He let out a chuckle with a bitter tinge. "How could it not? But I'm not sorry that it's made me cautious. I won't let anyone hurt my girls like that again. Put them at risk—"

"Or hurt you," I interjected. Because as much as Calder was trying to shield his daughters, he was trying to protect himself, too. When the woman you loved turned on you, it left scars. I simply hadn't realized just how deep they'd been carved into Calder.

His grip on the coffee mug tightened, knuckles bleaching

white under the restaurant's bright lights. "I just don't want to ever go down that road again."

"Opening yourself up to finding someone doesn't mean that's where you'll end up."

"But there's always a chance. So, I'm not going there."

The flash of fire in Calder's gaze told me that this wasn't a conversation worth pursuing right now. I held up both hands in surrender. "It's your life. But Everly isn't you. She wants a connection, a person to be with. She's just scared of what that means she could potentially lose."

"She's smart to realize that now. But I don't want you getting caught in the crossfire if she bolts."

"Everly will always be worth that risk for me."

Calder set down his mug with a thud. "I hope that's the right play."

It had nothing to do with right or wrong anymore. It was the *only* play. Because I'd given myself over to Everly without even realizing it. And I wouldn't change a damn thing.

Chapter Forty

Everly

TIM PULLED ME INTO A HARD HUG. "I'M SO GLAD YOU'RE okay. I mean, you are okay, right? They said you were, but you never know. I can't believe that happened at your house."

I patted his back and then stepped out of his hold. "I'm fine. Really. Hayes has a few stitches, but other than that, we made it out relatively unscathed."

Tim scowled at Hayes' name. "You'd think they would've had this figured out by now. You should really think about staying with me for a while. It would be safer in town."

Kelly made a tsking sound as she came out of the office area. "Please, she's locked up with Mr. Tall, Dark, and Sexy. I wouldn't be giving that up for anyone. Wouldn't matter how many bullets were flying." She gave me a quick hug. "Real glad you're okay, though."

I couldn't hold in my laugh. "Not even for bullets, huh?"

"Girl, that man is fine. And the way he looks at you?" She started fanning herself. "Break me off a piece of that."

Tim made a gagging sound and headed for his reception station.

"I think we might've been a little too much for poor Tim."

She waved me off. "He's just bummed because he has himself a little crush on you, and now you're taken."

"No, he doesn't—" I stopped mid-sentence, thinking back on all of our interactions so far and realizing that maybe Tim *did* have a small crush on me.

Kelly arched a brow. "See?"

"He'll get over it. I'm just fresh meat."

"True enough. Everybody always has to check out the new girl."

Miles bustled in through the back. "Morning. I brought donuts."

Kelly perked up. "I always said you were the best boss I ever had."

He smiled at all of us. "Sugar is always a good bribe in my book."

I took a strawberry donut and almost moaned when I took a bite. "This is amazing. Thank you."

"No one does it better than the bakery. And, good news, your paint mare and the mini-donkey will be ready to go home on Friday."

The bite of donut suddenly felt like a lead weight in my stomach. It was officially happening. The start of my sanctuary. There was no going back. This step almost felt as scary as those three little words I couldn't seem to utter to Hayes. But at the same time, they both felt right.

I glanced out the window and to the street. I could see where I'd had the run-in with my brother, where I'd been attacked. I could picture the hardware store just blocks away where my uncle had almost hit me. None of that was enough to scare me away. If I wanted the big, full life of my dreams, I would have to step into the unknown.

"I can't wait to get them there. Gabe and Shiloh are going

to help me check everything over this afternoon. And the barn should be done in a couple of weeks."

Miles reached out and gave my arm a squeeze. "You'll be giving this community an amazing gift. The animals. And the people, if you ever decide to open it for visits."

"I actually have an idea for an entire educational curriculum."

His eyes widened a fraction. "Really?"

"It's all theory right now, but I thought it would be a wonderful place for schools to take a field trip. If I can build it into what I have in my mind."

"Everly, I have no doubt that you will."

The only way we'd find out is if I moved forward into the unknown.

The faint sound of hoofbeats on the gravel had me looking up from pulling on my muck boots. Gabe and Shiloh, atop their mounts, crested the hill to the cabin. Gabe waved. "Beautiful day for a ride. Thought we'd take advantage of it."

"Sounds like a wonderful idea to me." I loved how Gabe was with Shiloh. He'd do whatever he could to spend time with her, but he also just let her be instead of forcing conversation. He would take whatever she was willing to give.

"I bet they could use some water. Hold on a sec." I jogged over to one of the new storage sheds we'd built with all of our helpers and pulled out a plastic water trough. Walking back to the fence where Gabe and Shiloh had dismounted, I filled the bucket from the newly extended water line.

Gabe grinned, running his fingers through the stream of water. "It even works. I gotta be honest, I wasn't sure. It had been a while since I laid new pipes."

Shiloh chuckled. "You know, Mom thought it was going to end up blowing up in your face."

"I might just have to send her a video of how nicely it turned out."

I shifted on my feet. "How's she doing with everything going on?"

Gabe's smile faltered a fraction. "Better, I think. She's always going to be a worrier. Nothing will ever change that."

"Time," I said. "Time will change it, eventually. We have to hope it will."

He patted my shoulder in the same fatherly way he did to Shiloh and Hadley. "Right you are. Now, tell me. When do the animals arrive?"

"The mare and the donkey are coming on Friday. We need to make sure everything's set up in their paddock. And the guy who owned them hadn't even named them, so we need names. Any ideas?"

Shiloh slid her saddle off Trick's back and balanced it on a fence rail. "We gotta get to know them a little bit first. Don't you think?"

"That's a great idea." The mare's sorrowful eyes filled my mind as I looked around at the land surrounding us. I hoped she would find rest here. The same peace I searched for. Maybe we could find it together.

"I'm thinking we should build a couple of hay feeders today," Gabe offered. "Having them ready to go as new animals arrive will make things easier on you in the long run."

I was starting to see it: all sorts of different creatures making their homes here. And for the first time, my excitement overtook my nerves and fear. "I think that's a great idea."

He clapped his hands together. "Let's get to work."

We spent hours assembling the feeders. When we finally finished, we towed one of them into the paddock where our new mare and donkey would be living.

Shiloh grinned. "I think they'll be happy here."

I bumped her shoulder with mine. "I think so, too. If you guys position this, I'll go get some hay so we can see how it looks."

"Sounds good," Gabe agreed.

I hopped back onto the four-wheeler I'd bought a couple of days ago. It was used, but the price tag had still given me the sweats. I headed for the hoop barn, pulling alongside the opening. I jumped out and went for just a single bale of hay. Even though I'd always been active, the work I'd been doing around the property had given me muscles I'd never known existed.

As I set the hay down in the bed of the four-wheeler, I heard rustling. Just what I needed—little critters making their homes in the hay. I turned to look, but before I could, there was a flash of movement and then blinding pain.

The entire world around me wavered and then darkened. But before I descended into the nothingness, I could've sworn someone said, "Sorry."

Chapter Forty-One

Hayes

I SCRUBBED A HAND OVER MY FACE AND THEN BLINKED A few times as I stared down at the map again. No matter how long I stared at the damn thing, the little Xs I'd marked off where each attack had occurred, nothing became clear. I pushed back from my desk and stood, stretching my back. It might be time to walk the streets. I'd been locked up in this damn office for too long.

My cell phone buzzed from somewhere on my desk. I patted down the map and other papers until I found the device. I swept my finger across the screen. "Easton."

"Hayes?" Shiloh's voice was pained, with a shaky edge to it.

"What's wrong?"

"We—Dad and I—we're at the cabin with Everly. She went to get hay and didn't come back for a while. So, I went to look for her, but she's not here. The bale of hay is on the back of the four-wheeler, but I don't see any sign of her anywhere."

"You checked the cabin?" The question was automatic, as if my response were preprogrammed. Because there was no way Ev could disappear. There was an explanation, a simple one. There had to be.

"I checked, and Dad's looking in the barn now. But I don't see her—" Shy's voice cut off.

"What is it?" I was already moving, grabbing my keys and heading for the door.

"Her phone. It's on the ground."

"Don't touch it."

"I won't."

The desks in front of me blurred as I tried to weave through them. "I'm on my way. Don't touch anything. Stay with Dad."

I hung up before she had a chance to say anything else. I pulled in a ragged breath, willing myself to hold it together. Ruiz was talking with the front desk officer, a new guy whose name escaped me. He took one look at me and froze. "What is it?"

"Ev. She's gone."

"Where?"

I spent the next seconds relaying all the information I had. Each breath I took seemed to claw at my insides, begging me to move, to get to the cabin, to find Everly. "That's all I know. I have to go."

Ruiz reached out a hand, resting it on my shoulder. "You can't work this case, Hayes."

I shook off his hold. "I'm not working it as the sheriff. But you know damn well you can't stop me from looking for her."

"Don't do anything stupid."

"I'll do whatever it takes to find her. Don't think I won't."

I turned on my heel and headed for the lot. Vehicles were already taking off, lights flashing, headed for Everly's property. I jogged to my SUV and climbed in. I wasn't above using my lights, too. I didn't give a crap if it was an abuse of department resources since I wasn't on this case.

By the time I pulled up into Ev's drive, I'd gone completely numb. It was necessary. If I didn't, I'd lose it and would never be able to get it back. I pulled to a stop in a spot I knew I could get out of quickly. Switching off my engine, I hopped out of the SUV and jogged towards my sister and dad.

Shy had her arms wrapped around herself. "I'm so sorry, Hayes. I should've gone with her. I never should've left her alone."

"Hey." I grabbed her shoulders, and Shy jerked back. I let my hands fall but bent to meet her gaze. "This isn't your fault. But I need you to tell me everything."

Shy and my dad walked me through their afternoon with Ev as officers pored over the area. Dad's jaw tightened. "I didn't hear anything. No scream. Nothing."

"Think. Did you hear an engine?"

His eyes widened. "No. And we would've. We were done using any tools. We were just placing the feeder."

"He's on horseback." I scanned the surrounding forests. There were endless places for him to go. Up into the wilderness, out into national forest land, to a farm we had no idea about.

"I'm getting Trick tacked up." Shiloh started towards her horse.

"Shy, stop. I have to call in Forest Service and our search and rescue teams."

Her hands clenched and flexed as she seemed to struggle to keep her breaths even. "And how long will it take them to assemble? I've got my rifle. I've got the sat phone and supplies."

"And I'll go with her," my father offered.

A muscle in my cheek ticked. I was so damn torn. I wanted to go with them. But I also wanted to make a trip out to the Kemper ranch.

Dad's hand came down on my shoulder. "We'll start the search here. When you're ready, get Calder or someone to have your back and take another direction. We'll cover more ground that way."

I knew he was right. But as I watched Shiloh put on Trick's

saddle, I couldn't make myself move. I'd failed my sister once. Turned my back and almost lost her. How could I let her go now?

My father squeezed my shoulder, bringing my attention back to him. "I've got her. I'll keep her safe."

"Okay." The single word was ripped from my throat.

"You find Everly. Love that girl like she's my own. And love her even more for what she's brought out in you."

My eyes burned. "She's everything to me."

"I know. So, you're going to get her back."

"I will." I clapped him on the shoulder and turned to head back to my SUV, but Ruiz stepped into my path.

"What the hell is going on? And where do you think you're going?"

I ground my teeth together in an effort to keep my voice calm. "Dad and Shy are taking the horses to search. I'm going to talk to some people who might have seen her."

Ruiz's eyes hardened. "Don't fuck up this case. We need to do everything by the book."

"By the book doesn't matter if we don't get to her in time."

"It will if we can't charge the asshole."

I knew he was thinking like law enforcement. The way *I* should be thinking. Only I couldn't. Because Ev's life was at stake. I'd never risk that for a conviction. "Do whatever you have to, and I'll do the same."

"You can't say you're there as the sheriff," he warned.

"I know that." I didn't need the letters of the department behind me. I just needed a clue. A direction. Anything that would help me bring Everly home.

Chapter Forty-Two

Everly

THE PAIN WOKE ME. THE BATTERING AGAINST MY SKULL. As if a hardcore metal band were practicing in my brain. My eyes fluttered the barest amount. Even the brief flashes of light those flutters let through hurt. I let out a low moan, rolling onto my back.

Something clanged, the sound ricocheting around in my head, picking up speed with the beat in my brain. God, everything hurt. Slowly, my brain started functioning again. Where was I? Had I been in an accident? Taken a fall?

I knew I needed to open my eyes. That was the only way for me to find answers. I tried again. The fluttering lasted for longer this time, but it still hurt like hell.

I got flashes of a room. Similar to my cabin but different. Rougher around the edges.

Finally, my eyes adjusted to the light. I had to squint, but I could see. It was a log cabin. Only one room, with a small kitchen that had a woodstove as a cooktop. There wasn't an oven or a dishwasher, just the bare bones. Another woodstove stood in the opposite corner, with two wooden chairs in front of it. And be-

My stomach cramped at that knowledge and what it could mean. I frantically searched to see what I was wearing, but all of my clothes were in place. Only on top of my jeans, on my left ankle, was a chain. And that chain was locked with a padlock. My gaze followed the length of metal to a bolt in the wall.

The meager food in my stomach roiled and pitched, but I swallowed the urge to lose my lunch on the floor. I needed whatever energy I had.

I pushed to a sitting position. The room around me wavered as if I were seeing it through water. I stayed still until everything righted itself.

Flipping through my memories, I tried to come up with an order of things. What had happened? I'd worked at the vet's this morning. Built feeders with Gabe and Shiloh. I stiffened as I pictured driving to get the hay, launching it onto the four-wheeler… and then the flash of pain.

My breaths came quicker but I forced myself to slow them again. To count in and out. To make them even and normal. Passing out would only get me hurt—or worse.

"Think, Ev." Tears sprang to my eyes as Hayes' nickname came to my lips. I let my eyes close for the briefest moment, picturing his face in my mind in all of its many incarnations. Pissed off and angry. Free and loose in laughter. The tender way he looked at me when he told me he loved me.

Tears slipped down my cheeks and off my chin. Why hadn't I said the damn words? Why hadn't I told him that he was everything to me, too? That for the first time, I had a place to truly rest—in him. It was the greatest gift I'd ever been given, and I hadn't told him.

I dug my fingers into my thighs, trying to pull myself together. I wasn't going to give up yet. Couldn't. I pushed to my feet and followed the chain to the wall. The bolt used to hold the metal looked more like something used in industrial construction than a mountain cabin. And there was no hope of me pulling it free alone.

I moved along the wall, peeking out one of the two windows in the space. I saw one other outbuilding, but other than that... nothing. Not a road, not another building, nothing but brush and trees.

I swallowed down the rising burn. No one would hear me if I screamed. No one would stumble upon me on their drive home.

I tried to move more, to reach the kitchen. If I could just get a knife—anything to defend myself. The chain pulled taut with a clang. I stretched my arms out as far as they would go but was still feet shy of the counter or any drawer.

I stepped back, letting the chain fall to the floor. At least when it was lax, it didn't weigh on my ankle as badly. I tested its bounds, moving in a half-circle around the space, seeing what I could reach.

Whoever had me had obviously done the same thing. And then had moved everything with any potential to be a weapon out of that sphere. The only thing I had in my space was a rug and the bed. The frame itself was heavy, made of thick wood. But it was also securely constructed. I wouldn't be able to break it apart. At least not without a lot of noise and pain.

I ran my hands over the posts and joints—no seams or lips I could grab hold of. Yet I kept moving my hands over the frame, not even entirely sure what I was looking for.

Hope. A little bit of that reckless hope was what I was desperate for.

I almost didn't notice the first time my fingers ran over the slightly raised nail. But I paused, backtracking more slowly. There it was again. A single nail that hadn't been hammered in fully. A mere millimeter of the head stuck up, but it was something.

I patted my pockets, looking for anything possibly left behind. There was no multitool, of course. No cell phone. All that was left was a penny and a dime—the remnants of my lunch change from picking up at Spoons.

I went for the dime first. Slowly and methodically, I worked it under the edge of the nail. My fingers cramped the longer I worked and sweat pooled on my brow. But, finally, I worked the penny under there, too. I had a coin on each side as I pulled.

The nail moved a quarter of an inch, but my penny went flying across the room. I bit the inside of my cheek to keep from crying. I'd made progress. I had to keep going. I tried with just the dime, but it was no use.

I tugged at it, and my fingers bled, a few tears slipping free. I grabbed at the quilt on the bed, finding a corner that was a bit thinner but still had a little padding. I gripped the nail as hard as I could through the fabric and pulled. Pain flared through my fingertips, but I didn't stop.

I heard a faint squeak and whine as the nail moved out another inch. I readjusted my hold and drew back with everything I had in me. It came free with a force that sent me flying back into the mattress, but I held onto my treasure.

Dizziness swept over me as I straightened into a sitting position. I had the nail, and it wasn't even bent. But before I could shift to work on the lock, the door swung open. I shifted on instinct, tucking the nail under the mattress but still within reach.

"Evie."

The voice, so achingly familiar and painfully gentle.

"I'm so glad you're awake."

"B-Ben?"

His cheeks heated. "Sorry about the chains. It's just until you're used to it here."

Until I was *used to it*... Bile crept up my throat. My childhood protector. My oldest friend and confidant. But everything had changed without me even realizing it. Only one question found its way to my lips. "Why?"

His expression gentled even further. "It's always been you, Evie. We're meant to be."

Chapter Forty-Three

Hayes

MY SUV BUMPED OVER A SERIES OF POTHOLES AS I made my way up the drive to the Kemper ranch. Pulling to a stop in front of the series of buildings, I forced my hands to release their stranglehold on the wheel. I flexed and fisted my fingers, trying to get a bit of feeling back in them. But they remained numb, just like the rest of me.

I couldn't feel a damn thing. From my fingers to my toes. Some part of me registered that my heart was still beating inside my chest, but I felt so removed from it that the organ might as well have not existed.

My gaze swept over the buildings and ranch roads, but everything looked eerily still. There were trucks and a beat-to-hell sedan parked next to the house, but I didn't see one sign of life. I flexed my hands again. Was Everly here? In one of these buildings? In a shed like Shiloh had been held in? Or worse, was I too late?

I shoved that thought from my head and pushed open my door. Mom kept saying when Shiloh was missing that she would know if her baby was gone. I had to believe I would know if Ev had left this Earth. I would feel it in my bones.

As I slammed the door to my vehicle, Allen stepped out onto the front porch of his house. "You're not welcome here."

"I don't care where I'm welcome. I have some questions, and you're going to answer them."

Allen's jaw worked back and forth. "We've talked to a lawyer. We'll be filing harassment charges against you and the department next week."

"Good luck with that." It wouldn't be the first suit Allen and his family had filed. They were always thrown out of court at one point or another, but they clogged up the legal system—sometimes for months. And the department would have to waste resources to deal with it.

The door swung open again, and Ian appeared, a sneer on his face. "Here to throw your bullshit papers around again? I already told you. I'll go wherever the hell I want. Talk to whoever I want. There's nothing you can do to stop me."

I rested my hand on the butt of my gun. "Where's Everly?"

Ian's face immediately blanked. "How the hell would I know? Can't keep track of your woman, Sheriff? That's because you don't take a firm enough hand with her."

My fingers tightened around the metal, the grip like an extension of my hand. Rage pulsed through me like a second heartbeat. I closed my eyes for the briefest of moments, trying to pull it back. "I'm going to ask you one more time, where is she?"

"Is Evie missing?"

The soft voice came from my right, and I whirled around to see Addie. Dark circles rimmed her eyes, and she moved stiffly. But even with those struggling movements, I hadn't heard her coming. "Yes. She was taken about an hour ago, give or take. Have you seen her?"

Addie's eyes widened, fear streaking through her expression. But it was Allen who spoke, his words cracking out like a whip. "Don't say another word to him, Adaline."

She straightened, but I didn't miss the wince of pain as she did so. "She's not here. No one's come or gone in over two hours."

"Adaline, be silent." Allen charged from the porch, but I stepped between him and his daughter, pulling my gun.

"I'm afraid I'm going to have to ask you to stay there, sir."

"This is my property, and that's my daughter."

"And she's answering my questions right now." I glanced back at Addie. "Who has been here recently?"

Addie tore at the side of her nail, a bit of blood springing up. "Ben. He came a few hours ago to talk to Ian."

"Is that typical?"

Her gaze flittered from me to Ian and back, always checking to see where her father was. "Sure. He comes by every few days, usually. But…"

"Addie, shut your mouth if you know what's good for you," Ian hissed.

"Tell me," I urged. "I can keep you safe."

Her expression went bleak. "No one can do that. But you'll keep Evie safe, right?"

"I'll keep you both safe."

Addie looked off into the distance, towards the seemingly never-ending national forest land that wrapped around our mountains. "Ben was agitated. He said Evie needed to come home, to be protected. He hasn't been himself since his wife died." She glared at Ian. "And Ian just gets him riled up. I couldn't hear everything they said, but Ben tore out of here pretty fast."

My rib cage gave a painful squeeze around my lungs. Ben. If he was the one who had her, that could be good or bad. He wanted to protect her, but it also sounded like he was in the midst of a mental break. I turned to Ian. "What did he say to you?"

"I don't have to tell you a damn thing. But maybe he'll be the one to finally teach Everly her place."

The urge to use my fists to get the information out of him

was almost unbearable. My fingers flexed and tightened around the grip of my gun again. "You're right, you don't have to tell me anything. But if anything happens to her, you can be arrested and charged as an accessory. I'll make sure that happens."

Ian scoffed and spat off the porch in my direction. "Your lies and trumped-up charges don't scare me."

I pulled out my cell phone with my free hand and typed a text to Ruiz, letting him know to pick Ian up for questioning. Then I looked at Addie. "Do you have any idea where he would go?"

She glanced in that same direction again, out to the national forest land. "He has a place out there. He would never tell me where exactly. It was his emergency place. But it'll be within a day's ride from here. Likely, half a day."

That was a hell of a lot of land to cover. And I knew this wasn't property Ben owned. He was squatting and hoping not to be discovered by the Forest Service. "Anything else you can think of?"

Addie shook her head. "Can I come with you?"

Her voice shook as she asked the question. But the bravery beneath the trembling meant I would forever admire this woman. "Of course, you can."

"You're not going anywhere," Allen bellowed, charging forward. "And you're going to answer for your insolence."

I shoved him back, tightening my hold on my gun. "Step back. Addie is an adult. And she is free to leave whenever she wants." I glanced at her. "Do you have anything you need to get?"

She opened her mouth to answer, but Allen cut her off. "If she removes anything from this property, she'll be shot for stealing and trespassing." His eyes narrowed on his daughter. "If you leave now, you'll be cast out. Dead to me and everyone else in this family."

Addie raised her chin. "It would be a sweet relief to be dead to you."

Allen's face turned so red, I wondered if he was having

a stroke. I motioned Addie towards my SUV. "Get in. It's unlocked." I kept my gaze trained on the two men as I waited for her to get safely inside the vehicle.

Allen's fists clenched and unclenched as he spluttered. "You're going to pay for this."

"You won't touch me or Addie. If you do, the department will come for you first. And this won't be something you can get out of."

Allen was silent but clearly raging as I walked backwards towards my vehicle. Opening the door, I climbed inside. "You know how to shoot?" I asked Addie.

"I know enough."

I handed her my gun. "Take this, just in case."

Her hands trembled as she took hold of the metal. "I'm sorry if I made trouble for you."

I started the engine and took off down the drive. "Don't be sorry. You were brave as hell."

"W-where are you going to take me?"

"To my mom. You'll be safe at our ranch, and your dad and cousin will likely think I have you at the station."

Tears slipped from her eyes and tracked down her cheeks. "Thank you."

I wanted to reach out and pat Addie's shoulder, to give her some sort of comfort, but I could tell any sort of touch wouldn't be welcome. I tore down the main road towards our ranch. It was still startling how close our land came to the Kempers'. A mere ten minutes' drive. But it might as well have been a world away. And I was beyond grateful for that at the moment.

My phone rang just as we pulled onto our ranch road. Ruiz's voice came through the speaker. "Tell me everything."

I recounted the events of the past thirty minutes, including the fact that Addie was with me. "We need to coordinate with Forest Service and get search parties in that area."

"We will, but we don't know he has her."

"It's a direction. A possibility. We have to try."

Ruiz let out a sound of frustration. "We split the teams. Half in that area, half working their way out from Everly's cabin."

It was a good plan. Sound. But it didn't mean I could rest. "Tell the teams I'll be in the area, searching. I don't want anyone to shoot my ass."

"Hayes…"

"It's public land. You can't keep me out."

"Fine. But be careful."

I noted an SUV parked in front of my parents' house that didn't belong to them. "I'll have Calder with me."

"Great, a smoke-eater watching your back."

"He knows how to shoot."

"I hope he does." Ruiz hung up without another word.

I turned to Addie, sliding my phone into my pocket. "You can hand me the gun now."

She did so instantly, her hands still trembling.

"You ready to go inside?"

"S-sure."

I climbed out of the vehicle and rounded the hood to open Addie's door. She didn't move for a few moments. "No one's going to hurt you here. You're safe."

More tears slipped down her cheeks. "He'll never truly let me go."

"He has to. And we're going to make sure of that."

Addie swung her legs around and eased out of the passenger seat. Pain flashed across her features as her feet hit the ground.

My hand went to her elbow. "Do you need a doctor?"

She shook her head. "I'll be fine."

"You let me know if you change your mind."

I led her towards the ranch house. As we walked up the porch steps, the front door flew open. My mom's eyes widened as she took in Addie. "Well, who do we have here?"

I had to give it to my mother. I could tell her nerves were frayed, her eyes were rimmed in red. Clearly, she'd gotten the news that Everly was missing. But she pulled it together and gave the woman in front of her a warm smile.

"Mom, this is Everly's cousin, Addie. Addie, this is my mom, Julia Easton."

Addie wouldn't meet my mother's gaze. "I'm sorry for intruding, Mrs. Easton."

"Nonsense, you come right on in. I'll fix you some tea. I bet we could all use some. And call me Julia."

We made our way inside to find Calder poring over a map on the kitchen island. Dad must've called him to tell him what had happened. His head lifted as we approached. "Any news?"

"We have a possible direction, thanks to Addie."

Calder took in the woman at my side, who had almost shrunk behind me at the sight of him. "Hi, Addie. I'm Calder, Hayes' best friend." He did his best to move slowly and didn't approach for a handshake.

"Nice to meet you," she whispered.

"I'll start on the tea," Mom said, moving to the stove. "How about some chamomile? I always think that's a good one for anxiety and stress."

"Sure, Mom," I answered when Addie was silent.

Her gaze was focused on the map. "I can help."

"You think you can show us where to start the search?"

She nodded. "We were taught to look for the same things when making shelter. He'll want trees, not brushland. A source of running water. If he built a true shelter, he might've wanted to bring things in. That means he's not up in the mountains."

Addie walked slowly towards the island, and Calder didn't move an inch. She gestured to the pencil in his hand. "May I?"

He extended it to her. "Have at it."

She studied the map, her brows furrowing. Then she used the

length of the pencil to measure miles. Doing a little math on the side of the map, she then drew three circles. "I think these are your best bets. You can trailer horses in?"

Calder nodded. "I've got the trailer hooked up to a ranch truck and two mounts ready to go."

She pointed to a forest road. "Drive in here until you get to mile marker eighty-two, then head east. That loop will take the least amount of time."

Calder smiled. "I'm thinking you should get a job as a park ranger."

Addie looked down, dropping the pencil as she turned away.

"Shit," he muttered. "I didn't mean to scare her off."

"It's not you. She's been through a lot lately." And I had a feeling I only knew the tip of the iceberg. I looked at my friend. "Are you sure you want to do this with me?"

Calder's face hardened. "Of course, I do."

But he had girls at home that he was an only parent to. Responsibilities that I couldn't dream of. "I can go alone."

"I'm going with you, so quit arguing. The truck is loaded with supplies. You ready to go?"

"Let's go." I could only pray that Addie's suspicions were right and that Ev could just hold on a little longer.

Chapter Forty-Four

Everly

"I BET YOU'RE THIRSTY." BEN MOVED FROM THE threshold to the small kitchen, lifting a bucket onto the counter. "I need to boil this before you can drink it, though. You've been living the city life for a long time. Don't forget, you can't drink straight from the creek. You'll get sick."

I watched as he stoked the fire in the woodstove in the kitchen area, then poured the water into a pot on top. I couldn't find any words. Ben. My sweet, kind, gentle Ben. He was the one who had taken me. *Chained* me.

My fingers itched to reach for the nail. At least that would be some sort of protection. But never in a million years had I thought I'd need protection from Ben.

"Did you try to take me before? Outside the vet?" I didn't know which would be better, that another psycho was running around, or that Ben had left me with a concussion and bruised ribs.

He stilled his movements, not looking at me. "I'm sorry you got hurt. That wasn't what I wanted."

"I know you wouldn't want to hurt me."

Ben turned, raising his gaze to me. "Not ever."

"This?" I lifted my foot that was chained. "It hurts me."

"You have your jeans protecting you."

"It doesn't hurt me physically, Ben. It hurts me here." I patted my chest. "It scares me."

"You don't have to be scared." He moved across the room.

I couldn't help my reaction. I skittered back on the bed.

His expression hardened to stone. "You don't need to do that. You know me. You've always known me better than anyone else. Now it's as it should've always been. You'll be my wife. That's why Liza died. I know it. Because it was always supposed to be you. I'll keep you safe. No one will find you here. Ian can't hurt you here, and no one else can, either."

I might've known Ben once. The boy who was my best friend. But the man before me now was a stranger. I studied his face as my heart hammered against my ribs. I wasn't even sure exactly *what* I was looking for. A reason why, maybe? A how? Had this sickness always been in him or had there been some sort of break?

"What happened to you?"

He stiffened. "What do you mean?"

I chose my words carefully. "I just mean… You're so scared someone is going to hurt me, but I've been taking good care of myself since I've been back. Ian hasn't hurt me once." Not unless you counted scaring the hell out of me.

"He wanted to. Was planning on it. *I* stopped him. He's the one who burned your barn. If it wasn't for me, you'd probably be dead. I have to keep you here. Keep you safe. And you'll see. We'll be married."

My stomach pitched as if I were on a Tilt-A-Whirl. Only there was no pleasant rush of adrenaline like an amusement ride. There was only nausea and fear. "If that's true, then you can unlock me. I'll stay here. I don't want Ian to hurt me."

Ben's eyes narrowed on me. "You're lying. I always know,

Evie. You don't see yet. But you will. You'll see the truth. You'll see that we're meant to be."

"Please, Ben." I wasn't above begging. My tears or trembling voice had always been his undoing. He'd hated the sight and sound of them. "I don't want to be locked up. We can figure out another way."

"This is the way it has to be."

The man before me might have been a stranger, but I knew that tone. It was the same one he'd had as a child. The one that said his mind was made up, and he wouldn't be moved. I sagged against the wall, needing time to come up with another plan—some other way. And I needed information.

"Where are we?"

He turned back to the stove. "It doesn't matter. All that matters is that it's home."

Helpful. If I got a chance to run, I'd be mostly blind. But if I could get to a clearing, somewhere with sightlines, I could use the mountains as my guide. I'd have to be faster than Ben. Because I was certain of one thing. He wouldn't have made a home here without knowing the land like the back of his hand.

I studied Ben as he moved around the kitchen, searching for any signs of injury. Hayes had thought his bullet had clipped his shooter, but I didn't see any evidence of injury. I needed a weakness, but there wasn't one in sight.

I let my eyes close for a moment, feeling the hopelessness of it all wash over me. But Hayes' face flashed in my mind. And I swore I could almost feel his arms around me. I wouldn't let this be the end for us. I refused.

My eyes opened as Ben moved the pot off the stove, placing it in the sink of sorts. He studied the liquid. "It'll take a while to cool."

"Did you try to take that other girl? Did you chase Hadley in your truck?"

His face reddened. "It was always only you."

The embarrassed hue of his skin gave me my answer. He had. The *why* of it, I didn't know. Would he have been content with one of them? My fingers twisted in the quilt. At least, it hadn't been Hadley. That would've broken the Eastons. If there was one thing I could be grateful for in this moment, it was that.

Ben strode towards the door of the cabin. "I need to water the horses. I'll be back."

The horses. God, he really was stocked for a future life here. But how long would that last? Because I would fight tooth and nail if he tried to touch me. And then what? The illusion of his happily ever after would be shattered.

As the door closed, I scooted up to the edge of the bed. My fingers quickly searched under the mattress for my nail. I prodded until I felt the little piece of metal. So tiny, yet I was counting on it for...I wasn't sure what. To save my life?

"Everything is a potential tool. A possible weapon." I whispered my father's words to myself. When I made a run for it, I would need every single one of his lessons.

I slid the nail into my front jeans' pocket and waited. Listened. I heard the sound of a horse whinnying. And then soft footfalls. I braced as the door swung open, and Ben appeared.

"I need to use a bathroom."

He studied me. "Is that the truth?"

I nodded. And that nod wasn't a lie. I could feel my bladder pressing down.

"I'm going to unlock you. But I have this"—Ben slid a gun from a holster at the small of his back—"so don't think of running. I don't want to hurt you, but I will if I have to."

I swallowed as the gun glinted in the late-afternoon light. "I won't run. I promise."

I would fly. That was what it would take. My feet would barely touch the ground.

Ben bent, pulling keys from his pocket and unlocking the padlock. He used the gun to motion me along. "I've got an outhouse made up."

I pushed to my feet but wavered a bit, my head swimming. Ben reached out to grasp my elbow. "Are you okay?"

I fought not to recoil from his touch. This was an opportunity. A chance for Ben to see me as weak. "My head. It hurts."

"I'll give you some tea my mom makes for headaches when we get back."

I gave him a wobbly smile. "Thank you."

I blinked against the light as we stepped outside. The sun was low in the sky. If I had to guess, there were only a few hours of daylight left. I did my best to take in our surroundings without being obvious about it.

There was a small corral with a shelter for the horses. There was even a wagon parked alongside the fence. A shed. And an outhouse. Other than that, I only saw trees. They were so tall and thick, I didn't have a chance to catch sight of my mountain. The one that might guide me home. To Hayes.

I quickly went inside the outhouse to do my business. Ben had even placed a bucket with water and soap inside. A hysterical laugh bubbled out of me. He really had thought of everything. That laugh turned into a most-pressing need to cry, but I swallowed it down.

I took a long breath, praying to anyone who would listen for my legs to be strong, for luck to be on my side. And I listened. I could hear running water. I would move in that direction when the time came. That would be my map.

I opened the door. "Thank you for the water and soap."

"Of course. See, it won't be bad here."

I didn't say anything. Instead, as we walked, I waited for my moment—the break in the trees I'd seen that would make for a clear path to run. Ben's hand stayed on my elbow, but his grip wasn't tight. He seemed to think I might have given in.

Twenty breaths. I just needed sixty seconds of bravery, one more time. I counted off my steps. And two before the break in the trees, I swung. My arm ripped out of Ben's grasp and came back with vicious force. The blow knocked the air out of him, but I didn't stop there. I whirled and brought his face down to my knee.

I missed his nose as he turned away from the blow. But the way Ben howled, I thought I might've broken his cheekbone. I didn't wait to find out. I simply ran.

Chapter Forty-Five

Hayes

"S O, ARE YOU GOING TO TELL ME WHAT THE DEAL WAS with that woman?" Calder asked as we steered the horses in the direction of the creek.

I was sure he was curious, but I knew more than anything that he was trying to distract me. I appreciated it, but nothing would take my mind off Everly in this moment. The woman I loved, possibly being held by someone mentally unstable—and whatever situation we might be riding up on.

I adjusted my grip on the reins. Soren didn't deserve me pulling on his mouth because I was about to lose it. "She's Everly's cousin. And I don't think she's had an easy life."

"She lived with the crazy uncle?"

"And Ian. I'm not sure who else. That ranch is a revolving door of people."

A muscle in Calder's cheek ticked. "I have a bad feeling about that place."

"It's justified."

My gaze traveled around us. Through the trees. Towards the sound of running water. There was nothing, but I was on high alert anyway.

Something about the energy of the air out here was strange. As soon as we'd gotten the horses out of the trailer, my skin had begun to prickle. Ev was out here. We just hadn't seen any sign of her or anyone else yet.

A team was assembling to start a grid search, but that kind of thing took time. They'd be at least an hour behind us. I looked up at the sky, sending up a silent prayer that we'd find Ev in time. There was no other option. As I dropped my gaze back to the makeshift trail in front of us, my gaze caught on something.

I squinted back at the sky. At first, I'd thought it was a cloud, but the shape was wrong. The color, too. I halted Soren's steps. "Calder. Smoke."

He stopped his horse and looked in the direction I pointed. "Hell."

I pulled my sat phone out of my saddlebag and dialed Ruiz. He answered on the third ring. "You find anything?"

"Smoke where there shouldn't be any."

"Where are you?"

I read off our coordinates.

Ruiz relayed them to someone in the background. "Stay where you are. We're sending backup."

"You know I can't do that." Nothing on this Earth could keep me from heading towards that smoke.

"Hayes—"

I hung up. I didn't want to hear his arguments. I glanced at Calder. "You okay with finding that fire?"

He checked the rifle attached to his saddle. "That's what we're here for. Let's go find your girl."

The tight weave of trees meant that we couldn't pick up to a gallop or even a damned trot. We had to plod a path through the obstacle course because we needed the cover. I noticed that we were following the curve of the creek. Maybe Addie had been right all along. Flowing water. Forest cover. It made for an excellent hiding spot. But the idiot hadn't thought about the smoke giving him away.

Calder held up a hand, and we both stopped. I strained to listen. It was something. Could've been an animal, but it could've been human, too. Whoever and whatever it was, they were running.

I pulled my Glock from my holster at my hip and slid from the saddle. I handed Calder my reins and made a motion for him to stay quiet. He wrapped my reins around his saddle horn and pulled out his rifle. We'd picked these horses because they had steady experience but were young enough to go the distance. I just had to hope they wouldn't spook at whatever we were about to face.

I crept forward through the trees, Calder and the horses on my heels. The sound of running grew louder, and then there was a scream.

Everything in me froze, my blood turning so cold it hurt as it traveled through my veins. The screaming picked back up, and then I heard the sounds of fighting. It was the only thing that kicked me into action.

I didn't think, I simply moved, crashing through the trees until I reached the edge of the forest. There, on the bank of the creek, was the woman I loved. She thrashed in a man's hold. He wrapped an arm around her neck and pressed a gun to her temple, stilling her movements. "I told you I didn't want to hurt you. But I will."

I raised my gun. "Don't move. Carson County Sheriff's Department." Ben froze. "Now, slowly lower your weapon and release Everly."

His hold on her only tightened. "She's mine. Not yours. You put her at risk. I keep her safe."

"If you want her safe, then you don't want her so close to that gun."

His finger was on the damn trigger. It would only take one wrong move for everything to be over. I met Everly's gaze. Tears spilled down her cheeks and over her chin, landing on the dirt below. I wanted to kill him for those tears alone.

Ben shook his head with a manic ferocity. "No, no, NO! You have to leave."

"Easy does it. Just calm down."

"No! You ruin everything. She's mine. She always was." His arm around her neck tightened, and Everly began to cough.

"She can't breathe," I gritted out.

He loosened his hold a fraction. Everly sucked in air. "Please, Ben. Let me go."

"No. If we're going to die, then it'll be together. Maybe that's the answer. It'll be in heaven, but we'll be together." He began backing up towards the edge of the creek.

I'd seen parts of Canyon Creek before, but it looked more like a river in this stretch. Even if he didn't shoot her, they could still drown if he took them both in. "Just wait, Ben."

He kept moving them backwards. "No more waiting."

I adjusted the aim of my gun, but I didn't have a clear shot. Everly's gaze shot to mine, and she mouthed three words. "*I love you.*"

I would've given anything in that moment to hear the sound those words made. To have them whispered against my skin while we were curled up in bed. To have them come out on a laugh as she tipped her head back—anything but this.

Her hand twitched, and she pulled something I couldn't quite make out from her pocket. In a flash, she lifted her arm and brought it down on Ben's thigh. He howled in pain.

I didn't wait. I went for the shot. And as it cracked the air, I prayed for it to hit true.

Chapter Forty-Six

Everly

THE CRACK OF THE BULLET WAS DEAFENING. EVEN against the water rushing behind me and the wind that had picked up out of nowhere. That sound cut through everything.

Yet everything seemed to move in slow motion. My body was already listing to the side, but my eyes never left Hayes' face. If I could just not lose sight of him again, I would be okay. I knew it.

I felt Ben's arm around my throat fall away, and the heat of him at my back simply disappeared. And I was falling.

I landed hard on the rocky ground, my hip and shoulder hitting first. I tried to keep my head from knocking, but it was useless. The force of my fall was too great.

The world went black for the briefest of moments, but Hayes' face was still there when light returned. And it was moving. *He* was moving—towards me.

He was on his knees in a flash, hands roaming all over my body. "You're okay. Are you hurt anywhere?"

"I love you." It was the only thing I cared about getting out. I'd been so dumb to hold the words back. Terrified and thinking I could protect myself from devastation if I simply didn't voice what was inside of me. But not saying it didn't change the truth. I loved this man with everything I had. He was my resting place. Somewhere I could lay my burdens and be who I truly was, no shields or false fronts—only me.

"Ev…" My nickname on his lips was a guttural plea as he framed my face. "Can't tell you what it gives me to hear those words. But I need to know if you're okay."

"I'm okay." I tried to sit, the world swimming a bit again.

Hayes was instantly there, helping me rise. "I've got you."

"I know."

As I sat, I couldn't bring myself to look behind me. I didn't know what I hoped to see. Even with everything that had happened, I couldn't find it in me to wish my childhood friend dead. "Ben?" I croaked.

Hayes' jaw hardened. "I don't know. My shot hit him, but he went into the creek. The current's strong here."

I turned towards the water that rushed and bubbled, swirling around rocks and fallen trees. I couldn't imagine him surviving that trek with a bullet wound. "I have to know. We have to find him."

Calder stepped out of the trees, two horses in tow. "I called in the team. They're downriver, so they'll watch for him." His gaze swept over me, assessing and concerned. "Are you okay?"

"I am now."

And that was when I broke. The first sob tore free before I even knew what was happening. Hayes engulfed me, wrapping his arms around me and absorbing each heave of my chest. He never once let go as I poured out the terror of the past few hours, the heartbreak of losing one of the few safe places I had growing up.

Hayes allowed me to let loose everything that was tearing me up inside. Not once did he try to tell me that everything would be okay or to stop. Nor did he make any sort of shhhing noise. He simply took it all in and gave me a place to lay it down.

I had no idea how long I cried. But Hayes was still there as the sobs eased. Holding me. He pressed his lips to my temple. "I'm here."

"You always are."

"And I always will be."

Instead of fear or uncertainty at that vow, I felt only peace. The ethereal feeling that had always seemed out of my grasp. It filled me now, and if I could experience that peace amidst the terror of today, I knew it would never leave me.

Hayes pressed a kiss to my other temple. "Think I can help you get up?"

I nodded against his neck.

Hayes slowly stood, carefully bringing me with him. I wavered a bit, and he steadied me. Then he started prodding at my head. "Shit, Ev. There's blood. Did he hit you?"

I brought my hand to my head, my fingers following Hayes'. There was a bit of tacky blood on the left side of my skull. "He knocked me out at the cabin. I didn't even see him coming."

"We need to get you to a hospital to get checked out."

"No hospitals. I just want to go home. With you." It was all I needed.

I got what I wanted. Mostly. After a slow ride back to the truck and trailer, a Forest Service team escorting us halfway, Hayes took me to his house since mine was a crime scene. He hadn't forced me to a hospital, but he'd had the town doctor check me out with Hadley serving as his assistant. I hadn't needed stitches, but I did have another mild concussion.

Now, after a shower that Hayes had demanded he take with me, I was clean and propped up on his couch with a world of people swarming about. Julia and Gabe. Shiloh and Hadley. And my Addie.

Hayes brushed the hair away from my face. "Are you sure you don't want to go to sleep?"

"No. I want to be right here." I wanted to bask in the light of the family I was making for myself.

"Stop trying to mother her, Bubby," Hadley said as she bustled in from the kitchen and handed me a ginger ale.

I took a long sip of the bubbly sweetness. "Thanks, Hads."

She gave me a wink. "Anytime."

"Chicken and dumplings are almost done," Julia called from the kitchen where she'd been cooking up a storm with Addie's assistance and Gabe hovering.

Hadley plopped down on the opposite side of the couch. "It's my favorite meal when I'm not feeling great. I'm pretty sure it cures all."

"She's not wrong there," Hayes said, lacing his fingers through mine.

I caught sight of Shiloh through the windows. She'd needed space since returning from searching for me. When she'd walked into the house, she'd made a beeline for me, hugging me tightly and whispering, "I'm so glad you're okay." Then she'd simply left.

"She needs to walk it off," Gabe had told me.

She was back, but she'd made her home on the front porch swing. I knew this had brought up hard things for her—ghosts and demons rearing their ugly heads. But Shiloh was one of the strongest people I knew. She would make it through this, too. We all would.

I pressed into Hayes' side. "I love you."

"I know," he whispered. "I knew before you could say the words."

I tipped my head back to take in his face. "Cocky."

The corner of his mouth quirked up. "No. You showed me without ever saying the words."

Everything in me warmed, and I burrowed into his chest, feeling only more of that peace. "I like giving you the words, too."

"I like hearing them. And, Ev?"

"Hmm?"

"I love you, too."

His words wrapped around me, only burying that peace into me. It was so deep now, I knew it would never leave.

Chapter Forty-Seven

Hayes

"THAT FACE LOOKS SERIOUS. BAD NEWS?" EVERLY ASKED from her spot in my bed.

I made my way towards her. I didn't want to tell her. I wanted to lie to keep the relief that had lived on her face for the past few hours in place, but I'd never lie to Ev. "They found him."

She visibly swallowed. "That's good. I mean, his family deserves closure—"

"He's alive."

"What?" She straightened against the pillows. "How is that even possible?"

"My bullet caught him in the shoulder. A Forest Service team found him downriver. He's in surgery right now, but they say he'll make it." I was trying not to be annoyed that it had taken Ruiz hours to call to give me the news. He was dealing with a storm and needed to work by the book.

I slid back under the covers, back to Everly and her warmth. I wrapped my arms around her and pulled her against my chest. "This doesn't change that you're safe. Young and Williams brought Ian in for questioning, too. They're holding him for as long as they can."

"I know I'm safe. I just…"

"What?"

She traced circles on the planes of my chest. "I don't know how to feel. On the one hand, I'm relieved that I'm not the reason he's dead—"

"You never would've been the reason. Ben's actions are what brought him to that place, not yours."

"I know that in my head…"

I pressed my lips to her hair. "But your heart's a different story."

"Yes."

And Ev's heart would always bleed for others. Her soul would take on more responsibility than it needed to. But I couldn't wish that away. Not when it was also her greatest strength. How she could reach people and animals in a way no one else could. The way she saw more than anyone else. Those were some of the things I loved most about Ev, and I couldn't wish them away. Even if I knew one of the downsides of her gift was pain. I would simply have to be there to ease that hurt.

I brushed the hair away from her face. "I love you, Ev. We'll get through this. You're so damn strong."

"And having you just makes me stronger." Her fingers moved from drawing circles on my pec to figure eights. "I realized something when he had me."

Just the words had images filling my mind, things that would haunt me forever, but I forced my muscles to relax as I held her. "What's that?"

"You're my resting place."

It wasn't anything I'd ever been called before, anything I'd ever aspired to. But in that moment, there was no higher compliment or calling.

Everly looked up at me. "I've never had that before. You helped me find my peace."

My throat burned as I stared down at the woman who owned me, body and soul. "I feel it, too. Never felt more at ease than when I'm with you. I think we created that peace together."

"Never felt anything more beautiful."

And we were never going to lose it. I would marry her tomorrow if she'd let me. But I knew that might be a bit much for her. I knew it would come, though. That day where we stood up and promised forever to each other. But forever had already begun.

Everly tilted her head and brushed her lips against mine. The feel and taste of her eased the bit of me that was still on edge. That fear still clawing at muscle and sinew, feral and vicious. Even holding her in my arms hadn't totally sated that beast. Because even though she was safe now, I'd still almost lost her.

Everly deepened the kiss, her tongue stroking mine, silently asking for more. It was all I wanted, and yet, I couldn't. I gently took her face in my hands, pulling away from the kiss with a groan. "We can't. You need to rest. Heal."

She wouldn't say it, but I knew Ev was hurting. I could see it in the way she'd moved up the stairs tonight. The last thing I wanted was to cause her any more pain.

Her hand pressed against my bare chest. "I need you, Hayes."

No other words could've broken my resolve. "I don't want to hurt you."

"You won't. But I need this. You. Us. I need to remember that I'm alive, and I haven't lost you."

My hand slipped beneath the borrowed t-shirt she wore, finding only bare skin. "You'll never lose me."

She looked up at me, almost pleading. "Then show me."

My fingers slid up the outside of her leg, between her thighs, searching. Everly's head tipped back as I stroked and explored. My lips found the column of her neck. I trailed kisses around the light bruises that had begun to form. As if my mouth could erase the marks, the memories, all of it.

I slipped two fingers inside her, stroking. Everly let out a low moan. The sound had me straining against the sweats I wore.

"Need you," she whispered.

Those words again. My undoing.

"Please."

My fingers slid out of her. I pulled down my sweats, my erection springing free. My hands went to Everly's hips, lifting her gently so she straddled my lap. "This is how we're gonna go. Nice and easy. You control the pace. If anything hurts, we stop."

The corner of Ev's mouth kicked up. "You're going to let me have control?"

I couldn't help the scowl that came to my lips. "I let you have control."

"Sure, you do." Her hands went to my shoulders, and all amusement fled as she sank onto me. Her forehead touched mine. "Needed this. Just you and me. Us."

She was right. When we came together, something was different. Every feeling and sense seemed heightened. If someone had told me that was possible, I would've called them a dirty liar. But it was the truth.

Everly began moving, rocking her hips. It was a slow and glorious torture. My hands slipped under her tee and cupped her breasts. She arched into me, taking me deeper and pressing her flesh into my hands.

I let out a groan as my hips rose to meet her movements. I'd tried to stay still, but with Ev, it was impossible. I always wanted more. To feel every inch of skin. To be planted in her as deeply as possible. To lose myself in the way she always made me feel— alive and at home, all at the same time.

Everly quickened her pace, and we found that rhythm that was ours alone, the energy that lit my blood on fire. My hands dipped to her waist, my lips finding the shell of her ear. "Need more?"

"Just need you."

My hand dropped lower, my thumb finding that bundle of nerves and circling. The space getting tighter with each pass.

"Hayes," she breathed as if my name were part prayer, part plea.

My thumb hit the spot where she wanted me most, and I pressed. Everly tightened around me, throwing me over that cliff that was the best high and the sweetest downfall. And not once did she let her eyes close as we fell. Together. I saw love and need and home in those eyes.

Her forehead came down to rest on mine again. "Love you."

"For the rest of my days."

Everly's hand found mine, twining our fingers. "It seems crazy to know this fast. But I feel the same way."

"Sometimes, the truth is the thing you know the fastest."

"I guess I can see that."

"You know that means I'm moving in, right?"

She straightened, scanning my face. "You want to move in with me?"

I cupped her cheek with my hand, stroking her cheek with my thumb. "It's important to you to make your sanctuary there, in every sense of the word. Of course, I'll move to be with you. This is just a house. What you're doing is important."

Tears filled her eyes, spilling down her face. "I haven't even been able to make myself walk inside the main house."

"I've been thinking about that."

She sniffed. "Thinking that I'm crazy to try to make living there work?"

"No. I think you just haven't found the right blend of the old and the new."

"Okay…"

"The main house is in rough shape anyway. I say we tear it down and come up with plans for something new. Something that's ours. You're fulfilling your promise to give that land good-ness again, but you're also building something that's *you*. Us."

Everly brushed her mouth against mine. "Have I told you lately that I love you?"

I grinned against her lips. "You might've said it a time or two today. But I'll never get tired of hearing it." Not today or tomor-row. Not when we were fifty or ninety-two. Those were the words I wanted to hear from her every day for the rest of my life.

Epilogue

Everly

ONE MONTH LATER

"THEY LOOK HAPPY," ADDIE SAID AS SHE GUIDED THE rocking chair back and forth on my front porch.

My gaze traveled from her to the paddocks in the distance. Not only were our paint mare, Dolly, and our mini-donkey, Donut, happily settled in their new home, but a pig and two goats had joined the sanctuary. And this weekend, we were getting three miniature horses.

"I think they are." I took a sip of lemonade. "So, what do you think? Whenever the house is done, you could live here in the cabin. You can stay as long as you want."

Hayes and I had already had the main house leveled. The day the demolition crew had taken the first swing, I'd wept. I hadn't realized just how much staring at the building I'd grown up in had been a weight. Just like Shiloh and the shed, I'd needed to start fresh. To tear it down so I could build the right thing in its place.

Hayes and I had met with an architect several times and were now waiting for the final plans to submit to the county. Addie had opted to stay with the Eastons instead of moving into the guest room in the cabin. I'd offered, but I also understood that it might've been awkward. The space was tiny, and we would've all been sharing a bathroom. But the Eastons had a ton of room.

Addie stared out at the animals. "Actually, Hayes said I could stay at his house in town when I'm ready. I'm not quite there yet. But soon. I want to stand on my own two feet."

I swallowed down the disappointment. I wished I could have my cousin closer, to look out for her, but maybe that was why she'd refused. And I was touched that Hayes had offered his home to her. He'd already decided that he didn't want to sell. This was the perfect use for the space.

I looked over at my cousin. She'd gained back a little of the weight she so desperately needed, but dark circles still rimmed her eyes. "It's an open invitation. If you decide you don't like living by yourself, this might be a happy medium."

She reached down and scratched between Koda's ears. He was fully healed now, and the Forest Service had caught the hunter who'd laid the trap that had broken his leg. The man was serving sixty days in jail. It wasn't enough, but it was something. Koda leaned into Addie's touch.

"Thanks, Ev," she said quietly. "I appreciate it."

Addie had taken to using Hayes' nickname for me. I'd visibly winced every time she'd called me Evie. It reminded me too much of Ben. The Ben who was currently in county lockup, awaiting trial. His lawyer was using an insanity defense, and I wasn't sure he was wrong. Ben was sick. And more than anything, I simply wanted him to get help.

Tires on gravel sounded as Hayes' SUV crested the hill. Just the sight of it had the chill at the reminder of Ben fleeing. Addie rose, and I followed. "You don't have to go. Why don't you stay for dinner? I can drive you back after."

Addie inclined her head towards Shiloh, who was walking up from the far paddock. "I'll just go with Shiloh. I'm supposed to help Mrs. Easton with some of the cooking."

"Okay...lunch tomorrow?"

"Maybe."

Even though I had my cousin back, she was still a hundred miles away. Because while Ian had been arrested, Allen was still walking around free. Addie refused to report any abuse she'd suffered at his hands, no matter how many times Hayes had tried to broach the subject.

I pulled Addie in for a gentle hug. "Love you. I'm here if you need anything."

Her arms circled me lightly. "Love you, too."

She headed for Shiloh's truck and gave Hayes a wave. Shiloh did the same. "See you guys tomorrow."

Family dinner. The tension with Hadley and Julia hadn't lessened any, but at least there were more people to distract both of them now.

Hayes waved to his sister and Addie and then climbed the porch steps. "Well, aren't you a sight for sore eyes?"

"I've got an extra glass just for you." I reached for it and poured a tall glass of lemonade.

"There any vodka in that?"

I looked up, taking stock of Hayes' features. "That bad?"

He bent to brush his lips across mine. "Better now."

"Tell me everything."

Hayes put down his gym bag and eased into the rocker that Addie had sat in as I pushed the glass of lemonade across the table between us. "Ben gave us everything we asked for. I almost feel bad for him. Ian knew that he was on the edge and used it to his advantage. Setting fire to the barn, carefully dropping warnings and innuendos."

In Ian's mind, no punishment was great enough for what he

thought I'd put my family through. But he'd likely always get joy out of causing me pain.

Hayes shook his head. "Ben's mind was already so broken, it was easy for Ian to plant those seeds. Didn't make it any easier not to throttle him, though."

"I'm glad you didn't."

"There *was* one weird thing."

"What's that?"

Hayes traced a design in the condensation on his glass as if using the action to puzzle something through in his mind. "He said he wasn't the one who chased Hadley down in her truck."

"Really?"

He nodded. "And I don't think he'd lie about that one random fact when he gave us the truth about everything else."

"Who was it, then? Someone with road rage issues?"

Hayes lifted a shoulder and dropped it again. "Maybe. Or someone who'd had too much to drink and was pissed off about something. But Hadley hasn't had any more issues."

At least, that she'd told us. And after the blowup with her brother, Calder, and her mom after that night, I wasn't sure she would. "Hopefully, that's it."

My mind drifted back to Ben and Ian, my stomach twisting. "What did the D.A. say about trials?"

"They're going to plead Ben out. Psychiatric ward of a prison instead of general population."

"That's good. Maybe he'll get the help he needs. What about Ian?"

A muscle in Hayes' cheek ticked. "He's taking him to trial for the arson, at least. It'll be an uphill battle for real time. But the good news is that the restraining order is permanent now."

I had to think any time in a prison had the chance to be a true wake-up call for my brother. At the very least, I wouldn't have to think about him for a while. I took a sip of lemonade and closed my eyes. I could feel the light breeze, smell the pine trees and the animals, sense Hayes next to me. That was all I needed to hook into my peace. As I opened my eyes, I looked at the man who'd become my resting place. "Now we can let it go. It's out of our hands. Now, we get to live."

His mouth curved. "That sounds like a great plan to me. And I think I've got something to mark the occasion."

"What?"

Hayes reached down into his gym bag and pulled out a cardboard cylinder. "I picked these up from the architect today."

I let out a little squeal and turned to move the pitcher and glasses to the side of the table. "Spread them out. I want to see."

He laughed and did as I asked. My gaze roamed over what I knew was the first floor of what would be our home. My finger traced the lines of the walls. The open kitchen and living space. An office for me that looked out at the animals. A massive garage and mudroom that would help us through the winter months and hold the snowplow Hayes had insisted on. I flipped to the second page and the upper floor. There were more bedrooms than I thought we'd need, a gorgeous suite for us, and even an attic space above we'd finish to use as a bonus room.

I looked up, smiling ear to ear. "It's perfect."

"I think so, too." Hayes pulled back the second page to reveal a third. "I asked them to consult a landscape architect for some possible designs on the back garden. I was thinking here would be the perfect place to get married." His finger circled the drawing of a pergola, but my gaze shot to his.

"Get married?"

Hayes pushed a small velvet box across the table. "Marry me, Ev."

I couldn't move. Couldn't breathe. Hayes picked up the box and rose. He crossed to me, settling on his knees between my legs. "You already know it's you and me forever. But I want to start that next chapter as soon as the house is done. I want to tie myself to you in every way possible. I want to make a family with you. You want that?"

"I want that," I whispered as tears spilled down my cheeks. "There's nothing I want more."

And as Hayes slid the gorgeous diamond onto my finger, I felt more of that peace I'd been looking for.

Acknowledgments

I'm a big fan of acknowledgments and as I'm sitting down to write these (at the beginning of 2021) it's been a rough few months. There has been so much pain in our world and some tough things in my own life. So, I want to take a minute to shout out to some women who have been an amazing support through it all.

First, in my writerly world. Emma, for being encourager, confidante, sounding board, and forever safe space. What would I do without you? Whatever it was wouldn't be good or fun. Grahame, for always being there to answer one question or fifty, for beta listening to all my books, for always being willing to toss ideas around or just cheer me on. Willow and Laura, what a gift you both are! Your positivity, light, and friendship mean the world.

Second, in my non-writer world. My STS sisters: Hollis, Jael, and Paige, you have been the bright spot of this quarantine. I love chasing dreams with you and sharing whatever might be in our hearts. Thank you for the gift of twenty years of your friendship and never-ending support. My Charshie. Oh, how I love you and am in awe of how you have walked through life these last months. You are an inspiration and force. And I love that these books have connected us when I couldn't be with you in person.

And to all my family and friends near and far. Thank you for supporting me on this crazy journey, even if you don't read "kissing books." But you get extra special bonus points if you picked up one of mine, even if that makes me turn the shade of a tomato when you tell me.

To my fearless beta readers: Angela, Crystal, Emily, and Trisha, thank you for reading this book in its roughest form and helping me to make it the best it could possibly be!

The crew that helps bring my words to life and gets them out into the world is pretty darn epic. Thank you to Susan, Chelle, Janice, Julie, Hang, Stacey, Jenn, and the rest of my team at Social Butterfly. Your hard work is so appreciated!

To all the bloggers who have taken a chance on my words… THANK YOU! Your championing of my stories means more than I can say. And to my launch and ARC teams, thank you for your kindness, support, and sharing my books with the world. An extra special thank you to Crystal who sails that ship so I can focus on the words.

Ladies of Catherine Cowles Reader Group, you're my favorite place to hang out on the internet! Thank you for your support, encouragement, and willingness to always dish about your latest book boyfriends. You're the freaking best!

Lastly, thank YOU! Yes, YOU. I'm so grateful you're reading this book and making my author dreams come true. I love you for that. A whole lot!

Also Available from
CATHERINE COWLES

The Tattered & Torn Series
Tattered Stars
Falling Embers
Hidden Waters
Shattered Sea
Fractured Sky

The Wrecked Series
Reckless Memories
Perfect Wreckage
Wrecked Palace
Reckless Refuge
Beneath the Wreckage

The Sutter Lake Series
Beautifully Broken Pieces
Beautifully Broken Life
Beautifully Broken Spirit
Beautifully Broken Control

Stand-alone Novels
Further To Fall

For a full list of up-to-date Catherine Cowles titles please visit
www.catherinecowles.com.

About
CATHERINE COWLES

Writer of words. Drinker of Diet Cokes. Lover of all things cute and furry, especially her dog. Catherine has had her nose in a book since the time she could read and finally decided to write down some of her own stories. When she's not writing, she can be found exploring her home state of Oregon, listening to true crime podcasts, or searching for her next book boyfriend.

Stay Connected

You can find Catherine in all the usual bookish places...

Website: catherinecowles.com

Facebook: facebook.com/catherinecowlesauthor

Catherine Cowles Facebook Reader Group: www.facebook.com/groups/CatherineCowlesReaderGroup

Instagram: instagram.com/catherinecowlesauthor

Goodreads: goodreads.com/catherinecowlesauthor

BookBub: bookbub.com/profile/catherine-cowles

Amazon: www.amazon.com/author/catherinecowles

Twitter: twitter.com/catherinecowles

Pinterest: pinterest.com/catherinecowlesauthor